I0562901

SCORCHED EARTH

TERRY MIXON

YOWLING
CAT PRESS

Scorched Earth

Copyright © 2017 by Terry Mixon

All rights reserved. No part of this book may be reproduced or transmitted in any form or by any means, electronic or mechanical, including information storage and/or retrieval systems, or dissemination of any electronic version, without the prior written consent of the publisher, except by a reviewer, who may quote brief passages in a review, and except where permitted by law.

This is a work of fiction. All names, characters, places, and incidents are the products of the author's imagination, or are used fictitiously. Any resemblance to actual persons, living or dead, events, or locales is entirely coincidental.

Published by Yowling Cat Press ®

Digital edition date: 6/21/2023

Print ISBN: 978-1947376076

Large Print ISBN: 978-1947376311

Cover art - image copyrights as follows:

Luca Oleastri

Donna Mixon

Cover design and composition by Donna Mixon

Print edition design and layout by Terry Mixon

ALSO BY TERRY MIXON

You can always find the most up to date listing of Terry's titles on his Amazon Author Page.

Note: the links below (ebook only, obviously) redirect you to my website where you can click a button to go to Amazon. This allows me to participate in Amazon's associates program and earn a little more. Sorry for any inconvenience.

The Last Hunter

The Last Hunter

Bonds of Blood

Alpha Strike

The Enemy Revealed

Command Authority

The Grand Conspiracy

Shield of Humanity

Fog of War

Ships of the Line

Operation Liberty

The Empire of Bones Saga

Empire of Bones

Veil of Shadows

Command Decisions

Ghosts of Empire

Paying the Price

Recon in Force

Box Sets

The Empire of Bones Saga Volume 1

The Empire of Bones Saga Volume 2

The Empire of Bones Saga Volume 3

The Empire of Bones Saga Volume 4

Humanity Unlimited Publisher's Pack 1

Humanity Unlimited Publisher's Pack 2

Want to get updates from Terry about new books and other general nonsense going on in his life? He promises there will be cats. Go to TerryMixon.com/Mailing-List and sign up.

DEDICATION

This book would not be possible without the love and support of my beautiful wife. Donna, I love you more than life itself.

ACKNOWLEDGMENTS

Once again, the people who read my books before you see them have saved me. Thanks to Alan Barnes, Jeff Brackett, Michael Falkner, Michael Goad, Cain Hopwood, Edward J. Knight, Kristopher Neidecker, Bob Noble, Andrew Olivier, Jon Paul Olivier, Bill Smith, Tom Stoecklein, and Jason Young for making me look good.

I also want to thank my readers for putting up with me. You guys are great.

1
―――――――

"**D**amn!" the young man guarding the gate at the Portland Expo Center shouted with a grin. "Are you ready for the apocalypse or what?"

Tom Morgan smiled down at him. "Not yet. Give me a couple of hours."

The rent-a-cop looked up at him. He didn't have much of a choice. Tom sat in an old Army two-and-a-half-ton extended-bed cargo truck that was over ten feet tall. His steering wheel sat almost seven feet off the ground. He called it the Beast.

"Where you going?" the kid shouted.

"The gun and prepper show, of course. I'm Tom Morgan with Adler Arms. My name should be on the list."

The kid grabbed a clipboard, scanned it, and nodded sharply. "Gotcha right here, Mister Morgan. Let me get you a pass. Vendor parking is around back."

Tom really didn't need directions. He'd been to this particular show many times, though rarely in association with a seller. He usually came to buy. Today was no different.

He'd arranged for an old friend to add him to the vendors' list as his employee. Picking up his newest purchase around back would make Tom's life a lot easier.

He took the paper pass from the kid and hung it on the rearview mirror. With a wave, he put the Beast into gear and headed towards the back of the Expo Center.

Cars towing trailers, trucks, and moving vans filled the parking lot. Thankfully, there was still plenty of space available. Maneuvering the Beast into a parking spot was out of the question.

Even though Tom had made some upgrades to the sturdy cargo truck—including rear wheel steering—the vehicle was still eight feet wide and over twenty-eight feet long, and that didn't even count the equally rugged ex-Army trailer he was towing behind it.

Together, the long-bed cargo truck and trailer stretched over forty-two feet and could carry almost eight tons of whatever he wanted. Far more than he could legally move on the public roads without a commercial license, in any case.

Tom parked lengthwise at the back of the lot, locked the doors with another aftermarket add-on, and opened the hood. It only took him a moment to remove the battery quick-disconnect and stuff it into his pocket.

He probably didn't need to worry, but he wasn't about to take any chances. All he needed was for some idiot to try to take the big truck on a joyride. That would be a disaster.

Of course, the odds of that were pretty low. Not many kids these days knew how to drive a stick shift, much less one in a nonstandard pattern. He just didn't feel like taking any chances. Not when the North Koreans might send them straight to hell at any moment.

The ramps leading onto the loading dock at the back of the Expo Center were busy with vendors moving their product inside or carting things back to their vehicles. A number of people stood around drinking coffee in the cool fall air while stinking the place up with cigarettes.

Tom ignored the stench and forged his way inside. He was pleased to see that there were no guards at the rear entrances or signs prohibiting the legal carry of concealed weapons.

With gun shows, the police always set up in front to make sure that no one came in with a loaded weapon, but they rarely checked in back. They just assumed the vendors would follow the Expo Center rules.

Shoppers packed the huge building, examining guns and gear of all kinds. Vendors at the gun and prepper show had everything under the sun that might appeal to folks like him. The preparedness angle was a new trend but one he wholeheartedly approved of.

Tom found Moshe Adler at his booth telling a story to a couple examining the pistols laid out on the table. Moshe knew how to tell some grand tales. Tom had used bits and pieces of them in his own work on occasion.

Moshe was about twenty years older than Tom with thinning white hair. He was also significantly shorter. Even though his old friend had lived in the United States for over thirty years, Tom could still hear his homeland in his voice. An Israeli accent was very distinctive, even when eroded by years living in a new place.

Tom gave his friend a nod and looked over the array of weapons while he waited his turn. There was quite a selection, both semiautomatic and revolver. A few of them looked interesting but nothing Tom wanted to pick up today.

The couple left without committing to anything and Moshe turned toward him with a smile. "You made it! How was traffic?"

Tom grimaced. "Portland traffic is bad at the best of times, but it's truly terrible when I'm driving the Beast. I was able to get up to about fifty miles an hour on the highway with the new tires, but it was slow once I got to town. Very slow. Believe me, I was popular."

Moshe laughed. "I'll bet. Have you already picked up that big purchase of yours?"

Tom shook his head. "No. I just got here. I'll come back around when I'm done loading it."

The older man nodded. "Sure, sure. Are you going to be able to get all that stuff into your truck by yourself? I could help."

"I appreciate the thought, but Randy Caldwell is going to help me."

Moshe nodded again. "Do you really think this North Korean thing is that serious? Your new stuff didn't come cheap."

Tom smiled without humor. "That depends. Do you really think North Korea and Iran need their own constellation of GPS satellites, or whatever they call them?"

The other man sighed. "I suppose not. You think they have nuclear weapons up there?"

"It's hard to imagine anything else. I know a guy in Washington, DC, that works in intelligence. The government is sure the North Koreans are putting up a mix of spy satellites and EMP devices. Probably to use as a threat rather than a preemptive strike, but you never know.

"Anyway, I'm hoping for the best and planning for the worst. If things turn ugly, you grab Rachel and head out to my place. You'll be safe there."

Moshe's daughter was a recent immigrant from Israel. Tom didn't know her that well, but he'd like to change that. She was both beautiful and tough. And far out of his league.

"We appreciate it," the older man said solemnly. "I hope we never need to, but I've read a few of your books. Scary stuff. How's the new one coming?"

"Pretty good. I figure I'll be done with the first draft in another week. I'll publish it in a month or two."

"Already? You just got finished publishing one. What is that? Seven this year?"

Tom shook his head with a grin. "Nine. I have a different one that'll be ready to go out next week. I'm on course to get a dozen published this year."

"I don't see how you can write that fast," the old man complained. "I can barely *read* a book a month."

"Slower doesn't mean better, Moshe. As an indie author and publisher, speed is my friend. I can write just as well without going through half a dozen revisions. Hell, that kind of stuff strips the author's voice right out of the story. I wish more people understood that."

Moshe shook his head. "If you say so. You go take care of your business, and I'll be right here when you get back. Oh, and I have a surprise for you. You'll like it, so don't sneak off."

"Why does that fill me with dread?" Tom asked his friend wryly. "This shouldn't take more than an hour. Don't do anything crazy while I'm gone."

"I'm an old man," Moshe called after him. "I'll take any crazy I can get."

Tom laughed and walked away.

Moshe was right about one thing. He was a lucky man to be able to make a living writing and publishing books. Not only did that allow him to set his own schedule, it gave him the freedom to do what he loved. In this case, that meant telling stories set in science-fiction universes and postapocalyptic fiction.

Not exactly the career field his late father had encouraged him to pursue but a surprisingly lucrative one nevertheless.

Tom found Randy Caldwell set up in a large booth at the rear of the Expo Center. That made sense. Solar panels took up a lot of space.

Caldwell was a slender and somewhat geeky young man. What else did one expect of an MIT graduate?

Tom raised his hand in greeting. "Randy."

The young engineer smiled. "Tom, it's good to see you. I have everything out back in a rental truck. I'll leave Jenna here to run the booth while we get it moved. Did you bring a big vehicle? The panels and supports are relatively large, and you ordered a lot of batteries."

He grinned at the engineer. "I wouldn't worry about that. You'll see."

The two of them made their way out to the parking lot. Caldwell laughed when he saw the Beast. "Oh yeah. You're not going to have any trouble moving this load. Christ, how much can that damn thing carry?"

"More than I can legally drive," Tom said. "It's rated up to ten thousand pounds of cargo on pavement and five thousand off road. Add in the trailer and I could conceivably move almost sixteen thousand pounds. I'd need a commercial license to fill it up."

"Wow. I never expected to see something like this up close. Okay, so what are you thinking? Solar panels in the vehicle and batteries in the trailer? How big is the truck bed?"

"Sixteen feet deep by eight across. The trailer can hold a bit more than nine feet depth-wise and almost seven across.

"If you'll bring your truck over, we'll get everything loaded. I'll drop the tarps to keep everything out of sight when we're done. I still have a few things to pick up inside, and I'd rather not have anyone try to abscond with all these solar panels."

The engineer raised an eyebrow. "Abscond? Those ruffians. Your writer is showing."

Tom laughed. "I can't help myself."

It took the two of them longer than Tom had expected to move all of the solar panels, struts, electric motors, and batteries from the engineer's truck into the Beast.

Once they finished, the young man used a handkerchief to wipe his brow. "That's a lot of solar capacity. You must have quite the house, particularly on the coast. It's usually pretty overcast there, isn't it?"

"There are plenty of clear days, but then you get dreary ones, too. Add in the occasional storm with hundred-mile-an-hour straight-line winds for a change of pace and you have the Oregon coast."

"Like the storm blowing in now?"

The other man meant the remnants of a typhoon that were going to hit Oregon or Washington State sometime in the next couple of days. It promised a lot of rain and some damaging winds.

If it actually hit the Oregon coast, it would be epic. Tom wanted to be home by then so he could button everything up tight.

Tom nodded. "Exactly like that. It's the price I pay for living in such a beautiful area. Don't worry about it, though. All the weak limbs and trees are already gone. I've got a protected location to install these. They'll be well shielded from the winds."

The other man shook his head. "Suit yourself. I'm a lot happier in Nevada where the sun is always shining."

"That's something of an understatement. I'll take the cooler weather, thanks."

Randy laughed. "Let me get the printed materials for you. The instructions are straightforward, and you shouldn't have any trouble getting everything set up. The sensors and motors will work together to track the sun as it moves, generating the maximum power. Even on overcast days, you'll still get some energy.

"With all those batteries, you won't have any trouble maintaining power for three or four days during bad weather. Longer if you shut down as much as you can. Hell, on the good days, you'll be selling energy back to the grid. You might even pay this all off in a decade or so."

Enough solar panels to power his house completely and charge far more batteries than he actually needed had cost him just over $40,000. Hype aside, he wouldn't be paying that back anytime soon.

Used in conjunction with the whole-house propane generator he'd picked up last year, this should keep the lights on for a very long time if the grid went down.

He needed to bite the bullet and finish filling the large propane tank he'd bought from a commercial company that had gone bankrupt over the summer. It could hold sixty-five hundred gallons, but he'd only bought fifteen hundred.

Propane wasn't cheap enough for him to do it all at once. Added to the five hundred-gallon tank he already had, he'd thought he had enough. That had been before the North Koreans and their antics. One more thing to take care of after he got home.

He'd dipped deeply into his inheritance with all these purchases, but in times like these, he considered it money well spent.

Honestly, the solar panels were more disaster preparedness than prepping. He might write about the end of the world as we know it—or TEOTWAWKI—but he was more concerned that the West Coast was overdue for a devastating earthquake.

It might happen next year, next decade, or long after he was dead. No one knew.

When it did, it was going to cut the Oregon coast off from the rest of the state. The roads that went over the mountains would become impassable, and the electric grid would vanish.

Odds were good that it would take years to restore access after it finally happened. They'd need to bring relief supplies in on the ocean side.

Tom knew the solar panels were an extravagance, but he wasn't a survivalist. He was a gearhead who liked to write about the end of the world. He didn't have anything close to the skills he often wrote about. If the world ended, only the equipment he'd collected would set him apart from the rest of the doomed population.

He looked up at the clear sky. The sun was shining and the birds were chirping. The end of the world seemed so unlikely. He prayed it stayed that way.

Well, if he wasn't on the road before evening rush hour, he wouldn't get home until long after midnight. He dropped the canvas top to hide his haul and headed back inside to see what kind of surprise Moshe had for him.

2

One of the women smoking on the loading dock called out to Tom as he went back inside.

"That sure is a lot of solar panels. Are you worried about them North Koreans? You need to come by my booth. I can fix you right up."

He gave the woman a polite smile. "I might just do that. You can never be too prepared."

She laughed. "From the looks of it, you can afford me. I've got the best stuff you'll find at this crappy show. Lots better than these other losers."

There wasn't a polite way to respond, so Tom inclined his head and walked past her into the Expo Center.

One of the men coming in behind Tom shook his head. "She's such a bitch. She makes the circuit fleecing people just trying to stock up and prepare for emergencies. She loves to talk trash about everyone else, too."

"Thanks for the warning."

Tom filed that information away and headed for Moshe's booth.

For once, the older man didn't have any customers demanding his attention. He gestured for Tom to come behind the table. "I've been keeping my eye out for something special that I know you want. When I saw this pop up, I had to snag it. You're going to love it."

Tom recognized the pistol case as the man took it out of one of the storage boxes. The big Glock logo made sure of that.

"I don't know. My collection of Glocks is pretty complete."

The old man smiled. "Don't I know it? I figure you must've bought most of them from me. No, this is something special. Just take a look and tell me you're not in love."

He took the case from his friend and flipped the hinged lid open. Nestled in the foam was a Glock, the model number prominently displayed on the long slide: 17L. Based on the packing, it was a new gun, not a used one.

Tom grinned. "You *do* know me. I'll take it."

The older man nodded. "I figured. I ran your background check with the information I have on file. I knew you wouldn't mind. And trust me, I'm only adding a modest markup for my trouble."

Tom laughed. "For something like this, you can take a little extra."

"Now who knows who?" the old man asked slyly. "You're not usually one to complain about price. Not with something you really want."

Moshe was right. Tom had been on the market for a brand new 17L for a while. The company only occasionally had limited production runs for this model, and he didn't want a used one.

Basically, it was their full-sized nine-millimeter pistol with about an inch and a half added to the slide and barrel, though the top of the slide had part cut out to save weight.

It had a few other tweaks, but that was the most significant change. That supposedly gave the pistol an impressive sight radius, and the added weight of the slide made for fast follow-up shots. The biggest draw was the fact he didn't own one.

He traded Moshe his bank card for the paperwork and quickly filled in the remaining blank spaces. A few minutes later, the pistol was his.

"Now if you could only get my other gun out of NFA jail," Tom said. "It seems like the government is taking longer and longer to process the paperwork for my toys."

The National Firearms Act made it a huge pain in the butt to buy automatic weapons, suppressors, or short-barreled rifles. Not only did the prospective purchaser have to pay a $200 fee for a tax stamp, they had to wait for the government to go through a yearlong approval process.

Every time he found something interesting, he'd arrange the purchase through Moshe and then wait on the government. When he added in the restrictions imposed by the Hughes Amendment—that restricted the purchase of automatic weapons to those manufactured before 1986—it was maddening.

The Sheriff had come to visit Tom a few times. Tom showed him around and let him look at all the tax stamps for his NFA items. The man hadn't been very happy, but everything was legal.

Moshe smiled at him. "I'm expecting the approval any day now. Maybe in time for Christmas. Wouldn't that be a heck of a gift? You should stop by the shop and visit."

Tom raised an eyebrow. "Are we talking about my gun or your daughter?"

The older man made a waggling gesture with his hand. "A little bit of both. It wouldn't break an old man's heart if you and Rachel got to know one another a little better."

"That seems like a little bit of wishful thinking. Your daughter doesn't know me. Besides, I'm sure she has a nice boy in her life already."

Moshe grunted. "You'd think so, wouldn't you? Doesn't she know I need grandchildren? Kids these days. So thoughtless. No respect for their elders.

"I don't like to say bad things about my own flesh and blood, but Rachel can be a little… blunt. I think she discourages any interest by being abrasive. But trust me, underneath all that, she's a good girl."

"And just how happy would she be to know that you're trying to set her up?"

Moshe leaned forward and whispered conspiratorially. "Why don't we just keep that between the two of us?"

Tom laughed. "Speaking of abrasive, I ran into this woman out back. Short, kind of overweight, with a bad attitude."

The older man rose up on his tiptoes and stared out over the crowd. "Is that her in the next aisle?"

Tom followed his gaze and saw the woman. "That's her. Her reputation must be pretty extreme if you knew who I was talking about based on just that. Does she have a name?"

"Here name is Debra Freeman and you have no idea. Her husband was a saint. He started their business fifteen years ago. She did nothing but harp and talk down to people. He spent half his time apologizing for her behavior.

"Now that he's gone, I can't imagine how she stays in business. Believe me, whatever she said to you was nowhere near as rude as she is to everyone else."

"How does she stay in business?"

Moshe shrugged. "God only knows. She has an eye for gear, I'll give her that."

Tom perked up a little at that. He was a gear hound. Oh sure, he'd picked up a few survival skills along the way as he wrote his postapocalyptic fiction, but he didn't have the same drive to really learn it that most folks prepping for trouble had.

He'd pick up interesting gear, test it out, and then put it safely away. Of course, it always found its way into his fiction. Honestly, it was like having his cake and eating it too.

Besides, he could afford the occasional splurge on cool equipment. Hell, that was what made life worth living.

"I might just have to check her out."

"Haggle," the older man said firmly. "That woman is guilty of usury. Believe me, if anybody knows what that is, it's an old man from Israel."

Tom laughed. "Well, if I get anything from her, I'll make sure and drive a hard bargain. Should I use your name as a reference?"

"Only if you want her to double the price. She doesn't like me any more than I like her."

"Thanks for the warning. Tell you what, let me take a walk around the place and then I'll head over to your gun store. I figure I can visit

Rachel and window shop for a couple of hours. Traffic should be better by then."

"You're making an old man happy. Bless you."

Tom smiled and headed off into the crowd. He'd return before he left to pick up the Glock. He couldn't wait to get home and try it out.

The rest of the vendors had a relatively normal mix of guns and gear. Tom had plenty of the former and a good selection of the latter. Still, if something caught his eye, he'd snag it up.

He picked up a few toys here and there and then made his way to the disagreeable woman's booth. Moshe was right. She had excellent taste in gear, including a couple of pieces that he wouldn't mind adding to his collection.

She had a radio repeater in a backpack for short-range work and a portable high-frequency unit in a case. The latter could connect with operators around the world. Very good equipment, but expensive.

Tom had a full-blown radio at home that he still needed to set up, once he built the large antenna it needed.

He'd downloaded a ton of information covering the various settings to use with the hand-held units in urban Oregon and Washington State, but these more portable versions would make excellent additions to his emergency preparedness gear.

Of course, to use them legally, he needed to get his radio license. That had been on his to-do list for quite some time, but he hadn't gotten around to it.

Unfortunately, she had really marked it up. If he remembered correctly, the suggested retail price for the repeater was around nine hundred bucks. She wanted twelve hundred and change. Considering she probably bought it wholesale, that seemed a bit extreme.

He'd just decided to give her a pass when an alert set his phone off. It only played that tone when he received a message from a select few individuals.

The text was from the guy he knew in the intelligence community. It was short and to the point.

NOAA just announced an incoming coronal mass ejection. Way stronger than the Carrington Event and headed straight for us. We have somewhere between half an hour and an hour.

Oh, shit.

He needed to get some critical supplies for the trip home right now. Thank God he'd already topped off the Beast and always carried spare cans of diesel with him. Otherwise, he'd probably be as screwed as everyone else.

Not that making a trip of over a hundred miles to the coast under these circumstances was going to be easy. He needed to grab anything useful before the lights went out.

Normally, he'd feel bad about what he was about to do, but this had just become a survival situation. Different rules applied.

Tom stepped up and smiled at her. "You weren't kidding when you said you had everything I need. I hope you'll cut me a good deal if I buy a few thousand dollars' worth of stuff. And by a few thousand, I mean more than twenty."

"That's a lot of money," she asked suspiciously. "How do I know you're not ripping me off?"

"You know Moshe Adler?"

She nodded. "Yeah. Stuffy bastard."

Tom turned and shouted over the crowd. "Moshe!"

When his friend turned toward them, he continued. "I'm about to spend twenty grand. Am I good for it?"

Moshe flashed them a thumbs-up. "He's good for it."

She flashed her yellowed teeth at Tom. "He'd never lie about something like that. You pick whatever you like and I'll give you a real special price."

"If you don't mind, I'm going to start pointing things out and let you tally them up. My schedule is incredibly tight. I have to be gone in half an hour."

Her smile got wider when he opened his wallet and pulled out his platinum card. "We'll have you out of here in twenty minutes."

"That would be awesome. I'll start with the radios. Both the high-frequency kit and the repeater pack. I know it comes with four handsets, but I'll take the deluxe version I see there with two radios and all four single units. That should be ten hand-held radios.

"I want every extra battery pack you have for them, too. In fact,

I'll take every battery you have, period. Next, those night-vision goggles. All six sets.

"Then those water containers and every bit of freeze-dried food you've got. Toss in the MREs and the energy bars. I don't need the ball ammo, but I'll take all the self-protection hollow points you have there in 9mm, .40 S&W, and .45 ACP, and 10mm, too, if you have any."

He went down her table selecting anything that looked like it might be useful. He almost passed on a set of handcrafted knives with a machete, but it was just so damned beautiful. He had a bunch of this kind of stuff at home already, but he wouldn't be getting any replacements for a while.

There was a good chance the CME—the coronal mass ejection—would wreak havoc on radio communication, probably adding a lot of noise and significantly reducing the transmission range. That should only last a few days, but the effect was inconvenient.

Tom reassessed what she had available and pulled out his other card. He'd max them both out and get everything he could. The Beast could easily haul it home. He'd hit the ATM while she gathered it up and withdraw some cash. He already had some in the Beast, but he could always use more. Plastic was probably about to become useless.

With the ATM withdrawal limits, he should use what he had in his bank account, too. This was now a case of use it or lose it. Thankfully, he could use his phone to move money from his savings account to his checking.

Once he reached his limit, he'd have to play hardball and demand some extra stuff to balance out her prices. He should be able to shave some off the bill. Everything he got might mean the difference between life and death in the next few weeks or months.

With the available balances on his two credit cards and his savings, he had almost thirty thousand dollars available. If the world didn't come crashing down, he was going to feel the burn. He'd be writing for a decade to pay off the new debt.

It took twenty long, agonizing minutes for him to select everything. The exuberant woman quoted him a price. He countered for a steep discount, truthfully pointing out how much he was spending.

Five minutes of haggling got him an acceptable concession. He used it to get more supplies. He didn't argue over the prices of the new items. Time was running out.

Tom handed her his cards and held his breath. The first charge went through, but the second had a problem.

She scowled at him. "Declined."

3

T om had expected some trouble. After all, he had fraud protection.

He checked his email and found a notice from the credit card company. He followed the link and declared he was making the purchase.

"Try it again."

This time it went through. The card to his checking account also sent a popup to his phone asking if he was making the charge. He approved it as well.

The massive purchase was complete. He was broke, but now he had a chance. He'd only left enough in the account to withdraw money at the ATM inside the Expo Center.

Needless to say, she was quite pleased with her haul, even after the discount that Tom had leveraged. Some of those additional items might only be marginally useful, but they'd make decent trade goods if things went that far south.

People would still accept cash for a little while, but that would stop when the depth of the catastrophe settled in. Money had the "full faith and credit of the United States of America" backing it. If that vanished, so would everything it propped up, like money and the rule of law.

Tom felt guilty about taking advantage of her, but with his life on the line, and possibly those of his friends, he'd do what he had to do. With survival on the line, that limited the ethics and morals he could allow himself to have.

In any case, he was taking the news from his friend in Washington, DC, at face value. If the disaster didn't happen, she would make a *lot* of money.

While she gathered Tom's purchases, he rushed over to the ATM and stood impatiently in line. He could feel the clock ticking down. When his turn came, he withdrew the maximum amount his bank allowed. His relief when it dispensed the bills was profound. He was officially broke.

Since he was at the back of the Expo Center, he headed toward Randy Caldwell's booth again. The couple was a long way from home. If the grid went down, getting back to Nevada might be impossible.

He brought up the browser on his phone and went to the National Oceanic and Atmospheric Administration website. He'd been checking it regularly as he made his purchases, but nothing had mentioned the supposed CME. Now he found an important notice at the top of the page confirming it was real.

Tom let out a breath he hadn't realized he'd been holding. He hadn't colossally screwed up.

The details of the notice mentioned the strength of the plasma field. It was indeed significantly stronger than the Carrington Event had been. More than double, in fact.

Rather than being a major inconvenience, it was about to screw over the entire world.

Randy looked up from his laptop as Tom stepped up to the table. "Hey, that was quick. Is something wrong?"

Tom nodded grimly. "Read this." He handed the engineer his phone.

After ten seconds, Randy frowned. "I remember reading something about something like this in the 1800s. This is bad, right?"

"It couldn't be worse. You know I write about the end of the world for a living. This is a civilization-ending event.

"It's not the same as the nukes that North Korea has in orbit. It's going to affect the entire planet. The grid is almost certainly going down. Just to be safe, you might want to unplug that laptop."

The engineer speedily did so and shut it down. He called out to his wife to do the same. She looked at him strangely but did so.

"If the grid goes down, that means we lose the ability to refuel," Randy said.

Tom nodded. "Have you gassed up? You need to get moving."

"Yes, but isn't this thing going to affect the cars, too?"

"Not as much as an EMP attack," Tom said. "It's possible that some vehicles will have issues, but no one really knows. With the Carrington Event, they experienced auroras as far south as the Caribbean. This one might reach all the way to the equator. Total coverage.

"Any long conductive surfaces are going to be electrified. Power transmission lines, pipelines, and things we haven't thought of. Things plugged into the grid are probably going to suffer, too.

"You might want to start packing your gear. Once the lights go out, everyone's going to be moving. Traffic is going to be amazingly bad. You'll want to be out of the metro area before then."

The engineer nodded. "Are you going to be able to maneuver that big truck of yours through traffic?"

"I hope so. If nothing else, I'll head to my friend's gun shop. I can stay with them until it gets dark out. Traffic will drop at night, and the authorities might have gotten the disabled cars moved out of the way by then. You might want to do the same. The place is called Adler Arms."

Tom grabbed a pen and jotted directions on the back of a flyer. "It's less than a mile away from here, almost due south. If you stick to the main roads, there might be more lanes for people to get around stalled cars or accidents."

"Do you think there's going to be a lot of those?"

Tom shrugged. "I guess we'll find out. Are you going to go there?"

The younger man glanced at his wife, who was working with the potential customer, and nodded. "Yeah. Better safe than sorry. I'll start getting everything together. Thanks for the warning."

Tom headed back to Moshe's booth, stepped behind the table, and drew the man back a little. "Do you trust me?"

Moshe frowned. "Of course I trust you. Why? Do you need me to front you some cash?"

"Start packing. You're going to want to be ahead of the rush. Trouble is coming."

The older man's eyes narrowed. "You think something's going to happen here? Like a shooting?"

"Something a lot bigger than that. Call Rachel. Tell her that she needs to lock up the shop and get ready to head out of town. I think you might have to come visit me for a while. Time is short. This is going to happen fast, and the phones will probably go down in a few minutes."

Moshe eyed him for a moment and then took out his cell phone. He entered the number, held it to his ear, and watched Tom as he spoke. "Rachel, this is your father. I have it on good authority that the power is going out very soon. Maybe the phones, too. Close up shop and start packing for a trip. Grab the important stuff."

Tom heard her start to argue, but Moshe cut her off. "No time to explain. I'm getting ready to leave now. Look for me in an hour."

The older man disconnected the call. "I'll start packing. You can explain what's going on while you help me."

While his friend opened up carrying cases and brought out dollies, Tom started talking.

"Coronal mass ejections are huge clouds of charged particles that can wreak havoc with the grid and radio communications. We've had a few good ones in the last couple of decades. They caused widespread power outages in Canada and the northeastern United States, but they weren't in the same league as what we have here."

The older man paused to consider him. "What would be?"

"Back in 1859, an intensely powerful CME called the Carrington Event lit up the United States. It was so powerful that it generated a current in the telegraph lines that shocked the operators, started fires, and even allowed them to send messages with their batteries disconnected.

"Back then it was a curiosity. If the telegraph hadn't been in wide use, it wouldn't even have had the limited impact it did.

"In the modern world, another Carrington Event will probably bring down the grid for years. It might very possibly fry a large number of critical transformers that can't be easily or quickly replaced."

Tom paused for a moment to let that sink in before he continued. "The word I saw indicated something a lot more powerful than the Carrington Event. Something the world has never seen before."

Moshe shook his head. "I've read some of your books. Not my preferred reading material, but you talked about this a little. I remember you said that all the critical services in the modern world are interlinked. Without one, the rest will come crashing down. Without power, we lose food delivery, the financial sector, communication, and transportation."

Tom nodded. "It's exactly that bad. You'll have to pack up on your own. I need to grab the stuff I bought. I don't want that woman vanishing when the lights go out. We need those supplies.

"Pack as fast as you can and be sure to try to start your truck before you load it. It's remotely possible that the CME will disable it. Not as likely as with an EMP attack, though.

"If that happens, start loading things into the Beast. It doesn't have any computerized electronics. It'll be a much bigger pain in the ass to drive with all the other possible issues on the road, but we'll make do.

"Also, I invited the guy that built my solar unit to come to your shop. He and his wife are here from Nevada. They're never going to make it home in this nonsense."

The old man shook his head. "I should have read more of your books. Thanks for the warning."

Tom made his way through the oblivious crowd to where she was piling Tom's purchases on a large, flat dolly.

She flashed her yellowed teeth at him. "I figured I'd let you borrow my dolly to get the stuff out to that big old truck of yours. It might take you three or four trips."

"It takes what it takes. Thanks for the loan. I'll run the first load out now and come back in for the rest as quick as I can."

He reached for the dolly handle, but the lights went out before he touched it.

As the crowd began calling out in surprise, he mentally cursed. That had come at least ten minutes earlier than he'd expected. The grid had fared worse than he'd hoped. They should've had more time. The charge should have had to build up before things started going out.

He pulled the small flashlight from his belt and lit up the dolly. Just like his gun, he carried a light with him everywhere he went. Judging by the number of other lights coming on around them, he wasn't alone.

"Well, light or dark, I still need to move this to my truck," Tom said. "I'll be right back."

Word would probably seep out shortly that this was more than a normal blackout. He probably still had enough time to get his purchases loaded and to help Moshe.

One glance to the east convinced him that things were significantly worse than he'd feared. The Expo Center was less than five miles from the Portland International Airport. A significant cloud of black smoke was rising from that direction.

A CME shouldn't have affected airplanes like that. It certainly shouldn't have dropped them out of the sky. That was more like an EMP attack, though most aircraft would still get down safely if that happened. What was going on?

It took him six trips to get all of his purchases out. He worked as fast as he could. Debra Freeman had started packing and wasted no time, bitching that he was taking too long. He promised to speed it up.

He was unloading his last load when Randy Caldwell walked up. "Our car won't start. It looks like it was disabled."

Tom grimaced. "Damn weird. A CME shouldn't damage cars. Or airplanes."

"I'm not sure it was a CME," the engineer said quietly. "I heard a couple of people inside say that their phones died. One of the other vendors lost his computer. It was a laptop on battery power, not even connected to the grid. Honestly, this seems like an EMP event."

That didn't make sense. NOAA didn't make mistakes like that. If they said that a huge cloud of charged plasma was racing towards the earth, that was pretty much what they meant.

Yes, he'd been worrying about those satellites that North Korea had put up. Could the CME have caused one to go off? He had no idea.

If it had—and if the North Koreans had positioned a warhead over the central United States—that was the crappiest luck ever. It also meant that they still had an incoming CME to deal with.

"Forget your car," Tom said. "Move everything into my trailer. I have enough space for it. Only take the important stuff. Leave the tables and other standard items behind. We need to get moving."

He dug out his cell phone. It still indicated he had a connection to the cellular system. That hadn't come down. Yet.

He dialed his friend in Washington, DC. He half expected the call to fail, but it rang on the other end.

"Webster," his friend said.

"That was no CME. We just had an EMP strike in Portland."

"Here in DC, too. Probably the same high-altitude detonation. The North Koreans set off something right over the center of the country just before NOAA thought the CME would hit. Maybe they were afraid it would fry their little toy and decided to set it off early."

That was really adding insult to injury. Piling one disaster on top of another.

"I'm stuck in Portland," Tom said, "but I've got the Beast with me. I'm about to grab a few friends and head back to the coast. You probably need to find shelter. Have you got my satellite number?"

"I've got it," Webster said. "No telling what condition the satellites are in, though. A lot of them are hardened, but some aren't."

"If it took out the one providing my service, it probably took out most of the satellite coverage in the US. I haven't tried the phone yet, but I know that my network also has a satellite over Alaska. The

Pacific Northwest is right at the fringes of its coverage area. I'll try giving you a call on it a little later."

"Let me give you a secure number. It's on a hardened network, so it should stay up even if the normal telecommunications system goes down."

Tom grabbed a pen and jotted the number down. "Thanks for the heads up. You might just have saved my life."

"Call it enlightened self-interest. I might have to fly up there to ride out the apocalypse."

Tom laughed. "Good luck finding a flight. I hope to God you have a cabin out in the middle of nowhere."

"I've got a place. No idea if I'll get there. Thankfully, my department has a hardened bunker. We can ride this out.

"Do yourself a favor while you have a connection. Download all the offline data for the roads in the Pacific Northwest. You probably have paper, but it might come in handy."

Tom nodded. "Good idea. I also have a GPS with all that data, but you can never have too many options."

He hung up and started his phone's mapping app to downloading the offline data for Oregon and Washington State. Better safe than sorry.

Then he dug out his sat phone. It connected, but its signal was substantially weaker than he'd expected. The normal satellite must be out.

Rather than try his friend now, he decided to wait until after the CME had struck. He needed to know if he was going to have the ability to communicate after the other shoe had dropped.

Tom headed back toward the Expo Center and saw Moshe loading his truck. The crew cab was running, so the EMP hadn't taken every vehicle out. That was good news.

He walked over and helped him move the heavy boxes into the back of the vehicle.

"The truck started, but there's something funky going on," the older man said. "Some of the gauges aren't working."

"Things got more complicated," Tom said. "I'm done with my

stuff, so I'll come help you get the last of yours. We need to get a move on.

"There'll be a run on stores. I want to stop at one of the big ones and grab a bunch of food and water. Probably some other things that'll come in handy, too. Toilet paper, first aid supplies, and that kind of thing.

"Hell, we're going to snag every bit of toothpaste, shampoo, soap, and other hygiene stuff that we can. If this goes on long enough, bad hygiene is going to be what kills people."

Moshe nodded. "I read about that in some of the history books. Sickness killed more people during the Civil War than fighting. Good idea on the toothpaste. I suspect dentists are going to be hard to find for a while. If one of your teeth goes bad, it's going to be whiskey and a pair of pliers."

Tom shuddered. "Dental floss just moved up the list. I don't suppose you know any doctors or pharmacists. Getting our hands on some antibiotics and medical knowledge would be a really good thing."

"There's a clinic in my neighborhood," his friend said. "I can't guarantee anything, but the lady that runs it might be able to help us."

"Then we'd better get the rest of your stuff loaded and get on the road. Once it gets dark, I wouldn't be at all surprised to see rioting and looting. People go crazy when the lights go out."

He returned Debra Freeman's cart and helped his friend move the last of his inventory to his truck. Randy and Jenna Caldwell helped with the last load.

The crowd was getting antsy and streaming out. Other vendors had decided to pack it in, too. From what Tom knew, they wouldn't know that the CME had struck until dark. The lights of the aurora weren't strong enough.

That would change when the sun set.

During the Carrington Event, people had been able to read newspapers at night by the light of the aurora. He imagined this one was going to be even brighter.

He dialed Webster's number on his satellite phone. It took so long to connect that Tom feared his satellite connection had dropped, but it finally rang.

Webster picked up almost immediately. "Morgan. I'm glad your satellite phone is working, buddy. Unfortunately, I have more bad news for you. Listen up.

"That little shit in North Korea set off EMP bombs over Europe, Russia, the Middle East, China, and South America, too. They tell me that the dick hit just about every industrialized nation hard. Now the CME is causing even more disruption. Civilization is going down, buddy."

"Tell me something I don't know."

"The president decided that North Korea wasn't going to enjoy winning. He pushed the button."

Tom's heart flew into his throat. "Oh shit."

"Ain't that the truth? An Ohio-class sub off the North Korean coast just punched his ticket. Unfortunately, with all the damage to the satellites, ground radar sites, and communications networks, we think the Chinese just launched a retaliatory strike against us.

"Maybe they thought we were going to hit them. Who knows? That means we're probably going to launch at them. My gut tells me that Russia will jump in, too."

Tom tried to wrap his mind around this news. Was Portland a strategic target? Seattle? Northern California? Was it safe here? If it wasn't, could he do anything about it?

"I'm going to have to run for the bunker," Webster continued. "There's no way I can get out of DC now. I'll just have to hope the planners really did build it strong enough to survive a nuclear blast or two."

Tom started to say something, but Webster cut him off.

"Hang on. I'm getting some fresh information. Shit. It looks like Russia *is* getting in on the fun. This is turning into a general exchange. I'd guess we have a little less than thirty minutes before the bombs start landing. Get to somewhere safe and hunker down. I'll be thinking about you, buddy."

"Good luck, Webster. Call me when this is all over."

Tom disconnected the call and looked at the people gathered

around him. They'd overheard enough to know that the shit was hitting the fan.

"We need to get to the gun shop. Moshe, lead the way. I'll be right on your tail. We're on a tight deadline."

His plan ran into a roadblock almost immediately. A literal one.

A small group of cars and trucks had bunched up around the exit to the Expo Center parking lot. It looked as though they were having difficulty getting out. And if they were having trouble, he'd never even get to the gate in the Beast.

4

R andy and Jenna Caldwell were wedged into the Beast's cab with him, so he put the big vehicle in neutral and set the brake. "I'll be right back."

Tom climbed down and walked between the cars. Irritated drivers honked their horns impatiently. He felt like asking how that was working out for them.

When he arrived at the gate, he saw the problem. A cement mixer had stalled right in front of the gate. There wasn't enough room for anyone to get around him.

A small horde of irritated men and women were bitching at the driver. The bedraggled man was trying to explain that he couldn't do anything, but of course, that wasn't good enough.

Tom wedged his way through the crowd until he was near the driver. He shouted to be heard above all the other angry voices. "I might be able to fix this problem. Pipe down."

Maybe a third of the people closed their mouths, but at least the driver was looking in his direction.

"Is this thing loaded?" Tom asked.

The man shook his head. "No. I was on my way to pick up

another load when it died. I can't get it to start. I tried calling a tow truck, but the circuits are all busy."

Tom held his arms up. "Everyone. Everyone! I can get him out of our way, but you're going to have to do exactly what I say. I need you to go back to your vehicles and clear a path so I can get up here."

He pointed at the driver. "You. Get inside and put the mixer in neutral. Steer it a little to the left as I push. You can straighten it out and get off to the side of the road once I get you moving."

The man shook his head. "Dude, you ain't gonna get this truck moving. Do you know how much it weighs?"

Tom smiled. "Just do it. Everyone else, get moving."

He wasn't going to explain why they had to hurry because that would only slow things down. He was counting on their desire to leave to get them in motion.

Once he got back to the Beast, he climbed inside and revved the engine a little. The rearmost of the vehicles began backing up to allow others to extract themselves from the pack around the gate. It took about five minutes to clear an opening wide enough for him to move forward.

Tom put the Beast in low and edged it forward in first gear. With the spout sticking out of the back of the cement mixer, he could only come in at an angle.

Very slowly, he brought the vehicles into contact. Once he was sure he wasn't going to ram the mixer, he gave the Beast a little more gas. Just enough to give the mixer some movement.

He could hear the groan of metal, so something was giving. It wasn't going to be the Beast. His bumper could take it.

The mixer began drifting forward and slowly picked up speed as Tom accelerated gently. Once the other vehicle had some momentum, Tom tapped his brakes to disengage them. The mixer rolled forward a few dozen feet, and the driver managed to get it to the side of the road.

There was enough room, so Tom brought the Beast around and waved at the other driver as he passed. The man wasn't going to be pleased when he saw the damage to the cement mixer, but he'd have bigger problems soon enough.

A glance in the rearview mirror showed Moshe right behind him.

There were more stalled vehicles scattered on the road, but it looked like there was enough of a gap to get around them. At least traffic wasn't ground to a complete standstill.

The government had done EMP testing a number of years ago. Not very realistically, in Tom's opinion, but it was better than nothing. They took a few dozen vehicles and began setting off small EMP blasts to see what happened. They kept raising the power until a single car failed.

From that data, they extrapolated that an EMP blast would disable around ten percent of vehicles, while sixty to seventy percent would experience some form of glitch but would still be drivable. From their experiments, many of the glitches went away if you turned the car off and turned it back on again.

A few particularly tough issues required disconnecting the battery and letting the system reset. Worst case, some of those glitches never went away.

Judging from the number of cars stalled in front of him, their estimates had been more than a bit low. Based on what he remembered of the traffic, fifteen to twenty percent of the cars driving at the time of the EMP blast had stopped. They were lucky today hadn't been a workday.

Their luck continued when there were no accidents ahead of them. He only had to use the Beast's bumper to move one other vehicle out of the way. If his insurance company survived the apocalypse, they weren't going to be happy with him.

The other driver certainly wouldn't be. There had been no one around, and the vehicle had been in park. Tom had simply pushed it out of the way, the other vehicle's tires leaving rubber as it skidded across the asphalt.

Once they got into the clear, Moshe pulled out in front of him. By weaving between stalled vehicles, they were able to pick up speed and pulled in to the strip mall where Moshe had his shop a short time later.

They'd gone south from the Expo Center, and Moshe's shop was on the other side of I-5. That was the biggest delay, getting through the underpass. Thankfully, someone had pushed the stalled cars clear, and traffic was slowly creeping along.

From down below, it looked like the main lanes were a parking lot. He made a mental note that taking I-5 out of Portland wasn't going to work. He'd need another route.

He followed Moshe around to the back of the building and pulled into the loading area. The buildings on either side came back far enough to provide some shielding.

A nuke over Portland would screw them, but a near miss might be survivable. Or one that hit the other side of the city.

He jumped out of the Beast and climbed into the back. He'd put the water containers he'd bought in last so he could get them back out easily. The water supply would still be working off gravity for a little while. They needed to fill these up while they could.

Randy and Jenna Caldwell took them as he handed them down. Moshe joined in, and they quickly had the dozen 3.5-gallon cubes unloaded.

A person needed at least a gallon of water a day to survive. This would give the five of them eight days of water. More if they could find some bottled water at the store. Less if they had to take any more people with them.

Moshe used his key to unlock the rear door of the shop. "I tried the car radio on the way over. I've never heard such terrible static and wailing."

"It's all the charged particles," Tom said. "Radio reception is going to suck for a while."

Rachel was waiting inside. The tall woman didn't look pleased.

"What is going on, Poppa? What kind of trouble is coming? How did you know it was coming?"

Her first language—Hebrew—dominated her accent more than it did her father's, but Rachel's grasp of English was great. She didn't use many contractions yet, but Tom knew that would change with time.

Moshe held up a hand. "We don't have time to discuss this. Just accept that I'm telling you the truth. The North Koreans set off a bomb in orbit. The electrical grid is down. We need to get out of Portland."

"The situation is worse than that," Tom said. "My contact in DC said that nuclear missiles have been launched. There's a possibility that Portland is a target."

Everyone stared at him in horror.

"Is this some kind of sick joke?" Rachel asked.

"I wish it were," he said. "The roads are filled with cars killed by the EMP. It happened just like my friend in Washington said. Since he was right about that, I'd recommend taking his warning seriously. We probably have less than ten minutes under a worst-case scenario."

Tom held up the three water containers he was carrying. "We need to fill these up while there's still water pressure. If you have something that can carry water, fill that up, too. Gather any bottled water or soft drinks that you have in your machine. Snacks, too. We'll need to take it all with us."

Rachel gave him a steady look and then turned to her father. "What is the plan?"

Moshe gestured toward Tom with one hand. "We do what he says. How many of the boys are still here?"

"I locked up the shop after the power went out. The way you were talking, I figured it was okay to let those who wanted to go home leave. Only Greg is still here."

The older man nodded. "Well, if I only had one person to choose from, Greg would be it. He doesn't have any family in the area, and he has some skills that might be very useful in a situation like this. I'll go talk to him.

"Tom says we're going to need to pick up a lot of things from the store. You go with him. Take the cash from the safe. All of it. Buy everything he says.

"We'll also have to make a stop by the clinic on the way out of town to see if Doctor Emery can lend us a hand with some antibiotics or other medical supplies. Maybe she'll come with us. Who knows?"

The older man hurried to the back of the gun shop.

Rachel eyed Tom somewhat suspiciously. "I have never known you to play games, so I suppose I must take you seriously. If there is really going to be a run on the stores, we need to go now.

"If a nuke goes off over our heads, we die. We need to prepare for the more likely problems we are going to encounter. I have bought some of your books. Grim reading. Is it truly going to be that bad?"

Tom shrugged. "You know what they say. Hope for the best and plan for the worst."

"They say something like that in the Israeli Defense Forces, too. Just not the hope part. There is a box store right next to us. They will have many things we can use. With the power out, it will need to be a cash transaction. If they are even still open. Grab your friends and let us get what we can."

Before he could move, she held up a hand and fixed him with a cool stare. "If you are wrong about this, you will owe me. Poppa would never make you repay it. I am not Poppa."

He couldn't help but smile at that. "If I'm wrong, I'll happily pay you back every cent and make you a character in a book, too. Only I'm not wrong."

She ducked into the office and returned with a metal box a moment later.

Tom gestured for the Caldwells to join them, and they made their way out through the front of the store. Rachel had closed a metal screen when she'd locked up earlier. It took her a moment to unlock it, slide it up far enough for them all to exit the building, and close it back up when they were out.

"When trouble comes knocking, some people think they can cause trouble," she said. "Not today."

It looked as though the box store was still open. At least people were going in and out. Of those coming out, a few had baskets full of stuff. It looked as if they were still accepting cash. He had no idea how they managed to tally up the amounts due.

Out of the corner of his eye, he saw something ominous. Low in the distance, the clouds glowed to the north. It wasn't a bright flash, but considering the distance between Portland and Seattle, he really didn't expect one.

Rachel stared at the sky. "Oh my God. Is that Seattle?"

"Probably. We should get inside and away from the windows. Keep your eyes on the ground until we're inside. Don't look at the windows. If you see a flash of light, throw yourself on the ground. Stay away from anything that'll hurt if it falls on you. Hurry."

5

A young woman with short green hair stood inside the entrance to the dark and gloomy cave that was normally a well-lit store. Beside her was a small table with clipboards and flashlights.

She smiled at them. "Sorry folks. With the power out, we're only accepting cash."

Tom nodded. "That's fine."

The woman handed him a clipboard and a flashlight. "Write down what you're grabbing, followed by how many and the price per item. We're kind of going on the honor system, but our checkers know our prices pretty well, so don't be that way."

"We'll be scrupulously honest. We'll all need clipboards and flashlights. We're going to be getting quite a bit of stuff."

"Also, I think you should move further into the store. If something happens, you don't want to catch a face full of glass."

She frowned at him. "You think it's that thing about the North Koreans? You really think they're gonna nuke us?" She looked skeptical.

Tom shrugged. "We passed a lot of disabled cars. I think they might already have used an EMP weapon. And there was a flash from up north just a minute ago. If that was really a nuke hitting Seattle, the shock wave will get here just after the sound of the explosion. Maybe ten minutes from now."

The woman shook her head. "I think you're taking this a little too far. It's just a power outage."

He smiled and nodded. "You're probably right. Still, you might want to move a little bit further inside and maybe not faced directly towards the glass."

The rest of them had grabbed clipboards, flashlights, and carts. He got his and led them deeper into the store.

"We're going to be filling more than one cart apiece," he said briskly. "Rachel, how much money do we have to spend?"

She opened the box she'd retrieved before they'd left the gun shop. "More than enough. We will have plenty left over in case we need to spend some on the road."

"Okay. I'm going to the pharmacy. I won't be able to get any prescription meds, but there are plenty of nonprescription things we could use. Rachel, grab a lot of water. I'm talking several carts full. As much as we can take. Water is life.

"Also get every bit of powdered drink you can. Tang, Gatorade, High-C, hot cocoa mix, whatever. Get it all. Everything except the cocoa will give us electrolytes and potassium, and all of them will make recovered water taste a lot better."

"And chocolate," she said firmly. "I am not going through the end of the world without chocolate. I need a reason to live."

He turned to Randy. "Paper goods. Toilet paper is going to be worth its weight in gold. Unless you want to wipe your butt with leaves tomorrow, stock up. Again, fill up as many carts as you can move."

"What about me?" Jenna asked.

"Canned meats, soups, and other food supplies that we can eat on the road. Get stuff that doesn't require refrigeration. Stuff we can heat up over a fire."

Jenna nodded. "Since you're going to the pharmacy, get every feminine hygiene product they have. I'm not kidding. Grab it all. You have no idea."

As a man, that need hadn't even occurred to him.

"Got it. Work fast, everyone. We want to have everything back to the gun shop before people converge on this place. Or, God forbid, a nuke goes off. If we have time, we'll come back for a second load, but shop as if this is going to be the only chance you get.

"If you see something that isn't on the list that I gave you, but it makes sense, grab it. Also, remember this mantra: two is one and one is none. Get spares in case we lose some. Also, whoever sees them first, clear out the batteries. Take all of them. Use as many carts as you need for this stuff. Cash will be worthless in a day or two."

They split up and headed for their assigned portions of the store. He couldn't help but see all the other people crowding the aisles. Most seemed haunted and looked as though they were barely suppressing their panic. He feared most of them would be dead in a few weeks.

He noted that someone had locked the pharmacy up tight. The metal screen was down, and he didn't see anyone inside. There were a couple of loose carts in the area, so he herded them together and started filling them.

When he grabbed something he wanted off the shelf, he emptied that item into a basket quickly. He wrote down what the item was, the number he'd taken, and the price. He made certain that it was neat and legible. He didn't want to slow the checkout process down.

Since Jenna had mentioned it, he went to the feminine hygiene section early. He'd never bought pads or tampons before, so he just grabbed everything. There were also some medications for various feminine ailments, so he stocked up on those, too.

Next were the pain meds. Tylenol, ibuprofen, and everything else. Box after box went into a cart. He was certain he'd get crap for it, but he grabbed all the Midol and everything that looked like it. Anything he could do to make that time of the month a little easier for the ladies would pay big dividends.

The supplements aisle yielded tons of multivitamins. Most people didn't think about how their diet was going to change in a disaster situation. If they didn't get the right supplements, it would hurt them in the long haul.

He grabbed all the vitamin C, too. Scurvy would be bad. He grabbed everything that made sense.

It didn't take him long to fill up the carts he had with him. Getting them back to the front was a challenge.

The other three were there already. It looked as though they'd found a few extra carts as well. Randy had found a pallet jack and stacked the sturdy wooden platform with toilet paper and other paper goods. He obviously didn't want to be using leaves to wipe his butt anytime soon.

Rachel had swapped her cart for a flatbed version and stacked it high with water bottles, jugs, and boxes of everything under the sun. He made a mental note to do the same if they got back for another run at the supplies.

Looking at the sheer amount of stuff they were getting, he felt a stab of guilt. What they took would not be there for someone else. People would die because they didn't have food or water.

Yet he knew those people would most likely die anyway. It might look like a lot, but all these things would have been gone by tonight. He had to think of his people first. He couldn't save society. It was already too late for that.

He hadn't heard anything inside the store, but something must've happened outside. The checkers and everyone else were staring out the front glass, and he could see other people looking to the north. Some were also staring straight up at the sky above them.

The shock wave must've arrived. Now their time was really short. People would be dazed for a little while, and then they'd panic. At least no one had nuked Portland. Yet.

Jenna Caldwell was furiously scribbling on one of the clipboards. He glanced over her shoulder and saw that she was making a list of things that might prove useful. She was already thinking ahead to a second trip.

He nodded approvingly. Hopefully they had time to make it happen.

Her husband was tallying up the amounts. The woman with the green hair was nowhere in sight, but one of the cashiers was staring at all the carts with wide eyes and an open mouth.

Tom handed his carts off to Rachel. He left his paper sitting on top of one of them, saving a second sheet to write more purchases on. "Where did you find the flatbed?"

"In back with the stock," she said. "There are more there."

He headed into the back at a run. There were several flat carts, but he spotted something better. There was another pallet jack like the one Randy had snagged. Better yet, he spotted a pallet filled with dry cat food in his cats' preferred brand. Thank God.

Not exactly the kind of thing most people thought of as desperately needed during the apocalypse, but those people didn't have cats.

Cats didn't care if the world was ending. If you didn't feed them when they wanted, they'd be certain they were starving. There was no way he was going to fail in his duty to protect those under his care.

He guessed at the number of bags and tried to remember what he'd paid for it at home. That would have to do.

Thankfully, he had plenty of cat litter. It had a ton of potential uses. With this extra food, his cats would be in good shape for years. Hopefully things would have settled down by then, and he could trade for more if he had to.

He got back up front just as Randy was tallying the last clipboard. The man added the stuff from the new pallet and announced a total to the cashier.

Tom winced. That was a lot of money.

Rachel didn't bat an eye. She pulled out bundles of cash from the box and quickly counted out the amount to the stunned cashier.

Herding all the supplies outside proved challenging, but at least they only had to go up the sidewalk. Once he got outside, he saw what had gotten everyone's attention. The northern sky had a monstrous cloud rising from the horizon now.

Over their heads, all the clouds seemed shredded. The shock wave had passed over. He was moderately surprised that none of the big glass windows had broken.

"Back to the gun shop," he said. "We'll put the carts inside, and Rachel can come back to the store with me. You two see about moving everything into the Beast. Stuff it in as tight as you can. The truck can haul the weight as long as you can make it fit."

Rachel dug under the counter and handed him what looked like a set of earplugs with a curved plastic strip around them. She took one for herself and brought it around the back of her neck. That left the earplugs sitting at the curve of her throat.

"If you think you might have to use your gun, put these in. Your hearing will thank you."

She demonstrated by snagging one in either hand and popping them into her ears. It only took a second. Another second and they were back in their original position, hanging around her neck.

"They have noise-canceling technology built in," she added. "You will be able to hear while you are wearing them."

He nodded. He had earmuffs with similar technology back at the house. On those, he could crank up the volume and hear things that he wouldn't normally pick up yet still block the damaging spike from a gunshot.

Those might prove useful on their trip out. "Do you have any of the bigger ones?"

Rachel nodded. "Let me tell Poppa to pack some."

When she got back, they headed out the door and back toward the box store. Rachel had left the cashbox behind but handed him a wad of bills. She'd stuffed the rest into her jacket. They grabbed both the pallet lifters. If they had only one more load, they wanted to make it a big one.

The crowd in the parking lot had grown. From the way they were streaming into the store, Tom was willing to bet that they wouldn't be paying for whatever they took. The situation was just about out of control.

The green-haired woman was back at her post, trying to turn the crowd around. She kept telling people the store was closed, but they ignored her. The looting had begun.

Tom stepped over to her. "These people are going to get crazy very quickly. If I were you, I'd tell your people to get out now. Have them take whatever supplies they can carry for themselves, especially water and food that doesn't need refrigeration. This is going to get violent quickly."

The woman stared at the people who were already fighting over the food in the produce section. "I think you're right. Thank you." She turned to him and smiled. "Consider this trip on the house. Good luck."

Once she had vanished into the store, Tom looked at Rachel. "Go back and get more water. Also, get as many snack bars as you can, and grab stuff from the candy aisle. We're going to need the calories. Don't take any crap from these people. If they cause trouble, don't be afraid to show them your gun."

The tall woman shook her head. "I do not need to show them my gun. If someone gives me trouble, I will punch them."

He stared at her back as she raced into the store. He'd forgotten for a moment that she had just finished her service with the Israeli Defense Forces. She was probably better prepared for this kind of thing than he was.

Since the looting had started, he decided to head to the pharmacy first. If they hadn't managed to strip the place of drugs yet, he might be able to get some antibiotics. Those might save their lives.

He found a mob scene when he got there. A man was trying to pry open the screen with a crowbar. Judging from his appearance, he wasn't there to get antibiotics.

The situation inside the pharmacy had changed, too. There was a frightened older woman in there begging the man to go away. She wore a white lab coat, so she was either a pharmacist or a tech.

She'd be able to help Tom find what he needed as long as he could keep the looters from hurting her or stealing everything.

Since this might go bad, he put in his hearing protection. Then he stepped off to the side and drew his concealed pistol. He kept it pointed at the floor but was ready if the man caused trouble.

"You with a crowbar! Step away and throw it down. Now!"

The man didn't even glance over at Tom. "Screw you, asshole."

"I've got a gun, and I'll shoot you if you don't step away."

That at least got him to look. His eyes told Tom that he didn't believe Tom was a threat, but at least he stopped trying to pry the pharmacy open.

Instead, he hefted the crowbar like a weapon. "You think you're pretty big and bad with that gun? If you want to keep your head in one piece, you better get going."

The people nearby began backing up. Except for a guy with a tattoo of some kind on his neck. He stepped forward and smiled.

Tom's heart raced. It looked like crowbar man had a partner, and they wanted to dance.

6

The new guy was younger and bigger. He smiled, showing some scraggly yellow teeth. Without even a hint of concern, the guy reached around to the back of his pants and grabbed something.

Tom reacted before he even saw what the guy was reaching for. He brought his gun up and aimed at the guy's chest.

Just as he'd trained, he fired two quick shots. He'd intended to wait and see the results of the shots but quickly fired another two when the man didn't immediately fall down.

The guy squeezed off one shot from the pistol he'd pulled. It went into the floor as he fell over backward.

Adrenaline washed through him. His peripheral vision was gone. He felt clumsy.

He'd almost forgotten about the guy with the crowbar, but he turned to bring him back into view while still keeping an eye on the fallen man.

Crowbar man stared at his friend in shock. Then with a roar, he charged at Tom.

He hadn't taken more than two steps before Tom shot him twice: once in the chest and once in the throat.

The crowbar fell from the man's hand with a clang as he collapsed to the floor.

The people around them had ducked as soon as the shooting started. They now fled, screaming.

Tom stepped over and grabbed the fallen pistol. He didn't want the guy shooting him in the back. One glance told him that he needn't have bothered. The guy was dead. Crowbar man was well on his way to bleeding out, too.

As it looked as though the trouble was over for the moment, he pocketed the dead man's pistol and reholstered his own. His hand shook. He picked up the crowbar, too. It might come in handy.

"Don't hurt me," the woman inside the pharmacy pleaded. "You can take whatever you want. Just let me go."

Tom turned so he could see her while still keeping an eye on the rest of the store. If there were more hostiles, he wanted to know they were coming. The same for the police.

"I'm not going to hurt you," he said. "If you want, you can come out and get the hell out of here before the police show up. I was just looking for antibiotics and stuff like that. Not trying to get high. I can leave money."

She eyed him for a moment. "Why do you need antibiotics?"

Tom smiled sadly. "I don't know if you've figured it out yet, but this is the apocalypse. The North Koreans set off an EMP device, and somebody nuked Seattle. If I don't get supplies like that now, they're going to be impossible to find inside a day. They might just save the lives of my friends and me."

After a moment of obvious indecision, the woman unlocked the door. "Come in."

Before he could move, Rachel came racing up with her gun out. She took in the two bodies at a glance and lowered her weapon.

He expected that to terrify the older woman, but instead she seemed to relax a little.

"Rachel!" the older woman said. "Oh, thank God. Is your father with you?"

The young Israeli woman shook her head. "He is at the gun shop. Are you okay?"

The older woman nodded. "I was just grabbing the insulin before the looters got here. That didn't work out so well. Do you know this young man?"

Rachel inclined her head. "Doctor Annie Emery, meet Tom Morgan. He is one of Poppa's friends. He lives on the coast. We are getting stuff together to go home with him."

Tom frowned. "Doctor Emery? Moshe mentioned a doctor and something about a clinic. He didn't say you were a pharmacist here."

"I'm not. Now get in here before everyone and their third cousins barge in to start looting. We don't have time to chat. Grab all the carts over there. We'll need them."

Doctor Emery locked the door behind him after he pushed all the carts in. She grabbed one and pulled it back to where the drugs were stacked on shelves. She had a large cooler open next to the refrigerator in back and a bag of ice. She'd obviously been loading the refrigerated drugs into it.

"Finish emptying the refrigerated stuff into the cooler, Rachel," the older woman said. "If we take enough ice with us, we might be able to get it to someplace with power."

Tom shook his head. "The grid is down. It's probably not going to come back up. Not for years, at least. You said you were here for insulin. Can you survive without it?"

The woman's expression told him that she couldn't. "Are you sure about the power? It's really important to me."

"I'm pretty sure. Moshe wanted to pick you up and bring you along to my place on the coast. I've got a backup generator there that can keep refrigerated stuff cold and enough fuel to keep us going for a long time if the EMP didn't fry it. You're welcome to join us."

A look of relief spread across her face. "You're a lifesaver. Watch the front while I get the really important stuff to bring along with us. It should only take me about ten minutes."

Tom took a few moments to swap out his half-used magazine for his spare. He'd need to fill that up later, but he didn't want circumstances to force him to reload after only a few shots if more trouble came calling.

Then he pulled out his cell phone and dialed 911. If the police were coming, he wanted to make sure they knew he was a good guy. The call failed to connect and told him that all circuits were busy.

"It looks as though the phone system is overloaded," he said. "If we can get out of here in ten or fifteen minutes, the police may not get involved at all. I'd imagine there's widespread trouble all over the city."

Tom stiffened when he saw someone else running up the aisle with a rifle. He relaxed a moment later when he recognized the young guy from the gun shop.

"Is Rachel okay?" the man demanded. "I heard shots."

"I am back here, Greg," Rachel called out. "Get the pallet of water I left on the aisle with the food bars. Finish loading it up as high as it will go and take it back to the shop. Do not let anyone steal it."

The young man nodded and loped off into the store.

With the doctor efficiently dumping entire boxes and large bottles of pills into carts, it took very little time to fill them. She threw a large stack of needles in boxes on top.

"I have a pallet lifter out there. We can fit four carts onto a pallet."

Rachel shook her head. "It is easier to pull the carts. Use the lifter to grab something else."

Doctor Emery turned toward Rachel, who was just pouring the last of the ice on top of the refrigerated medication. "Are you ready? I've got everything that I think might prove useful."

"Get the less useful stuff. We won't get a second chance. We take everything we can."

People were starting to gather outside the pharmacy again. The sight of the dead bodies wasn't deterring them. Tom needed to get them moving soon.

Trying to think ahead, Tom grabbed a basket and dumped all the test strips he could find for the glucose meters into it. Then he tossed the meters themselves on top of them.

Doctor Emery nodded approvingly. "Good thinking."

With the carts filled to overflowing, they'd virtually stripped the pharmacy of prescription medications. Tom took the key Doctor Emery held out to him and unlocked the screen. The potential looters backed up when he drew his pistol.

Tom led the way out and grabbed the pallet lifter while the women maneuvered the carts. When a few people started grumbling, he waved his pistol. "Those people on the ground messed with us. Don't be like them. Go into the pharmacy and get what's left."

Once he felt relatively safe, he emptied a large box sitting on a pallet and took it back to the nonprescription aisles. The looting of the restricted area was well under way. Fine by him. They'd realize he'd stripped it soon enough.

The empty box was sturdy, so he filled it with everything he could grab. Bandages, ointments, all manner of first aid stuff. Once the box could hold no more, he headed for the front of the store.

The guy from the gun shop was waiting with the women. Based on the angry looks a big guy was giving him, he'd needed to recover the lifter at gunpoint. He might have taken some of the other man's loot, too. Greg was eating some beef jerky until Rachel stole it from him.

Tom found a large insulated cooler and packed it with ice. He repeated that with a second cooler. If they kept them closed, they might give them enough cooling power to keep the drugs cold until they made it to his place.

All of the employees had vanished, and the flood of people coming in to the store was increasing. They flowed around the guy from the gun shop, though. Tom supposed the sight of him carrying an AR around like that intimidated them.

They managed to get their haul safely out to the sidewalk and quickly hurried down to the gun shop. To his surprise, the green-haired woman from the store was standing beside the front door.

She gave Rachel a quick smile. "I know the system is probably down, but is there some kind of paperwork I can do to get a gun? I'm kind of scared. Things are out of control."

Rachael nodded. "Of course. Come in."

Once Rachel had opened the door, they all went inside. Tom had her grab him some hollow-point .40 S&W and found extra magazines his gun could use. He filled them all and topped off the partially empty one in his pouch.

He left Rachel and the woman to their business and pushed the lifter to join the carts in the center of the showroom. Randy and Jenna quickly jumped to grab the new material.

"Is everything okay?" Randy asked. "We heard shots."

Tom smiled a little. "Things are breaking down a little out there. Have you got everything else packed?"

The engineer nodded. "There was plenty of space inside the back of your truck. Excuse me, the Beast. All of this stuff can fit into it just fine. Mister Adler is getting his stuff together to load up last."

"I'll be glad when we get this done," Jenna complained. "I realize this is the apocalypse and all, but I'm beat. I need to drink some water and eat something. I'm starving."

"Where's Moshe now?" Tom asked.

Randy jerked his head around to point at the rear of the shop. "He's out back with the vehicles. He said somebody needed to keep an eye on them."

Tom rummaged through the new carts and pulled out a handful of food bars. "We have a selection for your dining pleasure," he said, extending the bars to Jenna. "There's more water here, too. For right now, that's the best were going to be able to do."

She took the bars eagerly. "That's good enough for me. I could eat a horse."

Tom grabbed a few bars and a couple of bottles of water. He made his way out the back of the store and found Moshe standing beside the Beast. The older man had a peculiar-looking shotgun on a strap around his neck.

He was staring off to the north. It seemed as though there were a grass fire off in the distance, but Tom knew the light and smoke were much further away than they looked.

"I never thought I'd live to see the day," Moshe said. "People have been talking about nuclear war my entire life. Now that day has finally arrived."

The old man turned to look at Tom, his expression bleak. "I suppose I should be happy that one of those things didn't go off here. Why Seattle and not Portland? Why not the other way around? How many people do you think died?"

"I think they might be the lucky ones," Tom said softly. "One minute they're walking along living normal lives and the next, it's over. I'm not sure I believe in an afterlife, but at least they didn't suffer. The ones that the nuke burned or the radiation poisoned, they're the ones I feel sorry for. And they're only the first.

"Some of the estimates I've read suggested that this kind of event will kill off ninety percent of the global population. With the power out, dehydration is going to take out a lot of people within a week, I'd imagine. Not here, of course. Portland has plenty of water. Dysentery and starvation will be the killers here."

"Realistically, what kind of chances do you think we have?" Moshe said.

Tom shrugged. "We have a leg up on so many other people. We've got food, water, and weapons. If we can get to the coast, I've got more. We can conceivably last for years, but a lot of that depends on other people.

"The violence is going to get really bad. Law and order are out the window. All of our civil structures will unravel very quickly. There are going to be lawless bands taking what they want by force from anyone who resists them."

He sighed. "I had to kill two men at the store. They attacked me. I know I had to, but I still feel like crap."

Moshe put his hand on Tom's shoulder. "In times of crisis, ethics and morality change. We have to live. You did what you had to do."

The rear door to the gun shop opened and Rachel stuck her head out. "I need both of you in here. I will stand watch over the trucks."

Tom glanced at Moshe. Rachel's expression didn't indicate anything good waiting inside.

"What's wrong?" he asked.

"The police are here. They have questions about some dead bodies."

7

Tom followed Moshe into the store, his stomach already knotting. He'd killed two men. The fact that the police had tracked him down probably meant he was about to go to jail. At the very least, they'd ask him some serious questions.

If they arrested him, the odds were good he was going to die here in Portland.

Rachel must have already opened the front door to the shop because two uniformed police officers were standing inside. One was a young guy and the other was a woman about Tom's age. She had sergeant's stripes.

He came to a stop a few feet away from them and inclined his head. He made sure to keep his hands in plain sight.

"Officers. My name is Tom Morgan. I've never been involved in anything like this before, so what do we do? It was self-defense."

The woman looked him up and down. "I'm Sergeant Reese and this is Officer McMillan. As we're standing in a gun shop and the world seems to be on fire, I'm going to assume that you're armed. Let's start by keeping your hands in plain sight and not making any sudden moves. Understand?"

He nodded. "I'm armed, but I'll do exactly as you say."

"Excellent. Since there appears to be a riot in progress next door, we haven't gone inside. It's too dangerous. Who were those people and why did you shoot them?"

"It was a guy with a crowbar and his associate with a pistol," Tom said. "They were breaking into the pharmacy. Doctor Emery here was inside. I told the guy to stop and his associate drew a pistol on me. I shot him, and when the first guy came at me with a crowbar, I shot him too.

"I did try to call 911, but it said all circuits were busy. It was getting crazy in that place, so I didn't want to stay inside."

The sergeant nodded. "Somebody finally managed to get through, and that pretty well matches up with what they said. Doctor Emery? Are you a pharmacist there?"

The older woman shook her head. "No, but I work with the lead pharmacist on occasion. I have her card. May I reach into my purse for it?"

"Do it slowly."

Doctor Emery retrieved a card from the wallet in her purse and handed it to the sergeant. The other woman examined it closely.

"I see that it has the pharmacist's name and number, as well as a statement that says you're authorized inside the pharmacy area. However, with the phones in the condition they are, I can't exactly call and confirm any of that. Why should I believe this?"

The woman with green hair cleared her throat. "Actually, I can confirm that. I'm Nika Andropov, the assistant manager. I sent all the employees home because it was too dangerous. I didn't see the shooting, but Doctor Emery is allowed in the pharmacy."

The male police officer had been looking deeper into the gun shop with his flashlight. "Sarge? They've got a bunch of shopping carts in here. Some of them are full."

"They paid for it," Nika said. "It was all cleared through me before the run on the store started."

The sergeant looked at each of them. "I don't know any of you except Mister Adler. You've always seemed like a standup kind of guy to me. Are these people telling me the truth?"

Moshe nodded. "I wasn't there, but I did send my daughter and

Tom here off with cash to buy what we needed. I've also known Doctor Emery for many years. She works at the clinic up the street. She helps at the pharmacy on occasion. She's old friends with the pharmacist."

After another long, tense moment, the sergeant nodded. "Okay. I'm not going inside that building with just the two of us. I'll make note in my report of what happened. Mister Morgan, I'll need to see your driver's license and your permit to carry."

Tom slowly retrieved his wallet, extracted the requested documentation, and handed it over. Sergeant Reese examined them closely and then handed them back. "Thank you, Mister Morgan. According to your license, you live over on the coast. Is that correct?"

He nodded. "That's right. We're going to head that way shortly."

She grimaced. "Traffic is a mess. I'd advise you to sit tight and wait for the power to come back on. There are dead cars everywhere, and there have been a ton of accidents."

"Thanks for the advice, Sergeant."

He had absolutely no intention of delaying his exit. Things would not be getting better.

His feelings must've been apparent based on his expression, because the woman smiled a little. "If I can't talk you out of making the attempt, at least let me make sure you don't waste your time. I-5 is completely fubared. You'll just get stuck in a traffic jam if you try to go that way.

"I suggest you strike out south. I don't know that the conditions are going to be any better down that way, but it stands to reason you might have less traffic."

She turned to Moshe. "Things are turning ugly out there, Mister Adler. I don't suppose we might impose upon you for some ammunition?"

"I'll give you as much as you can carry. Share it with your friends. Nine millimeter?"

She nodded gratefully. "Yes, please. And some shotgun shells, if you have them. Buckshot."

"Let me get some for you."

Moshe hurried off and returned with a small basket filled with ammo boxes. "I want to give you something else, too."

Reese cocked her head slightly. "Like what?"

"I'm taking a lot of things with me when we head for the coast, but I obviously cannot take everything. If things get as bad as I'm told they might, I want you to bring as many of the local police and people you trust back here and use what's in this shop to protect yourselves."

He pulled a key ring out of his pocket, took a large key off, and handed it to the sergeant.

"I hope to hell we don't need this," she said. "I'll make sure that some of the officers in the area use your shop as a base of operations. It's centrally located and easy to protect, considering everything you have in here. We appreciate you looking out for us."

She put the key into her pocket and headed for the door. "McMillan, you're with me."

The two police officers exited the shop and headed for their patrol car. They turned around and drove away from the riot in progress next door.

Moshe pulled down the screen and locked it with Rachel's key.

"I hope she and her friends make it back. Tom, why don't you give Greg and me a hand? I've been gathering some of the good stuff back in the stockroom. We'll take what we can. You know what they say. During the apocalypse, you can never have enough guns."

He laughed. "I don't know who said that, but I like it."

"I don't suppose I could impose upon you for a ride out of Portland?" Nika asked. "I can help."

Tom wasn't exactly sure what skills she had to offer, but he wasn't going to turn the woman away. Her support had kept the police from arresting him.

"Absolutely. That reminds me. We need to get clothes for everyone. I've only got what I have on my back."

"Actually, that's not true," Jenna said. "We found a bunch of underwear, socks, jeans, and T-shirts in one of the first carts. Both for men and women. I think we'll be able to get by for a little bit. I saw you picked up a bunch of soap, so we can stay clean. Someone grabbed some liquid laundry detergent that we can use, too."

So many things that they'd all taken for granted were going to be difficult to come now. He blessed Rachel's forethought for grabbing the clothes.

"Where is your place, Nika?" he asked.

"It's just up the street. If we're going south, we won't even have to turn off the main road."

"Then we'll stop and pick up anything you need. If you have anything precious to you, I suggest you bring it along. You probably won't be coming back this way."

The woman swallowed and nodded, obviously frightened.

Tom followed Moshe into the back. Greg Zimmer was already busy sorting through what looked like an incomprehensible stack of gun cases. There looked to be enough weapons to end a South American civil war.

"Good Lord! Do we really need all this?" Tom asked.

Moshe raised an eyebrow. "All this? You act as if these are a lot of guns. We've already moved a bunch of stuff out to the vehicles. Including, I might add, a pile of accessories that I'd bet you never thought of. Like ammo. How many bullets is enough for the apocalypse?"

Tom shook his head. "Are you planning on setting yourself up as a warlord on the coast? There's only half a dozen of us."

"Right now. How many people live on the coast? How many of them might join forces with us at some point? If someone else sets himself up as a warlord, exactly how do you plan on defending yourself?"

The older man shook his head. "The problem with you writers is that you get into your plot and then you forget about the twist. This time you aren't setting up the twist, my young friend. That ugly bastard called the real world is. Trust me on this one."

Tom held up his hands in surrender. "Who am I to argue? Are you going to leave anything for the cops?"

"Of course I am. They're not going to need many guns, so I'll take most of those. I'll leave ammunition for them. I have a bunch of it, so giving them a few cases of bullets won't to kill us."

Moshe grabbed a Glock case from one of the counters and handed it to Tom.

Tom opened the latches and peeked inside. The slide declared the pistol a Glock 18C.

He stared at it for a moment and then looked at Moshe in shock. "I can't take this! It's an automatic weapon. The feds will go—"

Moshe nodded as Tom closed his mouth. "I see that you've grasped my point. I don't think the government is going to be complaining."

The pistol was the same dimensions as a full-sized Glock, but it had a selector switch that allowed it to fire as many bullets as the shooter liked with one squeeze of the trigger. Moshe had allowed him to shoot it a few times with a nod and a wink from the law enforcement people that were getting the actual demonstration. The pistol was a wet dream.

Moshe grabbed a longer case off the bench. "You'll also want this in the cab of your truck, I'll wager."

Tom knew what he'd see before he opened it. The rifle he'd been waiting for the Feds to approve.

Nestled inside the padded case was an ST Compressor from Spike's Tactical. The short-barreled .300 AC Blackout rifle had a suppressor attached at the front of the barrel. A smaller suppressor sat beside it.

With its shortened length, the weapon was still handier than a regular AR, even with the longer suppressor attached. His friends called it "tacticool," but he loved its lines.

He'd fired it—under Moshe's supervision again—and the thing really lived up to its reputation. Rather than the standard 5.56 NATO rounds—or .223 Remington for the civilian side—his baby fired the larger .308 projectiles from a shortened case.

It didn't have the range or power of the full-sized .308 bullets, but inside a few hundred yards, it packed a hell of a punch. Best of all, if he used heavy bullets and kept the powder light, he could shoot subsonic.

Those were exceptionally fun to shoot, and that had been the point.

That's when he noticed that there were some parts inside the case. "What's this?" he asked.

"I made a modification to your gun," Moshe said. "I swapped out the sear with a fully auto version. Flip the safety past single fire and you can really lay it onto someone. The short suppressor is only rated for single fire, but the longer one will still work on automatic."

That would be badass. "Thank you."

"Bah," the older man said. "That might just save my life or my daughter's."

He gestured to a second case when Tom had secured his baby. "I picked up the .223 version, too. I knew I could sell it. It has both suppressors and the full auto conversion, too. Not nearly as quiet as the .300, but it might be useful."

Considering the scarcity of legal fully auto weapons, that was a gift worth tens of thousands of dollars. It really brought the situation home for Tom. They were in a fight for their lives.

One of the things that Tom learned as he helped load everything into the Beast was that Greg was ex-military and a qualified gunsmith. They made sure and stripped his working area bare of tools and equipment. Those were really going to come in handy.

The eight of them would be in terrific shape if they could make it to the coast. That outcome would take a lot of hard work and even more good luck, but at least they had a fighting chance.

It took them until after dark to finish packing everything.

No one had tried to break into the gun shop, but that was because one of them was always standing near the front with a rifle.

Sergeant Reese and her partner returned with backup just before they were ready to depart. Backup and what certainly looked like their families.

The handover of control was smooth and heartfelt. Tom really did hope that the dozen cops setting up shop held out when the city went completely crazy. They were unloading food and water, so it looked as though they were settling in for a siege. Good for them.

It was dark out when Tom and the rest exited the rear of the gun shop and climbed into the vehicles. He put Nika in the passenger side of the Beast, Greg joined Moshe in his truck, and Rachel loaded Doctor Emery and the Caldwells into her sedan.

The setting of the sun had revealed the aurora in all its glory. Tom had to admit it was glorious. He'd seen a couple over the years, but nothing like this.

The shifting curtains of light were almost unbelievably bright. Greens, reds, golds, purples, and blues shifted slowly above their heads, covering the sky from north to south.

Tom had a spot next to his seat where he could stash his new rifles. The .5.56 version had supersonic rounds, but he'd loaded the .300 with commercial subsonic ammo. It would be very, very soft.

He'd taken the time to load an extra dozen thirty-round magazines for each. When the time came to use them, he didn't want to have to reload empty magazines. Each set was marked will different-colored tape to prevent blowing up one of the rifles.

Once they'd all backed out and gotten on the road, Nika directed him to head south. After they grabbed her stuff, he'd try to get onto 99E heading south. It didn't cross I-5 for a long way, but there were only a few bridges to deal with according to his maps.

Those and the two rivers—the Columbia and the Willamette— were going to be his biggest headaches. He couldn't cross them without a bridge. One that was most likely completely blocked.

By taking 99E down, he'd have to cross I-5 around Salem. He only hoped his plans had some basis in reality. If things were impassable, he wasn't sure what they'd do.

Assuming that the stop at Nika's place took less than an hour, it would probably still be way after midnight by the time they finally worked their way clear of the city. If they managed it at all.

He fully expected that they'd run into trouble before then. The two men he'd killed earlier were probably only the first of many. That saddened him but also filled him with determination. Nothing was going to stop him from getting them to the coast. Nothing.

8

The drive to Nika's apartment building proved that getting out of Portland wasn't going to be nearly as easy as Tom had hoped. Word was obviously getting around that the end of the world was at hand.

The streets looked like something out of Beirut or Mosul, at least according to the news programs he'd seen over the years. There were a shocking number of burning buildings in the distance with no firemen in sight. They'd be lucky if the city didn't burn down around their ears.

The aurora provided more than enough light to see by, though he did use his headlights. It would be too easy to run into something unexpected if he turned them off. Hindsight being 20/20, he should've dug out the night-vision goggles.

Small groups of people seemed bent on fleeing the city with whatever they could carry. Many appeared to have given up on driving.

Some seemed inclined to either beg for help or take what they could by force. Greg leaned out of the truck in front of Tom and shouted for them to back off. In a few cases, he had to fire warning shots.

Those were far from the only gunshots Tom heard around them. He suspected the gangs were taking advantage of the chaos. Portland was more tribal than many people knew. It had lots of insular groups that would probably clash now that the pressure was on.

Within a couple of blocks, it became necessary for Tom to move the Beast up front. A major accident had blocked the entire street.

He started to move forward to push the cars out of the way, but Greg motioned for him to stop.

"This might be an ambush," the young man said. "I should check it out."

It didn't look like an ambush to Tom, but he wasn't a soldier.

Greg moved forward, ducking behind cars at every opportunity. Rachel advanced on the other side of the street with another AR in hand. Between the two of them, they had the front covered.

A glance in the rearview mirror showed that Moshe was watching behind them. That somehow made things more real for him.

After looking around the corner and dashing forward to aim his gun behind the cars in the intersection, Greg motioned for Tom to come forward.

He put the Beast into gear and edged forward until he was against the rearmost car in the pileup. With some judicious application of acceleration, he shoved it onto the sidewalk, making it flip in the process.

A couple of minutes later, he'd maneuvered through to the street beyond. He waited for the others to get back into their vehicles before he advanced.

It took almost forty minutes to get to Nika's apartment building. Under normal circumstances, they probably could've walked faster.

"It's this one," Nika said, pointing off to the right.

The building in question was moderately tall and looked to be in decent shape. A few of the windows were lit, so there were people still inside. He wondered how long their supply of batteries and candles would last. Surely, no more than a few days.

Tom pulled the Beast to the side of the road and shut it off. When the others followed suit, the silence was startling.

The hum of civilization was gone. He heard the sounds of a few engines moving around them, shouts in the distance, a few gunshots, and the wail of a child. The air stank of smoke.

They huddled together behind the Beast. When the rest looked to him for direction, Tom realized that he was going to be the one making the decisions going forward. That was a bit unsettling, but he supposed someone had to do it.

"Rachel and I will go up with Nika," he said. "The rest of you watch the vehicles. We can't afford to lose any of the supplies, much less the transport."

Moshe nodded and held out that strange looking shotgun to Tom. "Take this. You might need the firepower."

He took the weapon and examined it. It had some type of rotating cylinder under the barrel.

"This is a SRM 1216 twelve gauge semiautomatic," Moshe said. "The rotating cylinder has four tubes with four rounds of buckshot each. There's one in the chamber, so you have seventeen shots.

"It'll lock back when the tube feeding it is empty, but when you rotate a new one in the place it will automatically feed a round without you doing anything. Let me grab a spare cylinder so you have a reload. I'll show you how to swap them out."

It looked like an awesomely lethal weapon. After the demonstration, Tom felt confident he could manipulate it and even swap out the cylinders without too much trouble. Of course, even simple things became difficult when people were trying to kill you.

Before they went inside, he got back into the big truck and retrieved his binoculars. He might as well take advantage of being inside a tall building to look at their path going forward. If there were any obstacles, it would be better to avoid them.

Rachel put out her hand and stopped Nika from going into the building. She let the AR dangle across her chest on its strap and unholstered her pistol. She advanced into the building, with a tactical flashlight in her hand supporting the pistol.

With his hands full, Tom didn't have that option. If they'd thought ahead, he probably could have mounted something to the shotgun.

Tom followed closely behind Rachel, covering her back. Nika was equally close behind him.

Rachel searched out the lobby, probably to be sure that no one was hiding there. Once she'd done so, she edged toward the stairs.

"I live on the fifth floor," Nika said. Her voice echoed through the lobby.

Rachel gave the other woman a flat stare. "Perhaps you could keep your voice down," she said quietly. "Do not whisper. That carries. Just speak softly."

Without waiting for a response, she entered the stairwell. It was dark as hell in there.

Tom grabbed his everyday-carry light to provide some illumination and used that hand to support the front of the shotgun. He gestured for Nika to precede him.

Once they were on the stairs, they proceeded upward. Rachel didn't touch the doors leading into any of the other floors. She just covered them while Tom and Nika passed by. At the next landing, she again took the lead.

In this fashion, they made their way to the fifth floor. Once there, Tom pulled the door open, and Rachel advanced with her pistol already raised, sweeping the hall in both directions.

No one was there. It was spooky.

Nika's apartment was only a couple of doors down from the stairs. They covered the hall while the young woman used her key to unlock the door and then followed her in.

The apartment was tidy. Pictures covered the walls.

Once they'd made certain the apartment was clear, he examined the pictures more closely. The majority of them had either Nika or a young man up in the mountains. A few of them were from odd angles and showed the pair of them standing together. In many, they were rappelling.

She noticed his attention. "That's my ex-boyfriend and me. He loved to go mountain climbing and hiking. Me, too. We'd go all over the place and spend time out in the woods."

Tom was impressed. He liked hiking as much as the next guy, but using ropes to go up and down sheer surfaces wasn't his cup of tea.

"Do you still have any of the gear?"

The young woman nodded. "Sure."

"Bring it with you. We're probably going to be doing a lot of moving through the wilderness. The area just inland of where I live is rugged. Being able to climb safely might be useful. Bring anything that you think would be useful in a wilderness situation."

"While you pack," Rachel said, "we will go to the roof. Lock the door and do not open it without looking to make sure that it is us. Do not even open it for other people you know. It is not safe."

The young woman swallowed noisily and nodded. "I won't."

Once they'd made sure that Nika had locked the door, he and Rachel returned to the stairwell. When they arrived at the top, they found the door leading to the roof locked.

Of course it was. This wasn't the sort of thing that people just left open. There wasn't a padlock he could bash off, so he wasn't sure how to open the door.

Rachel holstered her pistol. "Keep watch on the stairs." She pulled a little pouch from her pocket and unzipped it. Inside was a set of lock picks.

"You can pick locks? I'm impressed."

"I can hotwire cars, too. Skills from my misspent youth."

He laughed softly and turned to focus his attention down the stairs. He occasionally glanced back as Rachel worked the lock. She held the tactical flashlight between her teeth and used both hands to work the picks.

Less than a minute later, she grunted in triumph. "Got it."

Rachel carefully put her picks away and pulled her pistol. "Open the door while I lead the way out."

She extinguished her flashlight, and they waited for their eyes to adjust. At her nod, he opened the door.

The roof was pretty much like he'd imagined: a relatively flat surface covered with tar and gravel. Water flowed down to the edges of the roof and out through spouts set at intervals.

A number of air conditioning units ran along its length. Of course, all of them were silent. Under the light of the aurora, they looked almost alien.

The moon was out. It was only a quarter moon, but without the normal light pollution from the city, it was more than enough light to see for quite a ways.

A number of the buildings around them had lit rooms. He could see a few with people moving around. Probably residents.

Off in the distance, he saw four large fires. One of them had engulfed several buildings. None in the direction they were going, thankfully.

He leaned the shotgun up against the short wall at the edge of the building. He didn't look down at the street. Heights were not his thing.

Using the binoculars, he was able to get a decent look at the streets leading away. The lenses acted like a poor man's night-vision goggles, gathering the ambient light and making for a decent view.

The streets looked to be in about the same shape as the ones they'd already traveled.

"It is a good thing that you have that monster truck," Rachel said softly. "We would be on foot if we didn't have something to push all those dead cars out of the way. There are fewer than I expected."

"People that write about the end of the world sometimes make assumptions," he said. "I've read a number of stories that went with the line that an EMP would burn everything out. All the cars dead, all the electronics gone.

"Then there are those that go by the research that the government has done. According to those papers, the EMP should have killed about ten percent of the vehicles. This is more, but not terribly so. I got it wrong in my books, which is surprisingly annoying."

She laughed softly, probably at the irritated tone he'd used. "There is wrong and then there is *wrong*. It seems to me that you are the only one who came into this ready for trouble."

"Oh, I'm sure that's not true. Working in a gun shop, I'd imagine you've seen all kinds of people that are ready for the end of the world."

Rachel shook her head. "No. I have seen people that *think* they are ready for the end of the world. They are not.

"They might have enough ammunition to start a small war and enough canned food to last a few months, but they do not have the right mindset to make it through. For that kind of thing, I am thinking you need a team. The apocalypse is not going to be kind to the people alone in their bunkers."

Tom wasn't sure about that, but it seemed impolite to argue.

"I wanted to ask you a question," he said after a moment. "You're an ex-soldier. You seem very tough. Why aren't you or Greg calling the shots?"

"Greg is a good man," she said, "but he is not suited to lead us. Once you know him better, you will understand. As for me, I considered taking charge but decided not to. I am new to this country and do not know the people.

"Also, you have done well. You have a deeper familiarity with the potential scenarios and skills we need. The snap decisions you make will take all that into account. I am satisfied in your leadership. If I change my mind, I will tell you."

Moshe was right. She was a tad blunt.

He opened his mouth to start explaining what he thought they should do next, but a shrill scream from somewhere below cut him off. It sounded as though it had come from inside this building.

Rachel headed back toward the stairwell at a run, her light coming on. Tom grabbed his shotgun and raced after her. Trouble had found them, it seemed.

9

The race down to the fifth floor only took a few moments, but it felt like an eternity. Tom clumsily stuffed his earplugs into his ears as they ran. When they spilled out of the stairwell, the door to Nika's apartment gaped open.

Rachel went in with her pistol raised and he followed on her heels.

Two guys were in the living room. One was struggling with Nika on the couch and the other was tearing open a suitcase beside her.

They'd caught the guy on the couch with his pants down around his ankles—quite literally—so Tom focused his attention on the other man.

Both of them were Hispanic, he thought. Not that it mattered.

The guy wearing all of his clothes had a pistol in his belt. He gawked at them for a moment and went for it.

That proved to be a fatal mistake. Both Rachel and he shot the man. He was sure she'd hit the man, but all Tom could see was the huge, gaping hole the shotgun blast made in the center of the man's chest.

The guy dropped, dead before he hit the floor.

The one that had been trying to rape Nika struggled to get free of the young woman's suddenly strong clutches. He had a pistol, too, but it was on the coffee table. Just a little bit out of his reach.

Tamping down the urge to watch what happened, Tom let Rachel deal with the rapist. He turned towards the rest of the apartment and the front door. If the guy had accomplices, Tom wanted to be ready.

It was a good thing he did. Two other guys came running out of the bedroom, guns drawn. Tom laid into them with the shotgun. The results were immediate, fatal, and gory.

He resisted the urge to go hunt for more of them and stood near the couch. If there was anyone else in the apartment, they'd come to him. He wasn't going to walk into their ambush.

Rachel prodded the rapist off Nika and backed him into a corner. "How many of your friends are in here?"

The man held his hands out, looking ludicrous with his genitals hanging out. Tom noted wryly that the moment seemed to have passed. Maybe this wasn't the kind of excitement the man had been hoping for.

"Don't shoot me," the man pleaded. "I can give you money."

"What you'd better give me is an answer," Rachel said coldly. "How many friends did you bring to the party?"

"Just the four of us! Just the four of us!"

Without another word, Rachel shot the man in the crotch. Twice.

She did it with cold precision and not one ounce of apparent regret.

Nika, on the other hand, snatched up the man's pistol and started pumping rounds into him as he lay thrashing on the floor. She only stopped when the slide locked back.

Tom felt cold inside. That was a big step beyond self-defense. Yeah, the guy had deserved it, but they'd just executed him in cold blood. That was going to prompt some soul searching on his part when they had time.

Rachel shook the sobbing woman a little. "You do not have time to fall apart. Were there only four of them?"

The green-haired woman nodded jerkily.

Tom looked away from her torn blouse. "Other than the two

suitcases behind the front door and the one on the floor, is there anything else here that you have to have?"

"No," Nika said, still crying. "This is all of it. I didn't let them in. They just kicked the door in."

Rachel nodded. "I am sorry we left you alone. We will not let that happen again."

She took the empty automatic from the woman's hands and snagged the fallen pistols off the floor. She spent a few seconds going through the dead men's pockets, apparently looking for extra magazines.

In the process, she grabbed a fresh blouse off the floor and handed it to Nika. "Put this on. We must go."

With three suitcases, it took them longer to get down to the lobby than it had taken to go up. Rachel covered the way forward and Tom kept watch behind them. Nika moved each of the suitcases from landing to landing as they went.

It felt like an eternity before they reached the ground floor. No one had come exploring to see what all the shooting was about.

Tom moved in a daze. The incredible violence of the last few minutes made him feel as if he were in a *Twilight Zone* episode. Or maybe an issue of *Judge Dredd*.

He was in shock, he realized. He'd been playing at surviving the apocalypse. He had to accept they were living it.

Moshe and Doctor Emery were inside the lobby waiting for them. The older man held an AR and was making sure that no one snuck up on them.

The doctor grabbed one of the suitcases and helped them pull it towards the front door. "We heard shots. Is everyone okay?"

"We're fine," Nika said harshly. "Let's get out of here before more of those bastards come looking for us."

Doctor Emery and Moshe shared a glance, and then everyone started moving out to the vehicles. It only took a few moments to secure the suitcases.

While they were doing that, Tom did something he should have done first thing. He climbed over the supplies and retrieved the radios and night-vision goggles that he'd bought at the gun and prepper show. He made sure to grab plenty of batteries for each and car chargers.

The instructions that came with the radios were basic but straight to the point. He quickly had the units up and working, though there was a lot of noise and static. It wasn't enough to render them useless, so he'd call that a win.

He handed them out. "If we need to pass information back and forth, we can do it without stopping. I have night-vision goggles, too. Does anyone know how to use them?"

It turned out that both Rachel and Greg were familiar with using night-vision goggles. They helped fit a set on him. Looking down the street through them was surreal.

Everything took on shades of green, but he could see the details clearly now. Without them—even with the aurora—shadows covered far too many areas where trouble might hide.

"Okay," he said. "We're a few blocks away from 99E. We're going to cut over to it and head south. I'll take the lead. I hope to God that we don't have to abandon any of the vehicles. Moshe, is your truck four-wheel drive?"

The older man nodded. "I wouldn't trust it going off road like yours, but I'm not afraid of the shoulder. Anyway, that might get us around some stuff, but it won't get us through the overpasses. You're going to have to use the Beast to push stuff out of the way."

"Or use the winch to pull things clear," Tom agreed. "This isn't going to be fast or easy, but we need to keep moving. I-5 is a no-go. We also don't want to be pinned against the Willamette. We're going to have to go south to Salem and then under the interstate."

Rachel looked up at the sky skeptically. "Do you think we can make it to Salem by dawn?"

He shook his head. "Probably not. If we can make it out into the wilderness, I suggest we set up camp and make firmer plans."

The young woman nodded her agreement. "We will be exhausted by then. We need to get off the main roads and set up camp. We really should have picked up camping gear, but the box store was not exactly the place to go shopping for that kind of thing."

"There's an outdoor store about seven blocks down," Nika said quietly.

Tom felt like slapping his forehead, but he resisted the urge. He hadn't even considered how long they were going to be out in the elements. There was a big storm coming in from the Pacific over the next few days. It was winter, and they were going to get drenched. Hypothermia was a real worry.

"Right," he said. "We won't survive without warmer clothes, shelter, and heat sources. We're going to have to take that chance.

"When we get there, some of us are going to have to stay with the vehicles and protect everything we have. This stuff is our lifeline. If we lose it, we're probably going to die in Portland."

He looked around at each of them. "Rachel, Nika, and I have already had to kill. You folks might have to do the same while we get what we need inside.

"I know the urge to help other people is going to be strong, but you have to remember that our little tribe comes first. We cannot afford to have the ethics we did yesterday. If somebody tries to beg something off you, send them away. With force, if necessary. Can you do that?"

In the end, Tom was only sure about Moshe and Greg. Randy Caldwell said that he could, but Tom had his doubts.

Doctor Emery was a firm no. "I can't. I swore an oath to do no harm, and I meant it."

"Okay," he said. "When we get there, the following people will come in with me: the Caldwells, Doctor Emery, and Nika. We'll gather what we can while the rest of you make certain that no one screws with our stuff."

"One other thing," the doctor said. "My clinic is between here and the outdoor store. A couple streets over, but not far. It would do us a lot of good to clean out my medical supplies.

"I take care of people that live on the streets. I've got everything needed to perform minor medical procedures. Even some major ones, in a pinch. There are basic medical supplies there, too. If I'm going to be a doctor in this new world, I need my tools."

Tom nodded. "We'll go there first."

Surprisingly, no one had broken into the clinic. With a number of them keeping guard, Doctor Emery quickly brought everything useful out to the vehicles. Even with everything they'd collected, the Beast was still more than half empty and nowhere near the weight limit.

Once they finished, the woman sighed as she stared at the building. "I suppose I'll never see this place again. That makes me sad."

"You might not see this building again, but you'll still be helping people," Tom said. "I'm sorry to rush things along, but we need to get moving."

She nodded and headed for Rachel's car.

Under other circumstances, driving at night with the lights off and navigating with the night-vision goggles would've been exceptionally cool. As it was, it was stressful.

He occasionally saw people looking out from the buildings. Some of them were armed. None of them could clearly see much detail about their little convoy. That was perfectly fine with him.

The outdoor superstore was a zoo. People were streaming in and out, carrying armloads of stuff. He saw one idiot with a bundle of tennis rackets. Another had a big-screen television. How much use were those going to be during the apocalypse?

He parked the Beast off to the side and a fair distance away from the front door.

"I'll have my radio," he told the rest as they piled out of the vehicles. "If you need assistance, just yell. We'll come running."

"You do the same," Moshe said. "We don't want to lose anybody."

Tom turned to Nika. "You've been here before. Take us to what we need, and we'll grab everything we can get our hands on."

"Hold it," Moshe said.

He quickly swapped Nika's pistol for one with a holster and helped her get it onto her belt. He then put spare magazines into her jacket pocket. The young woman looked both terrified and determined.

Moshe handed the Caldwells some regular-looking shotguns. "Put the spare ammunition into your pockets."

He then outfitted them with similar hard-sided holsters and

Glocks. That probably made sense. No external safeties to screw them up. Glocks were the ultimate point-and-click interface.

The group of them headed for the entrance at a jog. Tom doubted anyone was stealing the tents and camp stoves just yet, but one never knew.

A roar of engines announced the arrival of about a dozen motorcycles before they'd even made it to the front door. Whooping men in leather raced around the looters streaming out of the store. A few of them shot pistols into the air.

"Oh crap," Tom muttered.

One of the riders stopped, stood up a little, and stared toward where they'd parked the Beast. He turned his head and shouted at the other men. With engines revving, they shot toward Tom and his people with hungry grins.

10

Considering the way that the riders were brandishing their pistols—particularly the lead guy—Tom didn't hesitate. He raised his shotgun and shot him.

He hadn't gotten his earplugs in, so the shot made his ears ring. He pivoted slightly and shot at the oncoming threats as fast as he could.

They began shooting back. Some of them peeled off and raced around him. It felt as if they were playing cowboys and Indians. The vehicles were their covered wagons.

Tom's companions brought up their shotguns and began firing at the motorcyclists racing around them. Another automatic weapon opened up from the vehicles—one of Tom's friends providing covering fire.

That was the final straw for the biker gang. The survivors turned and raced away. Behind Tom, someone fired a single shot and then another. The rearmost biker lost control and crashed. All told, it looked as though only three or four had gotten away.

He'd just stepped past the revenge killing of the would-be rapist. The bikers hadn't actually done anything, though he was sure they'd been about to. It looked as though the new Golden Rule was "do unto others before they even considered doing it to you." So be it.

Tom charged toward the front of the store. The looters didn't want any part of him, so they scattered.

He found a treasure trove just inside the front door. Someone had a flatbed cart loaded down with tents, sleeping bags, a stack of camp stoves, and cases filled with small propane bottles.

"Doctor Emery, push that back to the vehicles. Randy, cover her. Get it unloaded and haul ass back with that cart while the rest get it put away. We'll be ready with more stuff as soon as you get here."

The looters still inside the store gave them a wide berth. Nika arrowed straight towards the back of the store. Tom and Jenna followed closely behind her.

Someone had smashed the ammunition display case and taken most of its contents. Loose rounds littered the area, gleaming bright yellow in his light. They all took care not to slip on them. A twisted or broken ankle would suck.

Nika grabbed a cart and started pulling cold-weather gear off the shelves: boots, socks, long johns, gloves, and everything else that one could think of.

Tom left Jenna to watch over her and started grabbing mats to put under sleeping bags. He hit the fishing rods next. They'd eventually have to get their protein the old-fashioned way. It would really help to have some decent equipment.

Not knowing anything about fishing, he grabbed an armload of poles and every lure and hook he could get his hands on. Several fishing tackle boxes filled out the pile he was putting on the floor.

He found an overturned cart that someone had abandoned and began filling it up. When he had his stuff loaded, he went in search of LED lanterns. A lot of those were gone, but he found the mother lode of lamp oil. He grabbed all the lamps he could find and put them into the cart.

Jenna appeared at his shoulder. "Randy is back. What can I grab?"

"Knives, machetes, any kind of camping gear we missed, you

name it. If it looks interesting or useful, put it in a cart. We're not going to get another chance like this.

"Send Nika to grab every rechargeable battery she can find and adapters for cigarette lighters. We'll also need water purification tablets and smokers for curing meat. I have a lot of salt already, but grab any food preservation stuff you find."

Next up for him: chainsaws. He grabbed three and loaded up on spare chains, sharpening implements, chain oil, and fuel mixture. When they got out into the woods, it would rock to be able to get fallen trees out of their way.

He also broke open the cabinet holding the binoculars. They'd be able to use all of these or trade them later.

The four of them quickly filled the flat cart and three regular carts with the most eclectic mix of outdoor gear he'd ever seen.

Looters had stripped the firearms area, but he knew the high-dollar items were usually locked up. They'd smashed all the glass cases and stolen everything in plain sight, so Tom went behind the counter and looked for secure areas that were less accessible.

There was a drawer under the counter. A few whacks with a small sledge broke the lock.

Inside was a treasure trove. There were a few guns, but the whoop he let out was because of the boxed scopes stacked inside. Everything from basic models to expensive long-range ones. In the back were a few infrared and night-vision models that would really help with shooting in the dark.

Tom took them all. He was about to order everyone out of the store when Nika stopped and pointed. "I want them."

He turned and looked at where she was pointing. Drones.

"Fun to fly I'm sure, but not exactly useful in a survival situation."

She gave him a stare. "The ones that come with cameras can link to handheld viewers or goggles. I see FLIR cameras in there. Forward-looking infrared, that is. Night vision, too. We could send them ahead and scout out places we'd rather avoid. There are some really expensive, capable models here."

Okay, that was a different matter. "You have any experience flying them?"

"Hell, yes!"

"Clean them out. Take everything. Especially all the batteries and chargers."

While she grabbed something to pry open the locked case, he raided the neat stack of gasoline cans. He had a hand pump and line in the Beast that he could use to get fuel out of underground tanks. With no power, there'd still be a lot down there. They'd need to gas up at least once on the way to the coast.

If they had to, he knew how to get fuel out of abandoned cars, but that was a lot of work. He'd much rather stock up at a random gas station. They'd be less vulnerable that way.

Once Nika had pulled out a number of boxes and stacked them onto the cart, they got the hell out of there.

He got another surprise when he got out to the parking lot. It seems the others had done some reorganizing. Rachel and Greg sat astride two of the motorcycles. Those would be good on the road, especially considering how littered with abandoned cars they were.

Where they'd run into problems would be rough country. Those were street bikes. It would be nice to have something that would be good for off road. Something useful for scouting.

He'd seen something inside that might work, if he could get them out of the building and find something to carry them.

Tom went around the back of Moshe's pickup and examined his bumper. It had a trailer hitch. Good.

"Someone help me siphon gasoline out of these bikes," he said with a gesture towards the fallen motorcycles. There were half a dozen of them. They would provide more than enough fuel for what he had in mind. At least to start.

He looked over at Greg and Rachel. "Grab some helping hands and go back inside. I saw some four-wheelers at the back of the store. Be sure to stock up on all the extra batteries, fuel filters, and other useful parts. If there are any spare tires, get those, too.

"There's a trailer in the back of the store that looks like it will hold them. Get enough tie-down straps to secure everything and some extra fuel cans. We'll have to stop at a gas station and fill everything up. Push them out the back door, and we'll come around and meet you."

Tom retrieved his hand pump from the Beast. With it, he was able to siphon the fuel out of the fallen motorcycles without getting that nasty taste in his mouth. He pulled about ten gallons in total.

The potential looters were still staring at them from the edge of the parking lot. Their numbers were growing, and it wouldn't be too long before they grew bold enough to go in again.

There was also the possibility that the surviving bikers would return with reinforcements. They'd be looking for payback. Tom wanted to be gone before they gathered themselves.

Moshe and Randy climbed onto the motorcycles. Good, they had more than a few people that knew how to use them.

He stashed the gas cans in the back of the Beast and climbed in. Doctor Emery got behind the wheel of Moshe's truck. Sticking together, they drove around the side of the store and pulled up next to the loading dock.

"We'll have to go back out front to get your car," he said to Rachel when he jumped out of the Beast at the back of the store.

She shook her head. "We already packed everything useful into Poppa's truck. I love my car, but it is a burden. Maybe if I had a Jeep."

"We grabbed new helmets. Some dark ones that do not smell like dead men. Ones we can use with the radios via built-in earphones and boom microphones."

Tom helped them maneuver the trailer behind Moshe's pickup truck and secure it to the hitch. He didn't bother connecting the lights. It would be better if the people around them had a more difficult time seeing them. With that in mind, he disconnected the lights on his own trailer.

They quickly rolled the four-wheelers up the new trailer's built-in ramp. It was snug, but both fit. They quickly secured them with tie-down straps.

While they were doing that, Tom retrieved more night-vision goggles. By the time he'd finished showing Moshe everything he needed to, Rachel and Greg had packed the trailer with the rest of the supplies they'd need for the new vehicles. Extra headlamps, spark plugs, and goodness only knew what else.

Greg was examining the night-vision goggles to see how they could use them with the helmets.

That was when Tom heard trouble in the distance. Motorcycles. Significantly more than had gotten away.

If the bikers knew which direction they went, they'd be able to catch them. Motorcycles were good at dodging through the stopped traffic.

The Beast wasn't the quietest vehicle in the neighborhood, either. All they had to do was stop and listen.

That line of thinking had apparently been playing out in Greg's head, too. He was eyeing a ladder that led up to the roof. "It might be best if we thin the herd."

The old Tom Morgan would've been horrified. The new one almost was, too, but that didn't matter. These people had come looking for blood, and he had to deal with them.

Tom reached into the Beast and retrieved both of the suppressed rifles. The satchel with the extra magazines was heavy, but he was able to slide the strap so that it hung off his back.

"The rest of you catch any stragglers that get around the side of the building," Tom said as he grabbed the ladder. "Take them down fast. Stay behind the concrete where you can. Watch the door leading into the building, too. You might get attention from people on foot."

It only took them a minute to get onto the roof and carefully rush toward the front of the building. Tom mimicked Greg when they got close and dropped to his hands and knees.

The two men peeked over the low wall and looked down into the parking lot. In the relative darkness, they'd be hard to spot.

That wasn't true for the bikers below. Half a dozen of them were checking the dead men. Another four were ransacking Rachel's car. Based on the number of motorcycles propped up on the kickstands, half a dozen of them had gone inside.

Most of them had pistols out, but a few had ARs.

"What kind of drop can I expect from the .300 at this range?" Greg asked quietly.

"The scope on it takes that into account," Tom said. "If you look on one side, you'll see a rabbit icon. That's for supersonic. The other side has a turtle. That's for subsonic. Use the turtle."

The other man nodded. "Suppressors don't mean Hollywood quiet. They're going to hear the shots. They just might not know where they're coming from."

Tom already knew that. "One thing to keep in mind is that while it shoots a .308 bullet, the subsonic rounds use a very light powder charge. It won't have the punch a supersonic bullet would have.

"Placement is key, or multiple hits. The magazines for the .300 have blue tape and mine have red. Don't mix them up or you might get a boom."

Greg nodded. "Here's what we're going to do. I'll start shooting the ones farthest away. Those closer in might not see them fall or might put the shooter out across the street. With the way things echo in the city, they're not going to have a clue. Those guys are the ones most likely to get behind cover. The ones out in the open are sitting ducks."

"What do you want me to do?"

"If it looks like the ones in front of the building have spotted us, start shooting. Single shot only."

The two men edged up against the front wall more tightly. Greg looked comfortable setting up to be a sniper. Tom wondered what he'd done in the Army.

Both rifles had scopes, so Tom was able to zero in on the people he was watching fairly easily. He took his eye off the scope so he could see them all. In the low light, it wasn't going to be easy to find people once they started running.

Too bad he couldn't have mounted the infrared scopes he'd snagged earlier. Or a red dot sight. One more task for later.

Greg lined up and took his first shot. The subdued blast was even softer than Tom had expected. Without the supersonic crack, he heard the action of the rifle tossing the spent brass more than he heard the shot itself.

He saw one of the guys out by Rachel's car twitch and collapse. Two more of them fell in quick order, though they took multiple shots. The last guy yelled a warning and jumped behind the car for cover.

Unfortunately for him, he assumed the shooting was coming from the other side of the road. Greg shot him in the back.

Meanwhile, the other six bikers suddenly realized that they were all alone out in the open. Tom dropped his eye to his scope, lined up on one with an AR, and slowly squeezed the trigger.

The rifle jumped in his hands. The suppressor cut back a bunch of the noise, but the AR15 was still significantly louder than the .300. His bullets were supersonic, too. The telltale crack echoed off every building around them.

The man Tom had been targeting clutched his chest and collapsed.

Tom quickly moved his point of aim to the right and shot a second man. He heard Greg firing on them as well.

One of the bikers jumped on his motorcycle and screamed towards the exit of the parking lot.

Tom lined up the crosshairs on his back and shot him. The motorcycle fell over onto its side and skidded to a stop in a sea of sparks.

Meanwhile, Greg continued firing at the remaining men. A "thwack" on the wall in front of Tom told him that the enemy had spotted them, but it didn't matter. The ex-Army man gunned them all down.

The two of them scanned for other targets as an automatic weapon opened up at the back of the store. The boom of shotguns and cracks of handguns quickly joined in. There was a battle raging back there.

Tom grabbed a few extra magazines and slid back from the edge a couple of feet before he stood and ran to the rear of the store. The gunfire continued unabated.

When he leaned over the edge of the roof, Tom could see that they were shooting primarily at the corner of the building behind the vehicles. Some of the bikers must have come around the side of the store.

He ran toward the corner of the building where the shots were coming from. Since most people never thought outside of the horizontal plane, he felt safe peeking over the edge to see what he was dealing with.

There were three bikers down below. One of them was firing around the corner with a pistol, trying not to expose himself. One of the others was reloading for him. The last guy was working with a rifle of some kind.

That was something he could deal with. Tom flicked the selector switch to the unmarked automatic position. Time to see if Moshe had gotten it installed correctly.

He leaned out over the side of the building and fired a burst into the back of the man doing the shooting. It was a nice, clean, three-round burst. The shooter stumbled forward and took hits from Tom's friends before collapsing.

Tom quickly switched his point of aim and emptied the rest of the magazine in a spray of bullets bouncing between the two remaining hostiles. The slide locked back a few seconds later.

The one reloading the pistol managed to fire at Tom before he collapsed. The shot came far too close for Tom's comfort. He was sure that it hadn't missed by more than a few inches.

He hoped to God nobody else had been hit. He raced back to the ladder while swapping the empty magazine for a fresh one. There were no shots from below. He carefully peered over the side of the building.

Rachel was looking up at him. "If you are finished playing around up there, we need to get the hell out of here."

He gestured for Greg to come back. He watched to be certain the man grabbed the satchel of extra ammunition and then went down the ladder.

There were three bodies just inside the door leading into the store. He let the rifle hang on its strap across his chest and drew his pistol before advancing to the edge of the building and peering in.

Three more bodies lay inside. That would be the six that had run inside from up front. It looked as though they'd tried to rush out and surprise his friends. That hadn't worked out so well for them.

Tom took a moment to grab their fallen weapons and tossed them into the back of the Beast's trailer. Everyone else looked okay, so he ordered them into their vehicles.

Rachel cursed. "Some ass shot my motorcycle. Hang on."

To Tom's horror, she ran toward where he'd shot the three men at the corner of the building. He raced after her and was relieved to see that no one else was hiding there.

"Have you lost your mind?" he hissed at her.

"No," she said calmly as she looked over the three motorcycles. The two at the rear were leaking gas. He'd probably caught them in the same burst that had cut down their riders.

While she looked at the last one, Tom made sure the men were dead and recovered their weapons. The rifle was a huge surprise. It was an antique, a Thompson submachine gun capable of fully automatic fire. It shot .45 ACP from either a magazine or a drum. Capone would be proud.

Tom found a second drum in one of the saddlebags, as well as a dozen regular magazines and extra ammo.

Rachel was apparently satisfied with the remaining bike. She climbed on board and started it up. "Hurry up."

He threw the saddlebags over his shoulder, held the Thompson and his AR awkwardly in front of him, and climbed on behind her. Only his arm around her waist kept him from dropping everything and falling off as she put the bike into gear and roared around the corner.

Tom climbed off the bike, put everything he'd collected away, and got into the Beast. He quickly brought it to life and stashed the AR beside him.

"Make sure you've got your radios handy," he yelled out at Rachel and Greg. "You're scouting ahead for an easy way forward. You've got to call back with statuses, or we might go down the wrong road. Also, you need to let us know if you run into any more bikers."

Rachel gave Tom a thumbs-up and put her night-vision goggles on under the edge of her helmet. She and Greg roared up the access road behind the store.

Nika was already in the passenger seat, so Tom handed her his radio. "Listen to that and tell me if anyone sends us a message."

He saw in the side mirror that Moshe and the rest were ready to roll. He put his night-vision goggles on, put the Beast into gear, and started up the road. Moshe was right behind him. None of them had their lights on. Hopefully they wouldn't attract too much attention from a distance.

"Turn right at the first intersection," Rachel said.

Nika told her they would.

They were on their way. Now all they had to do was escape Portland.

11

It quickly became obvious that 99E was a disaster. It wasn't as bad as I-5, but that wasn't saying much. Stalled cars and people trying to get out of the city had turned it into a parking lot.

While it was possible for their larger vehicles to drive on the grass beside the road, that would still be much slower than driving on pavement. Particularly considering obstacles like culverts and ditches.

Tom decided to stick to side roads. He was grateful that he'd downloaded the electronic maps of the area before the cellular network had crashed. Which it had. Even the data service and texting were gone now.

He called their scouts back, and everyone examined the possible routes on his cell phone. It turned out that Greg knew some people in the area. He pointed out a few shortcuts that might have less traffic.

At this point, everyone was exhausted. They needed to find a place where they could rest for a little while.

The farther they got from the city center, the fewer obstacles they ran into. There were places where traffic had to cross bridges. Those, by their very nature, were somewhat few and far between. So when one of them was blocked, they had to look for a different route or spend precious time clearing it.

That was the situation they found themselves in a few hours later. According to the map, they'd made it to the suburbs, at least.

In front of them was a bridge that went over a highway. According to the map, they'd have to go a couple of miles to either side if they wanted to take a different bridge. He'd prefer this one.

The problem was that someone had decided to set fire to the cars on it.

Greg eased forward for a look and returned with the news that there was no one on this side of the bridge. The ex-soldier said he could hear something from the other side, but he'd have to bypass the fire in order to scout it.

The highway the bridge went over was full of abandoned cars but also seemed quiet. Tom decided to join him in taking a look.

This would've been the perfect time for one of the drones, but they needed time to set them up. No one had thought to get the battery packs charging in the cars, either. He blamed himself for the oversight.

Tom and Greg eased down the embankment and moved slowly to the stalled cars. Each looked carefully up and down the roadway, but it seemed as though all the occupants had fled. The fire on the overpass provided more than enough light for their night-vision goggles.

Once they'd made it across, they eased up the far embankment.

Tom heard what Greg had meant. It sounded as though someone was having a party.

The two of them got down onto the ground and edged forward until they could just barely see what lay on the other side of the bridge.

There were fewer cars on this side, but someone had pushed them all together and set them ablaze, too.

It looked as though the men doing the celebrating had a few dozen people bunched up and under guard. It was hard to see a lot of detail, but Tom thought the crowd was mostly young women.

"What the hell are they doing?" Tom asked softly. "Portland was a law-abiding place twelve hours ago. How could it come apart so fast?"

Greg grunted. "The politicians don't like talking about it, but there's more than a few bad apples in the area. This whole damn city was a pot waiting to boil over. Everybody has a tribe, and every tribe has a beef with someone.

"I don't know who these people are, but I'll bet it's something like that biker gang. The criminal element thinks that the end of the world means they're in charge. In this case, it looks like they are."

Tom sighed. "As much as I hate to say it, the smart thing to do is to head back the way we came and go over to the next bridge. I don't like leaving those people to these bastards, but we were lucky during the last fight. One of us could have been killed so damned easily."

"The best fight is the one you never get into," Greg agreed. "We have people we're responsible for. We have to think of them first. This sucks, but we can't save the world."

They were just getting ready to ease back down the embankment when something happened in the crowd in front of them. Tom didn't see where she came from, but a young girl popped up out of nowhere with a younger boy in her arms. She bolted directly toward where Tom and Greg were hiding.

Several of the men shouted and took off after them. One guy back in the main group hefted a scoped rifle.

"Oh, hell no," Greg muttered. The young man already had his AR out. It spoke, and the man with the rifle fell over backward.

Tom grimaced and started targeting anyone with a gun. The people around the fire scattered, including the prisoners, who ran off toward the left. Any time one of the men tried to follow them, Greg or Tom shot them down. Since they'd already revealed their presence, they might as well do their good deed for the day.

With the fire at their back and the overpass ablaze, the people shooting at them probably couldn't see exactly where the shots were coming from. Also, Tom and his companion were down behind cover. The bastards were out in the open.

Tom wasn't certain where the two kids had gone. In all the excitement, the two of them had vanished again. He was impressed. If they hadn't made a run for it, the men around the fire might not have seen them sneaking away.

He tapped Greg on the shoulder, and they began backing down

the embankment. He grabbed the empty magazines and stuffed them into his pockets. They'd need them again soon if tonight were any example.

"We need to get across the highway before they get someone in position to shoot at us," Greg said. "We'll be sitting ducks down there."

"Go to the halfway point and cover me."

They leapfrogged across the highway, with one of them moving farther away and covering their retreat while the other rushed past.

Tom saw movement behind them as they were reaching their side of the highway. From beside a dark minivan, he shot at their pursuers. Greg took advantage of the covering fire and scurried up the embankment.

As soon as Greg opened fire, Tom charged up after him, praying that nobody hit him.

They certainly tried. He saw at least two bullets hit just in front of him, so he changed the angle of his retreat and started dodging a little bit. Not the easiest thing to do while climbing an embankment.

He managed to reach the top in one piece and rolled over the edge. Greg was there in a flash, checking to see if he was okay. At Tom's nod, the two of them turned and hurried away, bent over at the waist to reduce the chances of someone shooting them.

Everyone else had obviously heard the fight and was looking in every direction for possible threats. Rachel and Moshe moved to cover Tom and Greg as they ran for their vehicles.

"Head for the next bridge to the east," Tom shouted as he climbed into the Beast.

They'd parked far enough back so that they had the option to turn around. Rachel took her bike ahead while Greg kept watch on their rear.

Thankfully, the rear-wheel steering that Tom had installed on the Beast made reversing course at least possible. The turning radius on these old trucks sucked.

Moshe led the way, and Tom fell in behind him.

The radio crackled and Nika held it up where Tom could hear it.

"Looks like you picked up a couple of passengers," Greg said through the howling static. "I see two little faces looking back at me from your trailer. You want to stop while I evict them?"

That was an easy decision to make. "No. We'll find out who they are the next time we stop. Just keep an eye on them."

The kids were certainly going to have plenty of opportunity to escape if they chose. None of the vehicles was going very fast. When they had to dodge around stalled cars, they were easily going slow enough for someone to hop out.

Since he didn't hear anything from Greg, Tom assumed that the kids had chosen to stay where they were.

Rachel asked what had happened, so he gave them the short version while Nika held the transmitter. That got the Israeli woman to cursing. Nika looked sick to her stomach.

"I can't believe this is happening," the young woman beside him said. "This morning I had a normal life. Now it seems like every guy out there is going nuts. With a few notable exceptions," she said apologetically.

"No offense taken. These are rough times, and I can't blame you for being bitter after what happened."

She sat silently for a minute. "I'd seen the guy who tried to rape me before. He lived in my building. After what he did, I was so angry. I wanted to make him pay. Just like I hope those bastards behind us pay for what they were doing."

"The world we're entering isn't going to be kind to the meek," Tom said softly. "Don't feel guilty about killing scum like that. Be strong, just like you have been."

The next bridge they came to was miraculously clear of obstacles. It looked as though someone had pushed the cars out of the way. He wasn't going to count his blessings too soon, so once Rachel declared it clear, he drove over it quickly.

Nika consulted the map on his phone. She'd dug up a battery pack at her place that could keep it working for a long time if she only turned it on when they needed to see the map.

"There's a smaller road about three miles ahead," she said. "If we go east, we'll be farther from I-5 but also out into a less settled area. It'll mean more travel tomorrow, but it might be safer tonight."

He had to agree. There would be a lot of people streaming away from I-5 tonight. They'd have a better chance of finding a place to hole up if they got off the beaten path.

The farther away they got from the city, the easier navigation became. They were able to pick up speed. That meant turning the lights on, but he felt a little safer about doing so out here. They shut off the night-vision goggles to save their batteries.

He spotted a turnoff that had potential. The sign indicated there was some kind of campsite out that way. An additional sign hung underneath saying it was closed for the winter. Perfect.

"Tell them we're turning here," Tom said. "Ask Greg to tear down that sign and toss it into the bushes. The fewer people that know something is back here the better."

He doubted they'd be able to stay more than the night, but they needed rest. They also needed to repack everything they'd hastily shoved into the trucks. The critical items should be easily accessible.

That was a job best done during daylight hours. If so, they might wait until tomorrow night to travel any farther. Night seemed safest for movement.

Tom held out little hope that any organized government would survive the collapse. They all had to accept that the lights were never coming back on. He'd be thrilled to be wrong, but he knew he wasn't.

The campground was one of those that let people have little individual areas with trees, tables, and grills. It wasn't set up for RV camping but had plenty of space to toss up a tent. It was several miles away from the main road. Perfect.

There was a small shack where someone would normally collect fees, but it was empty. There was an arm down across the entrance to keep people from driving in, too. Rachel had already smashed the lock and raised it.

Tom drove in and headed back toward the rear of the property. It was on the other side of some trees, so they could camp there without fear of someone driving by and seeing them.

Once he pulled into a suitable spot, he shut the Beast down. "Nika, I want you to come talk to the kids. I'll probably scare them, so you need to get them to come out."

The two of them made their way slowly around to where they could look into the trailer. Tom kept his hands away from his gun. The temperature had been dropping all evening, and they had to be cold back there.

They'd found a blanket to keep warm. Good. They sat huddled under it and stared out at the two of them.

The girl was younger than he'd thought. She couldn't be much more than thirteen or fourteen years old. The boy was maybe ten. Both of them looked terrified.

"We're not going to hurt you," Nika said softly.

That's when Tom spotted the pistol in the girl's hand.

He wasn't sure if it was one they'd scavenged and tossed into the trailer or if the girl had gotten her hands on it before she escaped back at the bridge. In the end, that didn't matter. The situation had just become a whole lot more dangerous.

12

Tom kept his hands out in the open. "There's no need to be afraid. If you want, you can jump down out of the trailer and go. We won't chase you.

"Or you could let us fix you something hot to eat while we get to know one another. You don't know us, so I don't blame you for feeling nervous. My name is Tom Morgan. My friend here is Nika Andropov."

The little girl frowned. "That's a funny name."

Her voice was a little higher pitched and more childlike than Tom had anticipated. He might need to revise his age estimate down a little bit. Maybe twelve. Big for her age, but the girl definitely hadn't hit puberty yet.

Nika smiled. "My grandfather emigrated from Russia when my father was a little boy. I really wish you'd let us give you some food. Maybe we can find some extra clothes for you, too. You look cold."

The rest of his people had slowly gathered where the children could see them. All except Greg. Tom suspected the man was somewhere out of sight, probably with his rifle trained on the girl. He really, *really* hoped they didn't have to shoot her.

Perhaps it was because there were so many women standing

outside the trailer, but after a tense few moments, he saw the girl relax a little. "What kind of food?"

Tom opened his mouth to answer but realized he really didn't have any idea what they would fix. He had a ton of freeze-dried stuff he'd picked up at the Expo Center, but while filling, he wasn't sure that any of that would be enticing to a child. Maybe some of the canned soup?

"Do you like hotdogs and chili?" Rachel asked.

He turned his head and raised his eyebrows. "We have hot dogs?"

She shrugged. "I grabbed a few packages on the last run into the store. I also got some sandwich meat, sliced cheese, and bread. Hunk cheese and summer sausage, too. The meat and cheese are in the ice chests with the medicine."

"That would've been nice to know while we were driving around," he grumbled. "I've been eating food bars."

"Stop whining. We need to eat the perishable stuff in the next couple of days before it goes bad."

The girl had her brother climb out first and jumped down behind him. If he'd wanted to, Tom could probably have snatched the pistol from her while she wasn't looking at him, but that certainly wouldn't help the girl trust them. At this point, he had a feeling that this was going to work out.

One good thing about the camping area was that it had plenty of trees to block the wind. The air was still cold, but it wasn't biting. There was a wedge of trees between them and the road, too. They could build a fire without any danger that someone would spot the light.

He'd have to be careful to get dry limbs, though. Wet wood generated more smoke. While that probably wouldn't be a problem this late at night, it was best to start taking precautions. If they could find suitable wood, it would be smart to pack some away in the trailer. The next time they needed fire, it might be wet and miserable.

Yes, they had the camp stoves from the outdoor store, but he'd prefer to save them for when nothing else would do.

He'd mastered the art of starting a fire. He'd learned during the wilderness survival course he'd taken. It paid to know the skills his characters required.

Not that he practiced them very much. He'd find out shortly how badly that was going to hurt.

Tom decided to let the women handle the children. They'd be much less likely to feel threatening.

As soon as the kids were away from the trailer, he lowered the tailgate and looked at everything stuffed inside. It was a mess. He wasn't even sure the tents were in this part. They might be in the back of the Beast. Or in Moshe's truck.

"We need to get the tents up so that we can start moving things into them," he said to the rest. "I'm not sure what the weather is going to be like tonight, but it's pretty gusty. We might get some rain, and I'd rather not get our stuff wet.

"If we set up a tent right here by the Beast, we can move things into it as we unload. A lot of it will go back into the vehicles, but if we catch a sudden downpour, it'll stay dry. Does anyone know where the tents are?"

Greg materialized from the dim light cast by the aurora. He had an AR in his hands, but he wasn't aiming it towards where the women were settling the children in. Apparently, he thought the situation was under control, too.

"They're in the trailer with the four-wheelers. Should be easy to get out. We figured we'd need those pretty quick."

Tom walked back behind Moshe's truck and looked at stuff they'd stacked around the four-wheelers. They'd used tie-down straps and a couple of tarps to secure everything. Smart.

They must've picked up a couple of more tents when he wasn't looking, because he saw five boxes stacked together. Three of them were relatively small, probably big enough to hold three or four people. One of them was a bigger family affair with multiple rooms that could hold all of them in a pinch.

The last one was more interesting. It said that it was a refurbished General Purpose Medium Tent.

The only thing identifying it was a big tag tied to one of the ropes folding the huge pile of canvas into a tight square. There was a large box next to it labelled "poles."

"We found that in back at the outdoor store," Greg said. "The new ones are made of vinyl, but these heavy canvas jobs are really good. It was too good to pass up.

"Way more room than we really need, until you find yourself in a situation like this. We should be able to unload just about everything from the vehicles and get it under cover while we sort."

Tom scratched his head. "I'll make the guess that this is some kind of Army thing, but what exactly is a General Purpose Medium Tent?"

"A GP medium is a big tent with two center poles and a support beam that runs between them. There's a bunch of poles that sit along the edges to support the weight and hold up the sides. It's big enough to have cots on both sides and still leave the center aisle."

"How hard is it to get up?"

Greg shrugged. "Not too bad if you got enough bodies, impossible if you don't. You lay the tent out over the beam and support poles, stand the sides up, and then raise the center and tighten things down.

"It's got flaps for a couple of stoves to warm the interior. The two military stoves we found are dual fuel. Either liquid or solid. We can use wood if we need to sleep inside it."

Moshe shook his head. "Are the four of us going to be enough?"

"Should be," Greg said. "It'll take at least an hour."

"Well, we'd best get this started," Tom said. "Since you've done this before, tell us what we need to do."

They had sufficient open area to set up the tent, but Greg had them go over it with their flashlights, tossing any debris they found off to the side.

Only once the area was free of clutter did they fit the support beams together and attach the support poles. The four of them manhandled the heavy tent off the trailer and unfolded it over the poles. A lighter liner went inside the canvas.

Once they had it all fully stretched out, Tom realized the damned thing was huge.

"If this is a medium, how the hell big is a large?" he asked.

Greg grinned. "Think Ringling Brothers and Barnum and Bailey

Circus big. They set up chow halls for entire companies in those. This one is designed for a dozen people, but it can hold double that if you don't mind a little crowding."

They went around the exterior, setting the side poles under Greg's direction. They drove in stakes but left the attached ropes loose. Only when that was complete did they raise the center and get the tent square.

Once Greg was satisfied that everything was good and the ropes were tight, they rolled up the side closest to the trucks. That would make moving things in and out of the tent much easier. All told, it took them almost ninety minutes to get the huge tent up.

Tom called a break so they could eat. He'd smelled the hotdogs cooking earlier, so the women had gotten a fire going. He'd forgotten to check the wood, but it looked as though there was very little smoke.

It seemed they'd been able to generate some trust with the children. The pistol the girl had carried was nowhere in sight. He wondered if she still had it.

He took one of the prepackaged bottles of water, drank a bit, and then put some powdered drink mix into it. It was good. He snagged up a second one to have with his meal.

They'd built a fire in a square brick enclosure with a grate. Doctor Emery was performing the cooking duties. She opened a fresh package of hot dogs and put them on the grill to cook. There was a pot with some chili simmering beside them. Tom could see a couple of open packages of hotdog buns off to the side.

Once he sat down, he realized exactly how tired he was. Maybe unloading the trailer tonight was a bad idea. They were all beat. They'd had a hell of a day.

Rachel sat down beside him. She eyed the children across the camp as they spoke with Jenna Caldwell in soft tones.

"They have nowhere to go. It may be some time before we find out the whole story, but they were trying to escape Portland when those guys captured their family.

"Based on something the girl's father told her, I suspect that the men were convicts on a bus that overpowered their guards. They apparently rounded up everybody they could get their hands on. They marched the men off and didn't bring them back. There was shooting, but the boy didn't put it together."

It made Tom sick to his stomach hearing that. He wished he'd shot every single last one of the bastards.

"What about the mother?"

"It seems that she put up too much of a fight. They took her away with her husband."

Well, that certainly settled that. He wasn't going to abandon children in the wilderness.

"Does she still have the gun?"

Rachel nodded. "I would not worry. The safety is engaged, and it does not seem as though she knows how to shoot anyway. I am inclined to let her keep it. It makes her feel safe. She is not going to cause us any trouble."

"What are their names?"

"She is Nancy Baker, and her little brother is Adam. She will be thirteen in a few months. He is nine. Are you certain that we cannot drive back and kill every last one of those bastards?"

He smiled coldly. "Well, we do have to head back that way. If we happen to find them just sitting there, I suppose we might be able to do something.

"I don't want to go hunting for fights, though. We've been damned lucky. If our luck turns bad for just a little bit, one of us could die. Revenge is nice, but I've got to think about everyone."

She smiled at him. "You keep thinking about our safety. You seem to be doing a good job. Leave the revenge to me. I am very good at that, too."

Based on what he'd seen back at Nika's apartment, he didn't doubt her for a second.

"As soon as we finish eating, we need to set up the smaller tents," he said. "I think it's probably best if the guys sleep together in one and the six of you take the other two. Nancy and Adam don't know us. They're not going to be comfortable around men for a while, I suspect. Not after what happened."

Rachel patted him on the knee. "You raised that big tent. Finish your meal and rest. We will take care of the smaller ones."

Once she'd left, he gratefully accepted a paper plate with two chili dogs from Doctor Emery. He sat there eating the hot food in the cold night air, watching the gorgeous colors flowing over their heads.

How could utter disaster be so beautiful?

Well, it wouldn't last more than a few days. Possibly longer if there were additional coronal mass ejections. At this point, it no longer mattered if another one hit them.

Once the light show was gone, the night would be blacker than a pit.

Tom really needed to think about what their next steps should be, but his brain refused to function. He'd get a decent night's sleep and think about it in the morning.

13

Tom woke up groggy. He'd only lain down a few hours before dawn. Unsurprisingly, he'd slept poorly.

The thin mat underneath his sleeping bad kept him physically comfortable, but his dreams kept him tossing and turning. Lots of running, chasing, and shooting. More shooting than anything else.

That wasn't a big surprise. He'd killed over a dozen men yesterday. Maybe twice that number. Ironically, the lack of certainty disturbed him.

He wouldn't have done anything differently. Those people had deserved to die, given the circumstances under which he'd shot them. Their deaths still haunted him, though.

Greg had volunteered to take the first watch. The young man had told him that he'd wake Rachel to take the second watch. Tom wasn't certain who Rachel had tapped to go third.

He supposed it should have been him, but no one had woken him. Maybe that was because they'd gone to sleep so late.

Looking around the tent that the men had shared last night, he saw that Moshe and Randy were already up. Greg was still asleep, and Tom was inclined to let him doze while he could.

Randy should have spent the night with his wife, but the kids had bonded to her. She'd insisted that she stay with them in the women's tent.

Tom rose quietly and dressed. He really needed a shower—or at least to clean up—but it would have to wait until they had things moving.

He checked his watch. It was almost noon.

As he came out of the tent, he saw that everyone else was up. He'd been one of the last to rise. That shamed him a little bit.

They had the Beast's trailer unloaded. Its contents were in different areas underneath the protection of the GP medium. They were just beginning the process of emptying the back of the Beast.

Rachel saw him coming and headed out to meet him. "I decided to let you sleep in. Driving this monster all night really took it out of you."

"I suppose it did. Thanks, but let's not do this again. I need to do my share, just like everyone else."

"Fair enough. We dug a little pit out back. There is a red handkerchief tied to a bush beside it. That is where you can take care of your business. We will cover it when we leave. Breakfast is sandwiches."

Tom found the pit and relieved himself. Thankfully, the cold weather kept the smell down. He knew that in the summer months, things would be different. Smelly outhouses would be back in style.

Once he had his sandwich and bottle of water, he headed back to the tent. Rachel was looking at all the solar panels he'd bought from Randy.

"Are you planning on powering the entire West Coast? I do not think I have ever seen so many solar panels in one place before."

He smiled a little. "Well, the plan was to make sure that my place had more than enough power if the grid went down. This is probably more than I needed, but I figured we might have a bunch of days in a row where sunlight is scarce. That's also why I have all those batteries I bought from Randy Caldwell."

She gazed over at where Randy and Jenna were working together to get some boxes off the Beast. "He builds solar panels?"

Tom nodded. "That and more. He's an MIT graduate with an engineering degree. He designed these solar arrays and the motors that keep them pointing toward the sun. He and his wife lived in Nevada, so I suppose that made sense. I suspect getting back home won't be easy."

"If he is smart, he will not try," she said. "Water is going to be scarce, and without air-conditioning, it will be lethally hot."

He supposed she was right. Not even counting the difficulties of trying to get to Nevada, there wasn't much call for them doing so. For better or worse, the Caldwells would be staying in Oregon.

"Where are the kids?"

"Annie is examining them. They seemed healthy enough to me, but I suppose it does not hurt to be careful. What are our plans?"

He gestured at all the material they were unloading. "The first thing we need to do is get all of this sorted. We grabbed a bunch of stuff, so we need to take an inventory.

"Once we know what we have, we repack it in a way that makes sense. We have to be able to access everything we need in a timely fashion. That means that critical items need to be right there at hand. We'll pack the things that will be useful later deeper in.

"Also, we need to make sure and split up things like food and water so that we don't lose everything if one vehicle crashes or something. The same principle carries over to critical equipment. We don't need all our eggs in one basket."

Rachel looked at the Beast. "That is going to take the rest of the day."

"Then that's what it takes. It probably won't hurt us to spend an extra day getting ourselves in order and dealing with the emotions we're all feeling."

Rachel shook her head. "No. If we stop to think, half of us will fall apart. We need to focus on surviving."

She headed back to where she'd been working without another word. He didn't know what part of her past made her so certain, but he hoped she'd feel comfortable enough around him one day to tell him the story.

He finished his sandwich, drank his water, and threw the bottle away in a nearby trashcan. Seeing the other used plastic containers inside, he realized they should salvage those before they left. They could reuse and repurpose the bottles.

They'd need to look at recycling in a completely different way. Just about any piece of trash might be useful for some other task. Just one more thing to think about.

He joined the others, and they began really making progress on the Beast. Greg woke up about half an hour later and set off to scout the area around them. If they had neighbors, it would be good to know ahead of time.

Nika walked over to him and cleared her throat. "I hate to bother you, but you said we had a way to charge some power packs. I should really work on these drones while I have some sunlight. We might need them tomorrow."

He stretched his back. "Right. First, we'll need to finish emptying the Beast. I have an inverter generator up near the cab. It has a thirty-three-amp capacity and can produce AC power. It should be more than capable of charging everything you need without really denting its capacity."

"Won't a generator make noise?"

"It's not really a generator. It's a big battery that we can charge off the grid or some solar panels I have stored with it. I've got a couple of additional batteries that I can chain into it for another eighty-five amps."

She nodded. "That's plenty. Once we have it out, it shouldn't take more than a couple of hours to charge all the power packs that I think we'll need right now."

"Charge as many as you can, even if you don't expect to use them right now. The opportunity to do so might not come again until we get to my place."

Clearing out the back of the big truck took another hour. He set the power supply up in the family-sized tent that Doctor Emery had apparently decreed be used for common purposes. The little unit was light enough to go up on a folding table.

He left Nika unpacking drone boxes and attaching charging units to battery packs.

By the time they finished unloading Moshe's truck and the trailer with the four-wheelers, they were all exhausted and sweaty. With the trees blocking the wind, they'd been able to take their jackets off. Those would have to go back on now that they weren't working so hard.

The amount of supplies they had collected was impressive. He spotted any number of things that he'd never have considered getting before but that would prove useful. He hated the fact that he'd needed to become a looter, but all this stuff might save their lives in the months ahead.

The arsenal of weapons that Moshe had brought from his store was almost frightening. Tom was certain they could arm a Third World country. They'd almost certainly never need all the firepower, but having it at hand certainly made him feel better.

The older man walked over and stood beside him. "I pretty much cleaned my shop out. All the weapons, all the purchases that were waiting for people to pick them up, they're all here. About all I left behind was some ammo for the cops."

"What kind of stuff are we talking about? The rifles, I mean."

"Everything from .22 long rifles up to a .50 BMG. I also have all the automatic weapons, of course. Not just the ones you know about, but some stuff I've had in the back for years. Big stuff."

Moshe led him over to a couple of large boxes stacked on top of one another. At his gesture, Tom helped him move the topmost to the ground.

When his friend opened it, Tom gaped. "Is that what I think it is?"

"If you think it's an M2 .50-caliber machine gun, you'd be right. We don't have an infinite supply of ammunition, of course, but in a pinch this could really put the hurt on someone."

That it could. The Army had designed it to destroy equipment. It could chew through engine blocks, light armor, and any unlucky opponents hiding behind them.

"I have both the tripod and the vehicle mount. The Beast isn't set up for it, but I bet we can rig something up once we get to your place. Or we could mount it in the back of my pickup truck. We have all kinds of options."

Tom shook his head. "You're just full of surprises. What else do you have here?"

They moved the next box to the ground, opened it, and Tom laughed. "Somebody's been watching too much *Predator*."

"You can never see too much Arnold Schwarzenegger," the older man assured him.

The box contained a 5.56-caliber minigun with six rotating barrels. Spare barrels sat in the foam beside it.

"Damn," Tom said. "This will leave a mark."

Moshe closed the box. "I think you've seen just about everything else that's interesting, but I have one more thing to show you. A special order. I'd imagine the guy that's looking for this is going to be pissed if he's still alive."

Moshe went to the stack of rifle cases and selected one. He set it gently on top of the minigun box and opened it.

Inside the protective case lay a high-powered rifle. Tom had seen plenty of them over the years. This one had some extra device near the scope.

"This is a specialty gun for long-range shooting. That device is a built-in computer that calculates the distance, windage, and all of the other variables that a long-range shooter has to take into account. Even the rotation of the earth, if you can believe it.

"It was for an active-duty marine sniper. The company that makes these sells models that can shoot out to twelve hundred yards to the public for tens of thousands of dollars.

"This one is hush-hush and only for military and law enforcement. Its range is supposedly good out to two thousand yards. As you might imagine, it is obscenely expensive."

Tom was skeptical. Twelve football fields was a long way to shoot. Twenty was ridiculous. He knew that professionals were able to get hits at even longer ranges, but having a computer do it? That seemed a little too Terminator for him.

"Does it work?" he asked.

Moshe shrugged. "It's not as though I had a place to go test it for more than four hundred yards. It worked perfectly at that range. You line up the crosshairs on what you want to shoot, press the little button on the side of the computer, and it puts a little dot out on the view.

"That's where the rifle has to be aimed to get the bullet onto the target where you originally had the crosshairs. You can squeeze the trigger, but it won't fire until you bring the crosshairs onto the dot. Then boom.

"I watched a video review of it in which they gave one to a reporter who had never shot a rifle before. He was able to hit a man-sized target at a thousand yards with only basic training in how to correctly hold the rifle against his shoulder in a prone position."

Tom had to admit that was impressive. "We'll have to let Greg use it. He seems like the long-range shooting type."

Moshe laughed. "Greg thinks this thing is for cheaters. That's what he used to do in the Army."

"Really? I suppose it explains a lot of things about how good he is."

The older man nodded. "I can imagine this situation isn't doing him much good. He left the service with a few issues. I'm keeping my eye on him. If I get worried, I'll talk to him. I think he'll be okay."

The sun was starting to edge below the tree line. It was going to be dark again soon. He saw that Greg had returned and was over by the fire. He was probably fixing something to eat. That sounded good.

"I think we should all take a break. Then we need to figure out what we're going to do tomorrow. The longer we wait to get moving, the greater the chances that we'll run into trouble heading for the coast."

He really wished they could get moving, but the time spent repacking this mess wasn't wasted. He just hoped it didn't hurt them in the long run.

14

I t looked as though the evening meal was canned vegetable stew. It smelled delicious.

Once again, they all circled around the fire. Except for Greg. He'd vanished again. Probably out patrolling the area. Tom made a mental note to check with him and see what they should be doing going forward. The man obviously knew his business.

Someone had found metal mess kits for eating. There were plenty to go around. That made dealing with the hot stew much easier.

Once Tom had taken the edge off his hunger, he cleared his throat. "I understand that yesterday was intense. I'm sure you all have questions about what happened. Some of you know the full story. Some of you know almost nothing. Let me tell you what I know."

He laid out the background as concisely as he could. They looked numb by the time he'd finished.

"We've had the bad luck to run into some bad apples," he continued. "Unfortunately, people like that are going to take advantage of others during this crisis. The only thing they understand is force.

"I didn't sleep well last night. Frankly, I'm not sure that I will for a long while. It's no easy thing taking a life, even when the other person deserved it. It's worse when you have to do it wholesale. I'm sorry to say that I expect we'll need to do it again."

"It is distasteful, but we will do what we have to," Rachel said. "If I need to kill a hundred men like the ones yesterday, I will not lose one moment's sleep over it. Neither should you."

That just confirmed Tom's opinion of how tough Rachel was. They'd do well to emulate her.

"I'll understand if this is a little too Judge Dredd for you, but in this new world, we are the law," Tom said. "If someone crosses us, we need to cross them off. We're a long way from safety. Even once we get to my place, there'll still be dangers all around us.

"Civilization is dying. Between the EMP attack, the coronal mass ejection, and the nuke blowing up Seattle, all the modern conveniences are gone. Over the next week, people are going to go from scavenging to stealing what they need to survive."

Randy gestured toward the GP medium. "We're lucky we have all that stuff. You guys were really thinking ahead. It's like sitting on a pot of gold. So, if you don't mind, I'll think of you as the Collector rather than Judge Dredd."

Tom smiled. "Nice comic reference. I had a little bit of a jump on everyone else because I've been thinking about this for a while. I was also damned lucky in that I was at the prepper show and that I could use my credit cards to buy up a bunch of stuff before the lights went out. At this point, I don't even think cash is worth anything.

"The people in the cities that survived are almost certainly out of water by now. They'll start drinking from the rivers and any other place water gathers. That means people will start getting sick with waterborne illnesses. That'll cause a health crisis."

Doctor Emery grunted sourly. "You have no idea. Thirsty people will drink whatever they can get their hands on. The results will be ugly, but we're lucky here in Oregon. There's plenty of water to drink, even though it's going to make a bunch of people sick.

"Imagine what it's going to be like in Southern California. They have to import vast quantities of water just for the people that live there. With the power out, the death toll is going to be hideous. If someone nuked LA or any of the big cities down there, it will be even worse."

"That matches up with what I've read," Tom agreed. "The next few weeks are going to be awful in every big city still standing. People are trapped there and will use up every bit of supplies they have. Then they'll go to war to get what they need to fill their children's bellies.

"That doesn't even count the would-be warlords that are going to set themselves up. The motorcycle gang and the escaped convicts were just the first examples. Other groups will form. Once they get organized, it's going to make travel even more difficult."

He inclined his head toward the two children. "I'm sorry about what happened to you. I hope we can find your parents. If we can't, you're welcome to stay with us. We'll see that you get somewhere safe. As safe as anyplace is going to be."

Nancy nodded, her eyes glinting damply in the firelight. She knew they wouldn't find her parents. The boy just stared hopefully at him.

This was probably going to be hardest on them at first. They were young, though. They might adjust to the new world a lot faster than the adults did.

"What do we do tomorrow?" Nika asked. "We're not going to try to load the trucks and leave tonight, are we?"

Tom shook his head. "No. We'll let Randy and Jenna finish taking a complete inventory tomorrow. Once we have that, we'll pack everything up again. Randy, be sure to split the food and other critical materials up so there are some in all the vehicles, just in case.

"We'll leave the day after tomorrow. I'm not sure if we're better off traveling during the day or at night. Each one has pluses and minuses."

"Let me show you what we can do with the drones tomorrow," Nika said. "I'm betting you're going to choose daylight. We should be able to scout far enough ahead to see trouble coming."

"I'm looking forward to seeing what they can do," he admitted.

They were quiet for a few minutes. Doctor Emery was the next one to throw something out.

"I've been listening to a battery-powered radio. The reception stinks with all the distortion, and there aren't many stations still on the air. Most of those have switched to prerecorded emergency messages. It sounds bad.

"One with a human host confirmed that the civil unrest in Portland has spun completely out of control. Emergency services are gone. If there's a fire, it's burning until it runs out of fuel. A couple of big swaths of the city are smoking ruins.

"The police that are left don't dare come out and try to restore order. Frankly, I'd be shocked if they don't disappear in the next couple of days. Maybe things are different in small towns, but in Portland, it's everyone for themselves."

"Things won't be as bad in rural areas and small towns, but they're not going to be good," Tom said quietly. "They're going to get a flood of refugees and start closing up shop for outsiders. It won't surprise me to see local police turning people away. They have no choice.

"Even that's a stop-gap measure. They're going to run out of supplies themselves. There's a lot more self-sufficiency in the country, so it'll take longer. They'll hit rock bottom in a few months. Maybe six months tops. At that point, it's going to be the best prepared who come through.

"My place is pretty isolated, but we're not that far from the ocean. The fishing industry is going to survive in one form or another. I also have some seeds that we can turn into crops next year. I'm not saying it will be easy, but we have the tools to survive."

Tom glanced at his watch. "I realize that it feels as if we just got up, but we should get some more sleep. We'll get up at dawn and get to work."

He shook his head and smiled a little. "Listen to me. You guys haven't even said that you want me calling the shots. Is this okay with everyone?"

"When the shit hits the fan, you want to have one person in unquestioned command," Greg said from over near the trees. "You've got a good head on your shoulders, Tom. We'd be in bad shape if you hadn't led us this far. I think that's the way we should keep going."

The rest of them looked at one another and nodded, not saying a word.

"Then get some sleep. Greg, you know what you're doing tactically, so set up a night rotation. We need to have someone watching out for trouble at all hours. What do you think? Two-hour rotations?"

"That sounds about right," the man agreed. "We'll stick with experienced people tonight, and I'll start giving everyone training to do their part over the next few days."

Tom stepped over to where Greg leaned up against a tree, watching the people around the fire. "What did you find on your scouting mission?"

"There are a few houses up the road. Based on the lights in the windows, there are people home. There's lots of distance between folks, and none are too close. We should be safe here.

"I put the lock back on the gate and made it look as if everything was still secure. So long as we stay back here and don't make a lot of noise, no one will have cause to come looking."

That was good news. Possibly the first good news they'd had since this whole mess started.

"I've been thinking about scouting out ahead of us," Greg said. "While I like the motorcycle, it's noisy. I'm thinking it might be possible to have someone out front that other people don't hear coming from a mile or two away."

"What do you have in mind?"

"I tossed a couple of mixed-use bicycles into the trailer while we were at the outdoor place. They should be good on the asphalt and in the rough country. Those things move faster than most people expect, and they're quiet.

"If we take turns having people go two or three miles in front of the vehicles, they should be able to spot any trouble. Hopefully before trouble spots them."

Tom wasn't so sure that was going to work out as well as the ex-Army man thought.

"What if the scout runs into trouble? Help will be a long way away."

The man shrugged. "Life is full of trade-offs, man. All I'm doing is laying out options."

"Nika has an idea, too," Tom said. "She picked up a bunch of drones at the store. She says she'll put on a demonstration tomorrow. She thinks we can use them to scout.

"I'm interested to see their capabilities. Every time I check out something new like this, I find out that technology has taken it to levels I never would have dreamed possible. There's no damn telling what these things can do."

Greg seemed to consider that for a moment and nodded. "That might be true. If so, we should be able to combine someone on a bike being backed up by a drone checking out ahead of them. If the drone spots something, the scout can follow it up without exposing themselves.

"Only a couple of people are going to be able to ride a bike for any length of time. Me, Rachel, and maybe you. Nika looks fit. Randy and Jenna possibly."

Tom laughed. "I'm not in nearly as good a shape as you give me credit for. I'd be huffing and puffing inside of five minutes. Though it wouldn't hurt me to start losing weight—more weight—and getting in shape. That'll probably have to wait until we get to the coast.

"That does bring up an interesting subject, though. We need to get some cross-training done. I know how to drive the Beast, and you probably do, too. I'm not sure about anyone else. Rachel was in the IDF, so she might."

"She does. Moshe will know, too. He did his mandatory service in the IDF, too. Training is still a good idea, though. If we're going to do our traveling for more than a few hours at a time, it would be nice to switch off drivers."

The young man looked up at the sky. "How long is the color show going to last?"

"A couple of days, probably. Possibly longer if there are any follow-up CMEs."

The two of them stood in silence for a while and then Greg shifted. "I guess I should go find my replacement and give them a sitrep. I'm going to put you on the rotation for just before dawn. You can wake the rest of us up. You should probably get some sleep."

Tom nodded and headed for the men's tent. Maybe tonight he'd be able to sleep a little more soundly.

15

The third day of the apocalypse came early. Rachel shook him awake while it was still dark. He nodded in the dim light she had on, and she left him alone to get dressed.

He was getting ripe. It was long past time to break out the handy wipes. If they could've spared the water, he'd have loved a shower. Since he was wishing for the impossible, he upped that to a hot shower.

At least his underclothes were clean. They'd divided all the clothing they'd collected. He had plenty of new underwear, socks, and long johns. He had fresh outer garments, too, but he figured that those could last more than a few days before he swapped them out.

He had absolutely no idea how they were going to wash clothes while on the move. The simple answer might be that they weren't. That was one aspect of the apocalypse he'd never felt the need to research. Pity.

Once he had dressed and had his AR ready, he made his way out of the tent carefully. Rachel was waiting for him near where they'd banked the coals for the night. They'd dug a hole, put the hot coals into it, and covered them with a fireproof cover designed to keep them going.

"When the sky starts graying, Annie would like you to wake her up," Rachel said softly. "She is sleeping in the common tent with her gear. She figured if someone needed the doctor, they should not have to wake everyone else."

He nodded. "Is there anything I need to know about?"

She shook her head. "I heard a motorcycle going by on the main road about an hour ago. They must have really been going for the sound to carry all this way.

"There is no sign of anyone near us. It is easy enough to see around with the night-vision goggles, but I have been going easy on the batteries. If I hear a noise, I drop them down and look. I have seen a few animals that way, but no humans."

"Sounds good to me," he said. "Go get some sleep."

She headed into the women's tent without another word.

It was cold enough that his breath puffed in the air. He hadn't been paying attention to the weather forecast before everything went to hell. Other than the fact that the remnants of the typhoon were bearing down on the Oregon or Washington coast.

At this point, he supposed he'd be as surprised as everyone else was when the weather changed. It wasn't as though he could access the satellite feeds to see what was happening.

There must be some way they could access the raw data, but that was a question for Randy. They'd be wise to plan for rain today. Maybe rain for the next couple of days. That might limit the utility of Nika's drones.

If the storm went north, they might only get some scattered showers. If it hit Oregon directly, they'd probably get heavy winds and hard rain.

He set off walking around the camp to get the lay of the land. He used his night-vision goggles to make sure he didn't walk into anything. Nothing was stirring at this hour other than a couple of raccoons looking for a snack.

The campground was pretty bare bones, but he did find something interesting during his roving patrol. There was a well at the rear of the campground. It drew water up into a tank that fed out through a spigot. A couple of light taps indicated that the tank was full.

He finished walking his circuit and made his way to the GP medium. He had a portable shower setup for emergencies. One he could use the generator to heat water with.

Tom removed the generator from the larger common tent without waking Doctor Emery. It was weatherproof, so he carried it over to the tank water. It only took a couple of minutes to suspend the shower bag on the provided pole. A handy bucket was sufficient to fill it.

Tom knew from testing that it would take fifteen or twenty minutes to get the water nice and hot. He'd wake Doctor Emery once he'd gotten her water hot.

Alone in the dark, the aurora was beautiful. It made him wonder how the people up in Alaska and Canada were doing. The winter there was much harsher, but they were better prepared, he suspected.

When the sky began brightening to the east, he made his way back to the large common tent. He found Doctor Emery sleeping in one of the side rooms. He cleared his throat politely. She stirred immediately.

"You asked to be woken up early, Doctor Emery," he said softly. "It'll be dawn in about half an hour."

She sat up and brushed the sleep out of her eyes. "I think we're going to get to know one another well enough to set formality aside. I'd appreciate it if you just call me Annie."

"Of course. My dad raised me to be polite, so I can't help myself. I'll step outside while you get dressed, but bring some extra clothes."

She raised an eyebrow but didn't say anything.

It took her about five minutes to come out. He led her back to the shower.

"I found all this water that we're not going to be able to take with us, so I figured it would be useful for showers. The bag has a heater, but it's not infinite. Once you're out of water, you're out.

"There's a bucket right there next to the spigot that you can use to fill it up for the next person. Don't worry about it causing a problem running out. It has a shutoff for the heating element."

The shower had a privacy curtain on a ring. Tom had set up a folding table next to it with a selection of the soap, shampoo, and towels. There were also hand towels and a loofah.

She grinned. "This looks divine. How long does it take to heat the water up for the next person?"

"Fifteen or twenty minutes. Everyone will have plenty of time to take a shower, so don't be sparing. You can send one of the other ladies down once you finish. I realize that you cooked yesterday, but are you cooking today? I'm not sure who knows enough outdoor cooking to be useful."

"My husband used to take me camping all the time before he passed, and I've been on a number of long-term medical missions where we had to take care of ourselves. Cooking for this number of people is not a problem for me.

"I saw that you had canned and freeze-dried food. I'll be able to work with that and keep producing hot meals for everyone. It would be a lot better if we had more selection, but I suppose we'll have to make do."

He left her to shower in peace and went back to make one final pass around the camp. She finished her shower just as the sun was coming over the horizon. She ducked into her tent, put her dirty clothes away, and then went to send one of the other ladies to take a shower.

Since she'd lived out in the bush for those doctors' missions, it occurred to him that she probably knew how they could wash their clothes. He made a mental note to discuss that with her at some future point.

Tom woke the other men. He let them know that they'd have hot showers later but that the ladies had first dibs. As expected, they didn't have a problem with that.

Inside an hour, the camp was in full swing. Rachel chose to shower last and escorted the children to have their turns before her. Annie served some reconstituted scrambled eggs to everyone as soon as they were ready. He'd had freeze-dried eggs before, and they came out pretty good.

The older woman had also found a percolator capable of making coffee on the grill. That made her a very popular woman. She even had sugar and creamer to go with it.

He noticed that she took her coffee black and without sweetener. He supposed with her being diabetic, she had to be careful. Before too long, they'd probably all be taking their coffee that way.

Coffee was one of the things he'd stockpiled back at his place. He'd bought large bags of roasted beans and then sealed them in Mylar bags with oxygen absorbers.

The online groups he frequented said that the coffee would still be fresh for years that way. He'd figured coffee would make an excellent trade good. The ground coffee in stores got stale too damned quickly.

He'd picked up a lot of other things, too. People were going to want the common items that they no longer had access to in the new world. They'd be willing to trade things he needed for goods like coffee, cigarettes, and other everyday items.

Tom wasn't a smoker, but he'd stocked up on cigarettes and pipe tobacco. More so on the pipe tobacco because he could buy a lot of it for significantly less money than cigarettes. He'd bought up a bunch of cheap pipes, too. He figured that if people were desperate enough, they'd switch over.

If it took too much longer to get to his place, he was going to start worrying about his cats. As a precaution, whenever he left the house for any length of time, he put out large containers of dry food and water. Intellectually, he knew that they were good for more than a week—probably ten days—but that didn't stop him from worrying.

The cat boxes would be vile if it took that long. He used electric ones that moved the poop into holders that kept the smell down, but those would fill up in a week.

He'd make it home in time. He had to keep a positive attitude. That was critical in a crisis.

Once everyone had finished eating, the men took their turns at the shower. Tom waited until last. The hot water felt amazing. They were really going to miss this kind of thing until they got to his place.

Once he'd dressed again, he sought out Randy. He found the young man working with his wife to continue cataloging their supplies.

She was calling things out, and he was adding them to a spreadsheet on his laptop.

"Aren't you worried that we'll lose power and can't access that list?" he asked.

Randy shook his head. "Nope. I have a portable printer. Once I'm done, I'll print out several copies that we can stash in different places. We can make notes on the paper as the quantities change, and I'll update the spreadsheet when they become too messy."

Tom smiled. "I guess were lucky to have a techno geek with us."

"I don't know if that one particular thing qualifies me as a techno geek. I'm sure plenty of people at the show had portable printers. No, it'll be all the other gear I had with me that makes me one."

"Speaking of that," Tom said, "is there any way that we can access a raw satellite feed? We've got the remnants of a typhoon headed our way, and it would be nice to know if it's going to run over us."

Randy crossed his arms over his chest and frowned a little. "Hmmmm. That's an interesting question. The weather satellites will still be sending the raw feed, so long as the EMP didn't take them out. We'd need a satellite receiver capable of tuning into the signal.

"It *might* be doable, but I'm skeptical. I seem to remember reading that only certain large dishes can interface with them. If that's the case, they might have power for a while, but we can't talk to anyone with access."

Tom suddenly slapped his forehead. "We have a HF radio—high-frequency, that is—that's capable of interfacing with radio operators around the world. We should be monitoring that. We could find out so much by talking to people somewhere else. The CME might be too disruptive to actually use it, but it can't hurt to try."

Randy smiled. "Let me find someone to help Jenna with the inventory, and I'll get it put together. If I can find out any news, I'll start taking notes. I'm not a ham radio operator, so I'm not sure what the protocol is for interfacing with these people, though."

"I might be able to help you with that. I picked up a study guide for the operator's license test when I grabbed the radios. It might give you an idea of what you're supposed to do."

"I'm a quick study. Let me get cracking."

While he was walking away, Nika was walking up.

"Are you ready to get a drone demonstration?" she asked.

"You bet. Let's do this."

16

Nika had three drones laid out on a table near the GP medium. Two of them were quadcopter designs and one was like a little airplane with the propeller in the back. It was about four feet across. Of the quadcopters, one was fairly large and the other was tiny.

"Okay," she said. "Each of these has something to offer. Let's start with the fixed wing. It has the ability to stay in the air for about forty-five minutes. It also has a decent range on the controller.

"The company claims just over a mile, but depending on the circumstances, that might go up or down a little. With the CME making a hash of everything, I wouldn't count on half that distance."

"That's pretty good," he said. "We can probably work with that."

"I've got some higher-end controllers, and I can eventually modify these to use, but I've set them up using what the manufacturers supplied. Well, with a little bit of modification. The fixed wing has a controller that interfaces with your cell phone. That's okay, but I prefer using first-person-view goggles. FPV for short."

She held up what looked like VR goggles. Tom had never used anything like that, so he wasn't sure what the view would be like.

"The way I have this set up, more than one person can link in with their goggles," she said. "Think of those as receivers. That way multiple people can check something out."

He ran his hand along the fixed wing. It felt flimsy. "Is this thing really sturdy enough for us to use?"

She nodded. "It'll take a beating. I've seen them crash before. The wings will tear off, things will get scratched up, but it's very easy to put back together. Oh, and its top speed is about fifty miles an hour."

The fifty-mile-an-hour capability put it right in the same top speed as the Beast. Not that he expected they'd be doing that for long. It was just too dangerous, particularly when they got close to civilization.

"With only one propeller, it's quiet if you keep up high," she continued. "The software limits the ceiling to about five hundred feet. Once I have an opportunity to sit down with it, I'm pretty sure I can remove the restriction. At this point, I'm pretty sure the FAA won't mind."

Five hundred feet was good. "How hard is it to launch? Do we need much space?"

She grinned. "We'll need a little space for the landing, but launching it is ridiculously easy. Watch this."

Nika grabbed the controller and walked away from the tent. She pressed a button on the controller, and the propeller came to life. It was somewhat noisy from where he was standing, but he supposed it would be quieter at a distance.

She tossed it by the wing. The drone bobbled in the air for a moment and then took off. She wasn't doing anything with the controller, but the fixed wing rose up above them and began circling.

He put his hands on his hips and watched it. "I'll grant you that was damned easy."

"Right? Go ahead and put on your goggles." She took the set she had and slipped them over her eyes.

He followed suit and was instantly seeing the forest from the air. It was obvious the moment she took direct control of the drone because it straightened up and flew higher. To him it looked as though she was quickly rising to that five-hundred-foot control limit she'd mentioned.

If the CME was screwing with the signal, it didn't show in the seamless video. The view was astounding. He could see what seemed like forever. She put the drone into a bank, and he was scanning the area below it.

"I can control where the camera is pointed," she said. "Within limits, anyway. It's taking 4K video, too. When it comes back, we can recover it if we want to. Mainly though, this is useful for sending out ahead of us while we're on the road.

"We don't have to use it at full speed. It can glide along at about eighteen miles an hour. That also reduces its sound signature."

Nika turned the drone around and flew over the camp. Down below, Tom could see everyone moving around. No one looked up. He hoped that meant no one could hear the drone idling above them. He couldn't.

"Okay, point made about scouting ahead," he said. "Go ahead and bring it back in."

He took off his goggles and watched her bring the drone in for a landing. She touched another button, and it came in low and slow. When it was just a little way from them, the prop reversed, and it skidded onto the ground. The props folded back when it came to rest.

"That was easy enough," he said. "With this one, what do we need to use the others for?"

Nika smiled. "Come on."

She picked up the fixed wing and set it back on the table. Next, she grabbed the smallest drone.

"This one is special because you can put it away without disassembling anything." She proceeded to demonstrate by folding everything in. When she was done, the whole package was about the size of the bottle of water. Seriously. He could have stuck it in his pocket.

"That's small," he admitted.

"Yep. Greg was telling me about possibly scouting ahead on a bicycle. He could stick this and extra batteries in a small backpack. If he needs to look at anything, he can have it up and going in just a minute. It can go almost as fast as the fixed wing, but you can hover, too.

"The camera is independently controlled, and you can swivel it.

You can designate targets for it to focus on, and it will keep them in the center of your view no matter how you move the drone. That's not always guaranteed, but it works okay most of the time.

"Like I said, the big draw for this one is its portability. It's also got a ton of features we can use if we need them."

She unfolded the drone, set it on the table, and brought it to life. It was louder than the fixed wing, but the noise faded quickly as she left the area.

Once again, Nika demonstrated a deft hand as she controlled the device. Unlike the fixed wing, she could bring it down between gaps in the trees and look at things. She got too close to the camp this time, and people were pointing. Thankfully, they knew that Nika and Tom were testing the drones, so no one panicked.

She repeated the process of bringing it back in, and it landed right where she'd taken off. It had stubby little legs, so he imagined it wasn't going to be forgiving with tall grass.

"And finally we have the big guy," she said. "You'll notice that this one has *two* cameras. One of them is an excellent normal video camera. The second one on it right now is a FLIR camera. Forward-looking infrared. If we like, I can replace either of them with a night-vision camera.

"Rescue organizations use them for rescues and searches. Both cameras are individually controlled. That means one person could be controlling the drone while another keeps watch on the FLIR. My thinking is that this one would be useful for night scouting.

"Just like the little guy, this one has a much shorter flight time. I guess I forgot to mention that. The little one can fly for about twenty-five minutes and this one for about twenty. We've got plenty of extra battery packs, so bringing it back for a swap would be painless."

Tom could see the utility of all three drones. "You're absolutely right. These will be useful. I'll talk with Greg, and we'll see how we can fit them in with our travel plans. Excellent work."

She smiled. "We have multiples of each kind available. We could have one fixed wing scouting ahead of us as we drive and another watching behind us. I could control one from the truck with you, and someone else could run the other one from Moshe's truck. I have several chargers that can hold four batteries at a time. They run off of the cigarette lighter, so we can always be charging batteries for use."

"How hard are these to control for a beginner?"

"They're very forgiving for newbies. With the original controllers and software, they'll almost fly themselves. With the two quadcopters, there's always a risk of bumping into something. They have object-avoidance cameras, but they don't cover the sides. Or up.

"In any case, I can train someone else to control these while we have time today. They won't have the same level of experience as I do, but it should be okay. I'll work with Greg to show him how to control Junior. In fact, I'll work with anyone that's interested."

He left the young woman to take care of her drones, pleased with what he'd seen. The technology was unreal. Those things just might make the difference between getting home and not.

Randy waved him over as he headed back toward the big tent. The engineer had the high-frequency radio on a table nearby.

"What have you got?" Tom asked.

"Good news for a change. First, the HF radio is working. The other operators tell me the CME screwed them for a few days, but now they can communicate again, though there is significant noise. The important thing is that I can hear other people from a long distance away.

"Second, it seems as though the typhoon remnants are running north. I managed to connect with somebody that still had access to the weather satellites. A TV station in Idaho, of all things. We might catch a little wind and some rain, but the meteorologist said we're not going to be as bad off as we could be."

"That *is* good news," he agreed. "Are we getting any other word from around the world?"

Randy shrugged. "It sounds like Seattle got hit pretty hard. We're talking Hiroshima."

That wasn't a surprise. The mushroom cloud had been a dead giveaway.

"Any talk about other strikes?"

"Word is that San Diego and L.A. each caught one. That's just down the coast. News from out east is a lot fuzzier, but people say New York is gone. Same with the Dallas-Fort Worth Metroplex and Houston. Washington, DC, too, though not many people think of that as a negative.

"In fact, it looks like more than one country hit our capital. Maybe Russia and China. India and Pakistan clobbered one another. Big surprise.

"And you know that undisclosed location Dick Cheney used to run off to? It seems as though someone knew about it and wiped the parts of the government that managed to evacuate DC off the map. We're on our own."

Tom nodded. "That's not a big surprise."

"Somehow, Portland got missed," Randy said. "I mean that literally. A nuke went off on the other side of the Cascades. Hundreds of miles from anything worth a strike. I think something threw its guidance control off. Otherwise, we'd have been nuked, too."

It was hard hearing the young engineer say that. No one would have had time to get out of the cities. The death toll would have been in the hundreds of millions. The injured would be dying in terrible agony over the next week.

The United States of America was dead.

With Washington, DC, taking multiple hits, he wondered if Webster had found enough cover to save his life. He certainly hoped so.

"What about the rest of the world?" he asked softly.

"News from out there is spotty. People are saying that Moscow, Beijing, and a lot of other large cities got hit. Pyongyang is a smoking crater. So is Tehran. A lot of places in Europe bit the dust, too.

"It's really bad, Tom. The EMP blasts and the coronal mass ejection really screwed up all the power grids. The nukes removed any chance that someone could recover from this. Global civilization is literally toast."

"It makes me wish I had more engineering textbooks at my house," Tom said sadly. "Hell, any kind of science. All I collected were books that would be useful as source material. It makes me wish we could've taken Powell's Books with us when we left Portland."

"Books are important," Randy said softly, "but it's going to be the loss of all the knowledgeable people that hurts. When this is all said and done, you're going to find textbooks of all kinds lying around, only no one will have the time to spare to learn the information. All our attention is going to be focused on survival.

"All of the highly trained professionals in the sciences will pass on what they can to those who survived. Very few people will be able to spare the attention to pick it up."

They stared at one another silently for a minute before Tom gestured towards the radio. "Why don't you start giving me a rundown on how to use this?"

Randy gestured to the folding chair beside him. "Have a seat. It's not nearly as difficult as you think, and because of the disaster, the other operators aren't being nearly as ticklish about the rules."

Over the next hour, Randy gave Tom a guided tour of interacting with the other radio operators. The young man showed Tom some of the features of the radio that he hadn't known existed.

By the time they'd finished, he felt relatively confident that he could operate the machine by himself if he had to. Which was a good thing, since any of them might need to do so.

Tom stood. "As I told Nika earlier, I want you to cross-train everyone on how to use this. It could save our lives."

"You bet. I'll go grab someone now and start training them. Time is short."

He left Randy to his work and headed back to the GP medium. It seemed as though the inventory was far enough along that they could start organizing the repacking. At the very least, they could preposition some of the stuff they knew would be going back into the Beast.

First, he really needed to get something to eat. Somehow, the day was half over already. He needed to stuff a few ration bars into his pocket so that he could keep doing things he needed to do while staying fueled.

His handheld radio came to life. He'd set it to be just loud enough for him to hear the voice on the other end without the sound carrying too far.

It was Moshe. "We have trouble. Someone just stopped at the gate."

17

Tom eased into the trees and met up with Moshe where he was keeping an eye on the front gate. Even in the winter, the brush between the trees was sufficient to keep them concealed.

The clothes they'd picked up from the outdoor store were predominantly camouflage in nature. That proved useful in situations like this.

The visitors had arrived in a beat-up, older-model Ford. Its predominant color was rust. The men standing by the gate looked to be in about the same condition as the truck.

One of them took the lock they'd broken off the gate and dropped it. He raised the gate and gestured for his friend to drive inside.

"What do we do?" Moshe asked.

"We send them packing," Tom said grimly. "We can't let them see our supplies. That would make them do something stupid. Frankly, I've killed enough people already this week. I'd rather these two live to bother someone else."

Tom brought his radio to his lips. "Greg."

"Here, boss. I'm across the drive, watching them from the left."

He scanned that section of the woods but couldn't see the young man. Whatever he'd done, he'd hidden himself pretty well.

"I'm going to step out and send them on their way. I'd prefer not to kill them, but if they become threatening, take care of business."

"Copy."

Moshe had his AR, so Tom wasn't worried about backup from the side either. The older man was an excellent shot.

Tom hefted his rifle and slowly walked over to the road inside the campground. The men didn't notice him until he stepped out onto the pavement. That certainly got their attention.

The truck, which had been advancing, screeched a little bit as it came to an abrupt halt. Both doors popped open, and the men came out with rifles in their hands. To Tom's eye, they looked like beat-up lever-action 30-30s. Neither had a scope.

The driver stepped out a bit from his vehicle. "You just hold it right there."

Tom agreeably stopped walking. He had his AR across his chest, dangling on the strap. He could get it into action quickly if he needed to.

"Howdy," Tom said. "Anything I can do for you boys?"

That had sounded awfully Texan. Tom wondered if stress made his accent digress to that of his youth.

"I think we should be asking you that," the passenger said. "You're not from around here."

"Nope. Just passing through. I'm afraid that my friends and I are using the campground today. We'll be gone tomorrow. Sorry for the imposition."

Two men looked at each other. The driver shook his head. "That's a bit of a problem. We know the owner of this place. I don't think he'd take too kindly to trespassers."

"Might not," Tom agreed. "That doesn't change the facts, though. We don't want any trouble, but I'm afraid I'll have to insist you turn around and head back out."

The driver laughed. "You might have that fancy gun, but I don't see any of your friends. I think we'll come in and take a look for ourselves."

This was beginning to sound as though there wasn't going to be a positive ending.

"The way I see it, there are two options," Tom said. "The first is that you try to force your way in. If that happens, someone's going to die. I'm afraid to tell you that I don't think it's going to be me.

"The second option is that you get back into your truck and be on your way. No harm. No foul. Apologies for the lock, but we haven't damaged anything else on the property. I assure you that we'll clean up after ourselves. The owner doesn't need to concern himself with that."

Now both the men were laughing.

The passenger took two steps forward. "I think I can get my gun up before you grab that little toy of yours. You want to make a bet?"

Tom smiled. His stomach was churning, but he wasn't going to let them see him sweat. "Sure. I bet my life. Are you going to call or raise? Or better yet, fold while you can."

Before the man could respond, a shot rang out from where Greg had hidden in the woods. It blew a chunk out of the asphalt about two feet to the driver's left.

Both men jumped.

Tom raised his AR before their feet landed back on the ground. They'd helpfully pointed their rifles away from him.

"Well, it seems my friend threw a chip in the pot," he said. "It looks as if you boys can't cover the bet. Why don't you set those rifles down right there on the ground? Set them down and back up."

They hesitated but ended up complying with his instructions. Both raised their hands slightly.

"You got a lot of balls," the driver snarled.

"So I'm told. Keep backing up."

He could tell without looking that Moshe had done something to reveal himself because the men's eyes swiveled over in that direction.

"Yep, I have more than one friend. Play this smart and you still get to drive away. You've done the right thing so far, other than pushing me. Don't break your winning streak."

Since Moshe was coming up, Tom stepped to the side a bit.

The older man recovered the rifles without saying a word and then looked inside the truck. He held up a couple of boxes of reloads. Without coming between Tom and the men, he stepped back.

"Here's what we're going to do, boys," Tom said. "You come by tomorrow at noon. We'll be gone, but these rifles will be right behind the little shack at the entrance, along with your ammunition. You don't lose anything other than your pride.

"I'm not going to ask if that's okay with you, because you don't have a choice. Now, it's time for you to get back into your truck and drive away. Let me give you another piece of advice on the house. Don't come back looking for trouble. You'll find it."

The two men climbed into their truck, fury written across their faces. They drove off, tires squealing.

Moshe spat onto the ground. "Do you think they'll be smart?"

"They didn't look particularly smart. It won't surprise me a bit if we have visitors after dark. Hell, maybe before dark."

"So what do we do?"

"We turn this into Firebase Oregon," Greg said, materializing silently beside them.

Tom turned to face him. "What exactly does that mean?"

"I've scouted the woods. It's rugged out there, so that limits the possible routes they can come at us. The prime approaches are going to be from across the road here and off to our right. The main road outside the camp continues around. They could park up the road a bit and slip into the woods."

"All right," Tom said. "If that's the case, what can we do?"

Greg gestured towards the woods. "The first thing I'm going to do is set up a couple of booby-traps. Something I can easily recover in the morning if we have no trouble. Besides, I don't want to leave anything behind that would hurt someone innocently walking through the woods."

Moshe frowned. "You mean like a land mine? I didn't think we had anything like that with us."

"Audible tripwires. It'll scare the hell out of them, but it won't hurt them. If they go off, we'll know that somebody is coming. Maybe that will make them turn around."

Tom wished he were confident of that. He wasn't, but he might still end up pleasantly surprised.

"What else?" he asked.

"We set up a couple of foxholes out that way and also towards the road. We leave the women to guard the camp, and we spend the night in the trenches. If everything goes quietly, we finish tearing down camp in the morning and leave."

"All right," Tom said. "Moshe, you keep an eye up here while Greg starts scouting out locations for the foxholes. I'm going to head back to the camp and get them to loading things in the vehicles. If push comes to shove, we may have to bug out tonight."

Tom headed back to camp. It only took a couple of minutes to gather everyone and explain the situation. Rachel immediately took charge of wrapping up the inventory and repacking the vehicles.

"Do you want me to set a drone to circling the area?" Nika asked. "If they come back, I'll see them coming."

Tom nodded. "I think that's best. When it gets dark, switch out to the one that can do night vision and FLIR. That should allow us to see anyone trying to sneak up on us.

"Greg seems to think they're going to come in on the right side of the main entrance, but I'd rather not trust they're going to be so cooperative. Keep an eye out in every direction. If you see anything that looks wrong, call us."

She nodded. "In that case, I'd best go ahead and start with Big Daddy. The FLIR will work in the daylight, and I can swap the regular camera with the night-vision one in just a couple of minutes."

Tom went back out into the woods with a couple of collapsible shovels. The Army used to call them entrenching tools. These were higher-tech versions of those old standbys, but digging a foxhole with one was going to be a huge pain in the ass.

Once he caught up with Greg, the young man showed him the areas he thought might be best for their hiding places.

Thankfully, he wasn't recommending they dig something straight down into the ground. More like an area to lie behind fallen logs or other debris. They could use blankets to keep the ground from leaching away their body heat.

It took the men about an hour to get the hiding areas ready. Another hour and they had them concealed so well that Tom couldn't spot them from the front.

Thankfully, they didn't have any trouble before dark. Rachel reported that they had the Beast fully loaded just as the sun set. She indicated the women would start on the trailer next.

Nancy came out with some hot food. Tom was grateful. His stomach had been growling. She also had some food bars and water for later.

Randy called and asked if they wanted him to join them. Tom told the engineer not to bother. He wanted him back at camp in case the enemy snuck up on them from an unexpected direction.

Time dragged on slowly. They got the call a few hours after dark that the women had finished packing all of the vehicles. The only things still out were the cooking utensils and the tents. If trouble came knocking, they could quickly get moving.

Nika called them a few hours before dawn. "I see some vehicles approaching slowly from the area of the road that Greg was interested in. There are four of them."

"Copy," Tom replied. They'd found extra headsets, so he didn't need to take the radio off his belt to answer or worry that anyone else would hear the incoming call.

It looked as though those guys thought they could win the bet after all. Time to lay all their cards on the table.

18

G reg had shown them how to take dark blankets and attach local foliage to them. That meant they could stay somewhat warm while still breaking up their outline if someone looked in their direction.

Tom had his night-vision goggles on, so he could see the forest all around him. The creatures that had been making noises had gone silent. It was very spooky. They knew something was about to happen.

"They've entered the woods," Nika said. "I'm counting an even dozen of them. They seem to be moving in a group, but very slowly."

"They want to make sure that they stay together," Greg said. "They're going slowly to avoid making any noise. Can you tell what path they're taking?"

"It looks like they're headed about the direction you predicted."

The young man laughed softly. "Aren't they going to be surprised?"

The booby-traps were set up so that Moshe and Tom would be able to see the people that had tripped the wires.

Originally, Tom had positioned Moshe out by the road. About an hour ago, the young soldier had convinced him to allow the two men to switch places. He said that he had a plan that would add to their potential for victory, but he needed to be out by the road to make it work.

"Nika," Tom said. "Can you let me know when they get just short of the booby-traps?"

"If Greg was accurate in showing me their location, sure."

He slid a pair of the electronic shooter's hearing protection over his ears. These weren't the little ones that he could wear all the time. They were full sized.

With the press of a button on one side, the microphone sensitivity went up. He took it all the way to the max.

It seemed counterintuitive, but the things could amplify ambient sounds while still using a sound gate to prevent any loud noises—like a gunshot—from coming through.

Wearing them over the earpiece was going to allow some of the noise to bleed through, but there was nothing he could do about that. Randy thought he could rig up a connector to use the same plug the headphones normally used for their radios, but he hadn't had time to do it.

Meanwhile, it greatly increased Tom's ability to hear what was going on around him. For example, he could now hear slow movement of leaves off in the distance. That had to be the attackers.

He didn't expect the headphones would completely block the booby-traps when they went off. At least they were facing away from Tom and Moshe. The intruders were going to catch a hundred and thirty decibels of siren in their ears at point-blank range, though.

With the combination of his night-vision goggles and enhanced hearing, he easily spotted the intruders as they came into view. They were all bunched together and moving slowly, looking around them carefully.

"We have a problem," Nika said. "I just discovered a second group of them on the other side of camp. They came down a gully from somewhere up the road. There was enough gap in the trees for me to make sure it wasn't animals. It looks like eight people."

Well, that certainly complicated matters. He and Moshe could probably repel this attack. Greg was up by the road, so he could quickly move back to reinforce the camp. Together with Randy and

Rachel, they should be able to hold the other intruders back until Tom and Moshe could join them.

"Greg, I need you to head back to the camp," Tom said.

"Negative. I'm at the attackers' trucks, disabling them. When the ambush comes off, I'm going to make sure that none of them gets away. I can't get back to the camp in time to matter."

Tom cursed softly. That was not part of the plan. He and the young man were going to have some serious words when this was all over.

"Rachel."

"Right here."

"It's going to be up to you. Move everyone to a spot that's going to be safe from random bullets and set up an ambush for these guys. Make sure to get as many as you can."

"Copy."

He watched as the ambushers in front of him moved directly towards the area that Greg had seeded with tripwires. He wondered if they were going to spot any of them before they set something off.

A loud wail cut through the night as one of them set off a booby trap. The men about jumped out of their skin, and some of them began firing into the woods around them.

That was the signal he'd been waiting for. He flipped up his night-vision goggles and put his eye down by the FLIR scope. Both he and Moshe would have no trouble seeing the enemy.

Tom started firing at the men on the right, and Moshe began on the left. Since they could actually see what they were shooting at, their shots proved very effective. Still, the log he was lying behind soaked up at least one hit.

By the time the men sought cover, Tom had shot three of them. He had no idea how well Moshe had done. Knowing the old man, he'd probably gotten more.

His next target was a man peering around the side of a tree, looking for who was shooting at them. Tom put the crosshairs on the man's forehead and blew his brains out.

"I got four," he said into the radio.

"Five on my side," Moshe said with satisfaction.

"Figures."

That meant they had three mobile intruders. Tom could hear movement out there, but he wasn't seeing anyone.

"I see three people retreating from your area," Nika said. "It looks as if they're moving rapidly back toward their vehicles."

Once Tom was certain that was the case, he and Moshe could move forward and finish off any of the ambushers who were still alive. Then they could make a run for the camp and help defend it.

"Greg. What are you doing?"

"I just finished slashing all their tires. When they come out of the woods, I'll take them down."

"You'll have to handle that by yourself. Moshe and I will be returning to camp."

"Copy."

After a minute, Nika let them know she was sure those three were not going to be coming back. Tom and Moshe cautiously advanced on the fallen enemy. Tom turned his night-vision goggles back on.

"What about the other attackers?" he asked Nika. "Did the shooting get them turned around and headed back out?"

"I'm still bringing the drone around. I'll know in thirty seconds."

At close range, the siren was deafening, even through the hearing protection. Tom found two men still alive and squirming on his side.

He dispatched them quickly, even as one pleaded for his life. He'd have nightmares about that later.

All of Moshe's targets were dead, a tribute to the old man's shooting skills.

Tom found the switch on the booby trap and killed the noise. About that time, he heard three quick shots off toward where the men had parked.

"All hostiles down," Greg said. "Moving in to confirm."

"Return to camp as soon as you're sure," Tom said.

"Copy."

Even with night-vision goggles, it was a bad idea to try running through the woods at night. So Tom moved as quickly as he safely could back toward the camp. He was probably a hundred yards away through the woods when the shooting started.

He continued moving forward, staying next to Moshe so they didn't surprise one another. When the trees started thinning out, he saw the fight playing out in front of him.

It looked as though the intruders had rushed out of the woods toward the tents. Once they were in the open, Randy and Rachel had opened fire on them. At least half of the attackers were down.

His people had good cover behind the brick enclosure where they'd been cooking. Each one peered out from one side and fired at the remaining attackers.

They'd caught the men halfway between the tents and the tree line. It seemed as though they were using their dead companions as firing platforms.

Tom found a convenient tree and used it to brace his weapon. He was shooting from the side, so he had a decent angle. He quickly put two rounds into one of the men. Moshe opened fire moments later, hitting the next man out.

The surprise attack made the two remaining men turn and flee for the woods. Tom lined up the crosshairs on one man's back and shot him. Moshe apparently picked the same target. The bastard dropped dead.

That did nothing to stop the one man remaining from making it into the woods. He was going to get away.

A shot rang out in the woods. Then another. Finally, after a long pause, a third.

Tom advanced slowly and carefully toward the shots. He saw movement ahead and raised his weapon but kept his finger off the trigger.

Jenna Caldwell walked into the open, a pistol dangling in her hand. She looked as though she were in shock.

"I killed him," she said just loud enough for Tom to hear.

"That's the last one," Nika said. "I'm not seeing anyone else in the woods."

The attack was over.

Randy rushed out and took his wife into his arms while Rachel went from body to body to make sure they were all dead, including the man Jenna had dealt with. The lack of a follow-up shot told Tom the young engineer's wife had finished her man.

It looked as though none of them would survive this journey without drawing blood. Well, except for Annie and the kids. They'd each have their own kind of trauma to deal with.

Greg jogged into camp and Tom joined him. "Walk with me."

He led the ex-Army sniper a little bit away from the camp before turning toward him. "You put every single one of us in danger. You had a job to do and you decided to change the plan without consulting anyone."

"It worked, didn't it?"

"This time. Next time it might mean someone shoots and kills Jenna Caldwell. That could easily have happened tonight. She may not realize how much danger you put her in, but I do.

"I don't care how badass you are. If we can't count on you to be a part of the team, then we need to part ways."

The other man considered Tom, his expression blank. Slowly, he nodded. "I can see that I made a mistake. I should have done things differently. I'll work on it."

Tom let that hang between them for a moment before he answered. "That's all I can really ask for. Did you have any trouble with the three that got away?"

Greg shook his head. "No. They bolted out of the woods right in front of me, just like I planned. They never even made it to their trucks."

"We're going to have to get out of here as soon as possible. These men probably have vengeful friends and relatives. I'd prefer not to meet any of them."

"We can pack up the tents and be on the road in thirty minutes," Greg said.

Tom checked his watch. They had about ninety minutes before the sky started getting lighter.

"It'll be better if we can see when we take off. Come on."

Tom returned to the center of the camp. Everyone else had come out of hiding. Even the children.

He wished they didn't have to see the dead men lying there, but he supposed that was just part of the new world they all lived in.

"Break camp down," he said. "Pack the tents away and get all your personal belongings stashed inside the vehicles. Annie, if you'd be so kind as to make breakfast while we clean up, we can all get one final hot meal inside us before we hit the road. We leave just before dawn."

He gestured for the men to gather around him. "We're going to recover their weapons. We'll move these bodies into the woods. No need to look at them while we eat."

The men had a motley collection of firearms and knives, some of them excellent, most of them poor. In any case, they'd find use for them eventually. Greg and Moshe recovered the booby-traps and the weapons from the first group.

The trucks that Greg had disabled yielded more ammunition and a few extra bits of equipment that might prove useful, including a rather modern crossbow with a wide selection of bolts.

Greg gleefully claimed it. "I feel like Daryl from *The Walking Dead.*"

"No zombies," Tom declared. "We've got enough problems without zombies."

Nika finally located the trucks that the second set of intruders had used. Tom, Greg, Moshe, and Randy trooped around the road and found them stashed under some trees.

They were quite a surprise. Two brand new Hummer H2s sat under the trees. Both black vehicles had old military-style tanker trailers hitched to them.

Tom walked around to see how they'd done it. The trailers shouldn't be compatible with a normal trailer hitch. It looked as though someone had welded up a hybrid hitch that bolted in place like a regular one but still allowed the trailers to connect.

"These look old," Greg said as he climbed up on top of one. "I'm talking WWII old. Look at the manual pump with the hand crank."

It did look old, but someone had restored it with loving care. Even the paint job was perfect.

Tom tapped the side. "Empty."

"Yep," the ex-Army man said when he opened the hatch on top. "Doesn't smell like it's been used in a while." He sealed the lid and climbed down.

The second trailer was just as empty as the first. It seemed—based on the fresh-looking hitches and the lack of license plates—that the men had gone on a recent shopping trip.

Tom opened a storage compartment beside one of the pumps and found an original Army manual for vehicles from 1943.

It only took him a few moments to find the trailer. Six hundred gallons capacity. That might be useful if they could find a gas station to raid. One for diesel and the other for regular gasoline.

He looked inside the expensive Hummers and found a manual for them. The big vehicles could tow 8,200 pounds. A fully loaded tanker weighed 7,000 pounds. Perfect.

There was also an assortment of gear that looked stolen. It certainly appeared that these men had been preying on refugees.

One of the items was very interesting. It was a black moped with bike pedals. Apparently, the rider could utilize it in either mode. There were places to attach things that might be useful to the frame. It looked like the perfect scouting vehicle.

Based on the bloodstains, the men had taken it by lethal force.

Greg quickly got it started and headed up the road. It was a lot quieter than the big motorcycles.

A few minutes later, Greg came pedaling back. He'd shut the engine off. He coasted to a stop next to the Hummers.

"It's got a top speed of about twenty-five miles an hour," he said. "I can peddle it almost that fast. If we can keep the convoy down to that speed, I think this is the best way to scout ahead."

Tom nodded. "Sounds like a plan."

He called back to camp and let them know that they were returning with motorized vehicles. He didn't want anyone accidentally shooting them.

They climbed into the vehicles and headed back to camp. They'd probably have to abandon one or both of the big motorcycles. That sucked. They just didn't have enough capable drivers.

They'd have just enough time to wolf down some hot scrambled eggs and clean up before dawn. It felt ridiculous policing the area for trash during the apocalypse, but some habits died hard. Besides, he needed to recover the items that they could repurpose to other tasks.

Then they'd discuss the drive. It was time to head toward the coast. This time they were getting through, and God help anyone that got in their way.

19

The Hummers got a lot of attention from the group when they pulled up, as did Greg on the new bike.

"Where did you find all this stuff?" Rachel asked.

"It looks as though that second ambush group stole them from someone," Tom said. "The tanks are empty, but I think they had the right idea. The manual I found said that each of these could hold six hundred gallons. That could come in very handy. The only problem I'm seeing is that we're short on drivers."

The former gun dealer frowned. "How do you figure? You have the Beast, my truck, the two motorcycles, now these two Hummers, and that little bike. By my count, that's seven. Nika says that you want her to scout ahead with one of the drones, so that counts her out for driving. We have seven adults left. Seems like the perfect amount."

"We have three motorcycles, and every other vehicle is towing a heavy trailer. It doesn't seem as though that's going to be easy for all of us."

Moshe laughed. "As if the apocalypse is supposed to be easy. I don't know about you, but I'd prefer not to abandon anything we might need later. I say we try to take everything with us, and if we run into trouble, we can decide something different."

That made sense. "Okay. If Greg is going to ride the scout bike, who is going to take the motorcycles?"

Rachel raised her hand slightly. "I have one, and Randy said he knew how to ride."

Tom nodded. "I'm driving the Beast—for which I need to train some other people to back me up—and Moshe is driving his truck. That leaves Jenna and Annie to drive the Hummers. Is everyone all right with that?"

They all looked at one another, but no one raised any objections.

"Okay. Let's get on the road. Nika, you're going to be flying the fixed-wing drone ahead of us. Greg says that little bike has a top speed of about twenty-five miles an hour, so that's our convoy speed. We'll let him get as far ahead as the drone can communicate back with us through the distortion.

"You said the battery in that would last about forty-five minutes. Let's plan to swap it out every half hour. That way if we run into something that needs looking over at the last moment, we won't be out of power."

The young woman nodded. "Your big truck doesn't have the electrical system to recharge the batteries, but the other vehicles should be able to. Since I have multiple chargers, I'll get them set up in the other vehicles.

"The smaller drone has a longer-range transmitter. It supposedly has a maximum range of eight miles, but not in this mess. I took it out to three and still had a decent signal. Unfortunately, it only has a twenty-five minute flight time."

Randy scratched his chin. "You said that we can swap out controllers. I wonder if I could do something with the transceiver in one of the fixed wings. I've got a lot of tools for working on complex electronics in my stuff. It's possible that I might be able to take one of the spare fixed wings and boost its range."

"Well, that's going to have to be something you look at later," Tom said. "The people we killed are going to be missed, if they haven't already been. We need to get on the road.

"Greg, you're out front. If you start getting out too far, we'll let you know. Rachel, you'll be directly in front of the convoy. I'll keep the Beast in the middle. Jenna and Annie, you're next. Moshe, you're behind them. Randy, you're bringing up the rear."

He looked at the young engineer. "It's going to be your responsibility to keep an eye out behind us. Nika will turn the drone around every once in a while to see if someone is back there, but you're our first line of defense in case someone attacks from behind. You got that?"

Randy nodded. "Got it."

Tom looked at the two kids. "Nancy and Adam, I have a very important job for you both. I want you to ride with Moshe in his pickup truck. You'll be able to see past the trailer looking back. It's your job to help Randy. He can't be looking over his shoulder every second, so you keep looking past him and let Moshe know if you see anything back there. Can you do that?"

They both nodded seriously.

"We've dug out enough radios so that every vehicle has one. They've got plenty of range for the distances we're talking about. Nevertheless, whenever we stop, I'll be looking at the maps and designating rally points.

"Right now, we don't have a lot of choice but to go toward Portland. Once we get closer, we'll be able to pick between different roads. If someone attacks us, we might find ourselves proceeding separately. If that happens, head for the rally point. The rest of us will meet you there."

Tom paused for a moment. "Are there any questions or suggestions about how we can do this better?"

Everyone shook their heads.

"Then let's get moving."

He climbed into the Beast and got it running. It was going to take a couple of minutes for it to warm up. While it did, he made a final pass around the campsite to be sure they'd left nothing behind. He also recovered the items from the trash that they might be able to repurpose. They'd go into the back of the Beast.

He'd fully fueled the Beast while they camped. The other vehicles had varying levels of fuel but really needed to gas up. They needed to refill all the fuel cans, vehicles, and the tanks. Their first destination should be a gas station.

Tom pulled out one of his maps and figured out where the campground was located. There was a town a bit farther away from Portland on the main road. There would be filling stations there. Without power, the tanks would still have plenty to go around.

The problem was that towns had people. They might run into someone that recognized those two Hummers or the tanker trailers. That could be very bad.

It wasn't as if they had a choice. Without fuel, they'd be walking. They'd have to abandon all the gear and supplies they'd scavenged, and that was unacceptable. They'd have to take a chance.

He picked up his radio. "Everyone, we're going to be heading away from Portland at the main road. There's a town that way with gas stations. If we can, I intend to fill up every vehicle and the two tanks.

"We'll almost certainly run into people. We need to be cautious but not openly hostile. That all changes if any of you thinks we're about to be attacked. If that happens, shoot first. Greg, keep us informed of everything you see. Let's move out."

One by one, they got into motion. He saw Randy stop and close the gate as they left. Well, they had promised to put things back in order for the owner. He didn't expect the man to be happy with all the dead bodies, though.

A few minutes later, they arrived back at the main road. Surprisingly, it wasn't completely empty of traffic. They saw two cars heading away from Portland. It looked as though they contained families fleeing toward safer climes.

Once they headed out behind the refugees at a slower pace, it only took a short while to get to their destination.

"I'm coming up on the town," Greg said. "There are a lot of cars at the gas station. It's one of those big ones. Amazingly, no one seems to have looted it.

"There are a bunch of sheriff's deputies here, too. They seemed to be keeping the crowd orderly. There are hundreds of cars. This place is packed."

"He's right," Nika said. "Check this out."

The young woman was controlling her drone with the FPV goggles but held out the controller with an attached phone so that he could glance at it. Yeah, it was one of those big gasoline stations that serviced semis and heavy highway traffic.

It seemed as though the deputies were segregating the travelers as they arrived. The people in control allowed some to get gasoline but diverted most of them to a large lot nearby. Tom saw the cars that had passed them arrive. In moments, they were off to the large side lot.

He handed the controller back to Nika. "We should probably bring the drone in for a landing. We don't want them to know that we have that kind of capability."

They slowed to a stop, and Nika hopped out long enough to retrieve the drone. She stored it in the back of the Beast. The controller and goggles went into the box under her seat.

The deputies watched them closely as they pulled into the gas station. One of the uniformed men stepped forward and held up a hand. He only wore a pistol but had two other deputies in body armor with ARs backing him up.

Tom opened his door and stepped down to the ground. He left his AR inside the vehicle. He didn't want to raise the tension level any higher than it already was. Off behind the building, he heard a generator running. There were lights on inside the store, too. He smelled something delicious cooking.

The deputies had cautious expressions but didn't make any comment about his pistol.

"Morning," Tom said.

"Morning," the deputy agreed. "We're only letting people pick up gas that can pay for it. Cash only."

"We can pay."

The man grinned. "I wouldn't be so quick to say that. You haven't seen the prices we're charging. Twenty dollars a gallon. Or equivalent in trade if you've got some goods that are interesting."

That was indeed a lot of cash. Still, that's all it was. Paper. These idiots hadn't figured out yet that paper money was going to make terrible toilet paper at some point in the very near future.

He was sorry to see the police extorting money, but there had to be bad apples everywhere.

"That seems a little extreme, but we've got enough cash to fill up, I think," Tom said. "Without power, how are you getting it out of the underground tanks?"

"A couple of the boys have some hand pumps. Ain't the quickest, but it'll get the job done."

Tom motioned for Rachel to come join him and stepped away from the deputies. "How much cash have you got left? They want twenty dollars a gallon."

"That is literally highway robbery." She looked back at their vehicles. "Poppa's truck will probably take about twenty gallons. The motorcycles another couple each. The Hummers maybe twenty-five. How much does yours hold?"

"Fifty gallons. I filled up the tank, but I should refill the spares I emptied. How full are the other vehicles?"

"My estimates are based on the fuel levels I saw before we left the campground. We are looking at roughly one hundred and twenty-five gallons. Add the various containers we grabbed at the outdoor store and the ones you emptied, that will make it two hundred and twenty-five gallons.

"That comes to four thousand five hundred dollars. That is about how much cash I have left over from the store added to the money you gave me."

He nodded. "That won't do anything for the big tanks. Twelve hundred gallons would cost twenty-four thousand dollars. We'll just have to hope we find some empty gas stations further along the way."

From inside the Beast, Nika cleared her throat. "I might be able to help with that. I grabbed all the cash from the box store when I sent the employees home. I figured someone would steal it.

"I couldn't get into the safe. It was one of those that had a time lock and all that other security jazz. But the owner had a separate safe upstairs. I didn't know the combination, but I suspected where he'd hidden it."

The woman looked a little shamefaced. "I figured if things got really bad, I might need every bit of help I could get. I was going to bring it back if you were wrong about what was happening."

She held a backpack out the window to Tom. "I figure it's better you use it for what we need."

He looked inside the backpack and found a metal cashbox. A glance inside revealed a lot of money. He had Rachel hold it so that he could count the cash without flashing it to everyone around them.

There was enough to pay for all the gas they could hold, with a little to spare.

He nodded at Nika. "You did the right thing. This will help us survive what's happening. Thank you. We won't forget how you've helped us."

The young woman smiled. "I think you've helped me more than I've helped you. We're all in this together."

"That we are."

Tom took the cashbox out of the backpack, added the money Rachel had, and walked over to the deputies. "We think we need about a hundred and twenty-five gallons in the vehicles and another hundred for our spare gas cans.

"Since you have such big tanks here, we'll fill up the tankers, too. One with diesel, the other with regular gas. Six hundred gallons apiece. Let's go with the highest-octane gas you've got."

The man laughed. "My math skills ain't the greatest, but that's a lot of money. I don't think you got that in that little box."

"Let's see," Tom said. "Fourteen hundred and twenty-five gallons at $20 a gallon comes to $28,500. Does that match your figuring?"

Tom could see the avarice in the man's eyes. "That does sound about right. Let me see the money."

If the deputies meant to rob them, they'd make their move now. Tom edged his hand marginally closer to his pistol belt as he handed the moneybox over.

The men huddled together as the lead guy counted out the money in the box. The deputy grinned at Tom. "Looks like you got enough to gas up, with a little bit left over for snacks. Pull the diesel tank around back and get the rest of your vehicles in the line up front."

The man handed Tom just over fifteen hundred dollars back. "I'll keep the box. I warn you, the snacks are pricey too."

"Just tell me you got some of those chocolate things with cream filling. I'd kill for one of those."

"I think so. If I might ask, where are you folks headed? I saw you coming from Portland, so I assume you got a place in mind out east."

Tom nodded. He was more than happy to let the man think they were going east. That might save them a little bit of trouble down the way.

"My uncle's got a place out that direction. Just on the other side of the state line, but down south. We figure we can hole up there until things settle out."

"Good luck, then. I'll let you be about your business."

Tom pitied anyone actually driving east of here. He didn't know precisely where the missile that missed Portland had detonated, but it would kill anyone that got too close.

He climbed into the Beast and drove it around to where a man was pumping diesel with a hand pump. Jenna followed him with the big tank they'd designated for diesel.

Several deputies were standing close by. One of them held his radio up to his ear as Tom was pulling to a stop.

That deputy turned to the man with the pump. "Chuck says this guy paid up. Fill up his vehicle, the gas cans he shows you, and the big tank."

The man with the pump goggled. "You want me to pump that big old tank full of diesel? You are out of your mind."

The deputy frowned. "If you and your family want food tonight, you'll get your ass in gear. Food ain't free."

"It won't take much in the truck," Tom said. "I filled it up already. Let me get the spare diesel tanks out for you."

The deputy walked around back with him and looked on as Tom handed them out to Jenna.

"Looks like you hit the motherlode on supplies," the man said.

"We had a bit set aside. We also had some cash on hand, as our being able to pay for gas demonstrates."

Tom couldn't help getting the impression that the man was sizing up what kind of things they had stored in the back of the Beast and in the trailer when he walked around and peered into it.

It was definitely a good thing they weren't going east.

The man with the pump quickly filled the empty diesel cans and topped off the Beast. He then moved to the six-hundred-gallon tank behind the Hummer and began filling it.

Rachel, Randy, and the two kids came from around the side of the building. The young Israeli woman nodded toward the regular gas cans that Nika was standing beside.

"We came to get those. It will not take the guy long to top us off. Let me have the remaining cash, and I will get us some sugary snacks. It might be quite a while before we have another chance."

"Since they have power, get some ice, too. We should fill the coolers while we can. That extends the life of the…" he glanced at the deputy. "… food." He wasn't going to mention the medicine. That would only make the men greedier.

He dug out the remaining money, and Rachel stepped close to take it.

"We might have a problem up front," she said quietly. "I saw a couple of guys looking at the Hummer. They looked upset."

They might be associated with the men that had come to ambush them. That would be awkward.

20

One of the problems with stopping to refuel like this was that anyone who meant them harm could take a shot at them as soon as they left. Tom wasn't happy to hear that some of the locals might be affiliated with the men who'd tried to ambush them, but he couldn't say he was surprised.

He turned his back toward the deputy and spoke to Rachel softly. "The deputies have every reason to expect that we're going to continue heading east. If they're going to set up an ambush, they'll go that direction. Of course, once they figure out that we're not, they'll probably come hauling ass after us."

She nodded. "I think I see where this is going. You want to set up an ambush of our own."

"I think that's probably the best idea. If I'm wrong, no harm, no foul. If I'm right, we'll be set up to deal with whoever comes chasing us, be it law enforcement or other locals. The trick is going to be getting ahead of them."

"I will talk to Greg and see what he thinks we should do," she said. "When you are finished here, drive around front and we will settle the plan."

"Sounds good."

Rachel and the others took the empty gas cans and headed back toward the front of the gas station.

It ended up taking about twenty minutes for the tired man to finish pumping six hundred gallons of diesel into the big tank.

Once Tom verified that the man had filled it to the top, he dogged the hatch shut. He nodded to the man and the deputy as he climbed back into the Beast. He made sure that Jenna was right behind him as they turned and went around front.

He motioned for her to refuel and got behind the rest of their vehicles. It looked as though the man with the pump up front was just finishing the big tank on the other Hummer.

Greg jumped on the running board beside his window and handed him a bag. "Chocolate stuff filled with cream, as per your request. I also picked up some fuel stabilizer. We wouldn't want all this to go bad."

Nika came out of the store with bags of ice. A lot of them. She proceeded to the Beast and motioned for the others to help her drain the water out of the coolers. The fresh ice would make certain that the medicine stayed good until they got to the coast.

"Good thinking," he told Greg. "Did Rachel talk to you about our watcher problem?"

The ex-Army guy inclined his head toward the right side of the store. Tom glanced over and saw four men watching them intently. One of them was gesticulating strenuously. He had to admit, they did look as if they'd fit right in with the intruders.

Tom looked back at Greg. "The deputies think we're going east. If they're setting up an ambush, it's going to be off in that direction. That should give us a window to set up something of our own. How do you think we should go about it?"

"Once we get on the road, we're going to be going slow," the sniper said. "I'll work with Moshe on the ambush. Unlike the other vehicles, we can get his truck going fast enough to catch up to you when we're done."

"It looks as if they're about finished gassing up Jenna's Hummer, so the clock is ticking. Do you want to follow us out, or do you want to dash ahead?"

The other man considered that for a moment. "I think we'll follow you out. I don't think that they're going to attack us right next to the town. They don't want to get all these people disturbed by gunfire. They absolutely do not want them to riot."

The number of deputies that Tom could see was definitely lower than it had been when they'd arrived. Some of them were undoubtedly off to the east looking for a good spot to waylay them. It might be best if Tom waited a bit to let them get in place.

"Did you get anything other than the snacks? I don't suppose they had any sandwiches in there."

The other man shook his head. "I think we've about seen the last of lunchmeat for a while. They were frying up some chicken over an open fire off on the other side of the building, though."

So that's what Tom had smelled. No wonder he was hungry.

"See if you can use the last of the money to get everyone a hot meal. If we have to add something in to sweeten the deal, try to keep it light."

The other man grinned. "I was watching someone else negotiate. We've got enough cash left to get something for all of us. I'll use the last of it for more snacks. Let these bastards enjoy feeling rich for another day or two."

"We'll be over on that side waiting for you," Tom said. "Once everybody has their food and eats it, we'll hit the road. That should give the deputies more than enough time to embed themselves in their ambush spot. If, of course, they are actually ambushing us."

The other man shook his head. "Of course they're ambushing us. I've seen looks like that on people before. They want what we have. Don't feel guilty about what's going to happen to them.

"Actually, now that I think about it, once we head off in an unexpected direction, they might send someone to slow us down before their regular force catches up with us. I think Moshe and I probably will run out in front of you and set up the ambush after all. Once you guys pass us, we'll be ready for any pursuit. If there isn't any, we'll catch up."

They pulled around the building and edged closer to the road.

Tom kept an eye on the men who'd been watching them while Greg bought and distributed the chicken and snacks.

He and Nika wolfed down their chicken, washing it down with cold soft drinks. He was going to miss those. They used the supplied napkins to wipe the grease off their fingers and faces.

"Once we get out of direct sight, I want you to get the drone airborne," Tom said. "We'll want to know who's chasing us. And it would be nice to know if someone is ahead of us."

"I'll go get a fresh battery for it now. That way we can have maximum flight time. I'll swap the batteries in the controller and goggles, too."

She hopped out of the Beast and ran back to one of the Hummers. A minute later, she was in the back of the Beast doing her business there. Less than three minutes later, she had taken the partially depleted batteries back where she'd come from.

Nika climbed in and nodded to him. "They say they're ready."

"Well then, let's get this show on the road."

He made sure and watched both groups as Greg headed out onto the highway and turned west. That definitely got the deputies' attention. He saw one of them race to a squad car and yank out his microphone. Yep, they had indeed set up an ambush out to the east.

The four locals were watching them, but only one of them was slowly walking towards a pickup truck. He wasn't sure what that meant. Maybe the guy was going to follow them.

Once they were over the hill and he couldn't see anyone watching them, Tom slowed to a stop and let Nika out. Just like last time, it only took her a moment to launch the drone.

As soon as she was back in the Beast, she slipped on the FPV goggles and grabbed the controller.

"Let me get up to maximum height and look out ahead of us," she said.

Tom put the Beast into gear and got them into motion again. He wanted to get as much distance between them and the people that were going to be racing up behind them as he could.

Not that he cared whether the folks behind them rioted or not, but he didn't want to be trapped too close to town. The further away they got, the less likelihood that more people would chase after them once they repulsed the attack.

They made it back to the turnoff leading to the campground without any trouble. There was a good-sized hill half a mile ahead. On the other side of that, Greg and Moshe pulled off to the side of the road.

Tom waved at them as he drove past.

"Any sign of pursuit?" he asked Nika.

"Not yet. I'd expect it's going to happen fast. Cop cars are really fast."

"Swing around and take a look in front of us. I want to be sure we're clear."

He was coming around the curve as he said that and saw that they were not. Someone had pulled a couple of pickup trucks across the road and hunched down behind them.

"We've got trouble ahead," he said sharply. "Get down as low as you can. Signal the others to follow my lead."

Rather than pulling to a stop to get out and fight the ambushers, he jammed the gas pedal to the floor. The Beast roared and lurched forward. He couldn't say that it raced, because it just didn't have that kind of acceleration. Instead, it smoothly hit fifty miles an hour without any trouble on the slight downhill grade.

He aimed the vehicle at the center of the road and ducked down a little.

The good old boys had obviously expected some kind of hesitation. They had just enough time to see that he wasn't slowing down before they had to either fire or flee.

Most of them decided that diving into the ditches on either side made a lot more sense than shooting, but not all of them. One guy in the center just stood there with a look of fury written across his face and raised his rifle to fire.

A roar from behind the Beast distracted both Tom and the man. Rachel shot past Tom, her motorcycle screaming defiance. She had her pistol out and proceeded to empty the magazine at the man in front of her.

Tom had no idea if she hit him, but she sure as hell distracted him.

Rachel dodged to the right side of the road and flew past the blocking vehicles.

The man apparently couldn't make up his mind which of them to shoot, and that hesitation proved fatal.

The Beast struck the trucks and sent both of them hurtling aside. That's what happened when something heavy like the Beast ran into something light like a pickup.

One of the trucks smashed into the man hard enough to send him flying into the trees to the left. He wouldn't be causing anyone any trouble ever again.

The people in the other vehicles fired their pistols at the men on the sides of the road as they drove through the hole the Beast had blown through the roadblock. It sounded as though there was some return fire. Tom hoped the bastards hadn't hit anyone.

"Nika, what's our situation?"

She pulled herself up off the floorboards and manipulated the controller. "I don't think anyone is going to be driving those trucks after us. Some of the men are heading into the woods. The rest are just standing there."

"Get on the radio and make sure that everyone is okay."

As he'd driven through the ambush, he'd seen that the road went over a big hill in front of them. He'd be able to get a direct line of sight on those bastards from there. He wanted to make certain that Moshe and Greg didn't run into problems rejoining them.

"Have the deputies put in an appearance?"

"Not yet. Everyone else is reporting they're okay. I'm not sure about damage to the vehicles, though everyone says they're running fine.

"When we get to that big hill up ahead, we're going to be pulling over just past it. We'll wait for Moshe and Greg there. I want Annie to check everyone. If anyone is hurt, I want to know about it."

A few minutes later, they pulled over the big hill and found a place they could park.

Tom jumped out of the Beast and ran back to the other vehicles, personally checking each person to make sure with his own eyes that they hadn't been shot. In the heat of battle, people had died because they hadn't realized they'd been hit.

Then he started looking at the vehicles themselves. The only indication that he could find of a hit was on the trailer with the diesel fuel. There was a gouge across the top of one side. Not a hole. Just a dent in the heavy steel.

That was good. They didn't need fuel leaking everywhere.

Once he was sure that none of the vehicles were damaged, he went to look at the front of the Beast. The impact hadn't even dented the heavy bumper. It had smashed through the obstacles with only some scarring to the paint.

Annie took a moment to look him over. "No one is hurt. It's a bloody miracle."

"Thank God for that," Tom said.

"It looks like the deputies are making an appearance," Nika said from where she stood next to the Beast.

Tom took the extra pair of goggles she held out to him and slipped them on. Off in the distance, he saw what looked like a dozen police cars racing in a line toward where the drone was coasting. Amusingly, they had their lights on.

Just below the drone, he could see Moshe and Greg lying just off to the side of the road. They had one of the big guns in front of them, the M2 Browning machine gun.

This was not going to be pretty.

It looked as though Greg was going to do the firing. Moshe knelt beside the gun with something in his hands. Tom couldn't see it clearly, but it looked like one of the blankets.

As the police cars raced toward the two men, Moshe held the blanket as though he were shielding Greg from the sun, except the sun was on the other side of them.

It was like a scene from *Star Wars*. The machine gun rounds must have had some tracers mixed in, because he could see them racing down like laser beams to impact the police cars. The fire shredded the first car in an instant, and it swerved to the right before flipping over and crashing into the ditch.

The empty shell casings came flying out of the machine gun and hit the blanket, falling to the ground. They were collecting the brass. Tom supposed that made sense. They didn't exactly have a lot to reload with for the big gun. He'd have to have Greg whip up some kind of brass catcher for future engagements.

Greg just walked the machine gun fire down the line of police cars. Some of the ambushers tried to turn around, but it was far too late for that. The machine gun ground them up like hamburger.

Some of them tried to hide behind their vehicles, but the heavy bullets just punched right through. There was no escape from the merciless angel of death.

Inside two minutes, it was over. All the vehicles downrange were on fire. If there was a live deputy, Tom couldn't see them.

Tom watched Moshe bring the radio to his lips. "We've taken care of the ambushers. We'll be cleaning up and headed your way in just a couple of minutes."

He heard Rachel respond. "There are some people between us. We will take care of them. Wait for us to call."

"Got it."

Now that the fighting was over, the two men started breaking down the machine gun and putting it in Moshe's pickup truck. Then they carefully collected the spent brass.

Tom handed the goggles to Nika, climbed into the back of the Beast, and found the custom rifle case that Moshe had shown him earlier. He opened it on the hood of one of the Hummers. He hoped the computer that did the sighting was as accurate as Moshe had indicated.

He loaded the rifle with the rounds inside the case and headed back to the top of the hill. He lay on the ground and looked back at where they'd smashed through the two pickup trucks.

Two of the men were carrying the guy that had gone flying. They set him down beside one of the wrecked trucks. Tom counted six living people.

He lined the crosshairs up on one of them and pressed the button to the side of the scope. It gave him a range, and a dot appeared near the man. Just a tad more than a thousand yards. Longer range than he'd ever shot before.

Following Moshe's instructions, he squeezed the trigger. The rifle did not go off. Then he remembered he was supposed to keep the trigger down and drag the crosshairs to the dot. He did so.

The rifle slammed into his shoulder. Downrange, it seemed an eternity before the man grabbed his chest and fell backward. His companions stared at him in shock.

Tom couldn't believe he'd actually hit the man, but he didn't let that stop him from repeating the process with the first man to run to the other's aid.

They got the idea when he took down the third man. The other three threw themselves to the ground and scanned around for him.

Good luck hitting him at this range.

When he shot the fourth man, they seemed to realize where he was. The other two leveled their rifles at him and began returning fire.

Surprisingly, a bullet skipped up off the asphalt to his left, maybe five yards away from him. That was an amazingly good shot. He acknowledged the man's skill by shooting him in the head.

The last guy ducked as low as he could and tried crawling into the grass. It took Tom three shots, but he finally hit him.

Tom kept moving the scope around to be sure that no one was moving while Moshe and Greg drove past the danger zone. Only then did he allow himself to relax and start packing up the astonishingly accurate rifle.

He stood, watching the smoke rising from the burning cars in the distance. He wondered if that would stop the dirty cops from messing with anyone else.

Probably not. Some people didn't learn lessons easily.

Oh, well. That wasn't his problem.

When Greg pulled up beside him, Tom clapped the young man on the shoulder. "Good shooting."

"I'd say the same, but you cheated. I'm going to have to take the time to show you how to use a real sniper rifle."

Tom laughed. "I'm looking forward to it. Let's get the hell out of here."

21

The rain, which had been falling off and on all morning, became steady in the afternoon and then grew heavier. It looked as if they were catching at least some of the typhoon remnants.

If so, Tom could only imagine what Washington State was feeling. He wondered if a raging downpour would even dampen the fires the nuke had ignited in Seattle.

The wind wasn't too bad, at least not bad enough to stop the drone from flying. That was a good thing. They really needed those eyes to know what was coming up.

He'd originally planned to cross under I-5 at Salem, but the closer they got to the highway, the more convinced he became that route wasn't realistic.

The number of dead cars steadily increased the closer they came. So did the number of refugees they saw. These weren't like the people they occasionally passed who were driving away. These folks were on foot.

After a few encounters—some of them requiring threats to end—they changed course to avoid them. He didn't want desperate people swarming them. Guns were all fine and good, but a dozen men with makeshift clubs who didn't care about death could still overwhelm them.

They stopped every half hour to allow Nika to swap out the batteries in the drone. They took the opportunity to refresh themselves, use the restroom in whatever way they could manage, and connect with one another.

That proved more important than he'd ever considered before this disaster. He knew from his reading that he needed to keep his chin up. That became difficult when everyone was considering the sheer number of people they'd had to kill to make it this far and the probable fates of the refugees they encountered.

Everyone was depressed. Of course they were. It was the end of the world. Who could blame them?

Yet they didn't have time for a pity party. He had to keep their spirits up and keep them confident that they were going to make it. He needed to sound certain. No. He needed to *be* certain.

Because of the detours and the frequent stops, it was close to dark by the time they made it within observation range of I-5. They'd ended up closer to Salem than Portland, but not by much.

They'd have other obstacles once they'd crossed I-5. They still needed to cross the Willamette River. The nearest bridge north of Salem was at Newberg on 219.

Once they got past the Willamette, they could take 99W over to 18. That would get them to his place. They'd still need to pass through some towns, but he hoped they'd allow people moving through to keep going. If not, he'd need to find another way around any trouble spots.

The road he'd picked as their most likely avenue of advance across I-5 was as far away from any city as he could manage. He hoped they could make a crossing after dark and remain unnoticed by anyone.

That was not to be.

To his shock, the area was swarming with people. It looked as if a huge camp of refugees surrounded the overpass he'd intended to use.

"How many people do you think that is?" Nika asked. She was observing them through her goggles beside him.

"Hundreds," he said. "Maybe a thousand. It looks as if they're stuck on the highway. They had to abandon their cars, but they don't have anywhere to go. They're hoping someone comes to rescue them."

Counting on the kindness of strangers was no longer a good call. By the time these people figured that out, it would be too late for them.

"Send the drone up and down the highway as far as you can," he told her. "I'd like to know what the other overpasses look like."

They'd only be able to see one, perhaps two, based on the height of the drone. As it was dark out, they'd have to switch to the quadcopter with the night-vision and FLIR cameras shortly.

Nika quickly discovered that the clustering of people was not restricted to this one overpass. The two they could see to their south and the one to the north were all in a similar state.

He left Nika to watch over them while they set up camp. They'd pulled off the main road. They weren't lucky enough to have a campground close at hand this time. The best they could find was an old building they could hide behind. It didn't look as though anyone had used it in years.

"The lock is heavy duty," Rachel told him. "So is the hasp. Whoever owns this place does not want anyone breaking in. It makes me wonder what is inside."

"Go find out," he told her. "We have time."

He passed food bars and water to everyone. They couldn't risk a fire this close to so many people.

"It looks as if all the routes under I-5 have people around them," he said to the group. "We're not going to be able to just drive through like we'd hoped."

Jenna sagged a little. "But we have to get through. What do we do?"

"We come up with a different plan. One that lets us slip past all of these people. If they find out we're here, they'll come running. We've got to get on the other side of I-5 and away from these camps before they know we're here."

He looked around at each of them. "I'm drawing a blank right now, so if you've got an idea, I'd love to hear it. I don't care how crazy it sounds. This is brainstorming. Just throw everything on the table. No judgment. Any idea might lead us to something else, even if the original thought isn't workable."

They stared at one another silently for a moment. Then Nancy spoke up. "Maybe you could dig a tunnel."

Tom shook his head slowly. "I'm afraid we don't have anything to dig that kind of hole. Unfortunately, we can't fly over them either. We have to drive, and the overpasses are the only way through."

"Actually, they're not," Randy said. "We could cross the highway at any point. Only the *vehicles* need pavement. I hate to say it, but we might have to abandon the vehicles and supplies."

Tom really didn't want to do that. "Not unless we have no other option. Having said that, the Army designed the Beast for off-road travel. I'd have to adjust the inflation of the tires, but I can go cross-country."

He looked over at their other vehicles. "The Hummers have less clearance and bigger payloads, but they might be able to make a trip like that, too. It's conceivable that we have to abandon the fuel, though. They're right at the top of their towing capacity."

"My truck has four-wheel-drive," Moshe said. "It could make it, but what about the freeway? Those cars are bumper to bumper."

Greg finished wolfing down his food bar. "Cars can be moved. What we need to do is scout ahead and see if the land is passable. If it is, we might be able to drive to the freeway, move some cars out of the way, and push on to the other side while it's dark."

That sounded awfully risky. If one of the vehicles got stuck or broke an axle, they'd be screwed. Still, that was the only viable alternative anyone had come up with so far.

The two street bikes would have a harder time, but they were motorcycles. It was entirely possible that they could make the trip. Or, if the ground really was that bad, they could get the four-wheelers off the trailer and strap the street bikes in their place.

"Is this something we need to see in the daylight?" Tom asked Greg. "There's a real risk that those people will spot us. If so, we might end up in a confrontation that makes traveling through here impossible. I'd rather not have them know we're here at all."

"I've scouted plenty of places in the dark," Greg assured him. "I'll take the night-vision goggles and have a look. This land looks as though someone used it for pasture, so it's flat. The only things we really have to worry about are gullies. Something like that might make traversing the ground impossible."

The ex-Army sniper looked up at the waning moon. "The moon will be down in a couple of hours. The aurora is going to provide some light, but not enough to tip our hand. I'll head out then and see if I can find a way across that we can clear quietly. I'll have to look on the other side as well.

"If we catch any breaks at all, we might be able to make the push before dawn. The people in the camps would hear us driving, but they wouldn't know precisely where the sound was coming from. As long as we cross quickly, we should be able to keep them from catching up with us."

Tom nodded. "I'll go with you."

Rachel stepped out into the light of the fire. "It is a shop of some kind. It does not look as though it has been in business for some time. Someone was using it for storage. I found something interesting. Can you take a look, Randy?"

The young engineer rose to his feet. Tom decided to tag along with them.

The inside of the shop was a hot mess. Rotting benches, rusting tools, and the intense smell of mildew and something worse. There was something dead in here.

Tom walked to the back of the shop and found a large, heavily muscled man sitting in a straight-backed chair. He'd been dead for a few days. The gun on the floor and his ruined head suggested suicide.

The sight had surprisingly little emotional impact on him. That was worrying.

"You didn't think to mention him?" he asked Rachel.

"And spoil the surprise?"

He wondered if the man had just given in to despair. This was the easy way out. How many other people would choose to end everything rather than keep fighting?

"The door was locked with a padlock from the outside," Tom said as he pulled a handkerchief out to cover his nose. "How did he get locked in here?"

"There is another door in the front of the building," Rachel said. "He had the keys on him. Based on the pictures on the wall, I suspect he owned this place. But he is not what I called you to see."

Rachel led them to the back of the old shop.

"Is that an anvil?" Randy asked.

It was. In fact, there were several anvils of different sizes. There was also an array of hammers and other tools hanging on a wall rack. A bellows-driven forge of some kind sat off to the side. Unlike the other tools, these were in excellent condition.

"This is worth its weight in Twinkies," Randy declared. "Or whatever trade good you want to mention. Being able to turn scrap metal into tools will be a priceless capability. We've got to find a way to take this with us."

Tom stepped away from them and headed for the door. "I'll leave figuring that out to you. Just remember, we'll be leaving in about six hours. You have to be ready to move, and you can't overload the vehicles."

Rachel raised her chin. "I'll take that as a challenge."

"You do that. I'm going to go take a nap. Tonight is going to be a long one."

22

The moon had set when Greg woke him for their scouting mission. Tom rose from the sleeping bag he'd set up in front of the Beast and stretched.

He'd laid a tarp across himself to keep the worst of the rain off. He hadn't wanted them to sleep in the shop. The smell in there was awful.

To his surprise, the rain had let up. He'd expected it to get heavier. That was a lucky break. If the ground became too soaked, they wouldn't be able to traverse the fields.

Hell, it might already be too late. Just because the Beast could do off road didn't mean it was immune from getting stuck. That was far from true.

He still had his clothes on, so all he had to do was re-arm himself and put his boots on. Randy and Rachel had unpacked part of the cargo. They'd put a tarp over the back to keep the rain off them and the gear as they worked.

Their thoughts obviously ran along the same lines as his earlier ones. They'd swapped the street bikes for the four-wheelers. Even once they reached the other side of the highway, those would be able to keep up with the Beast.

He walked over to them. "Make sure you don't take too much out at a time. If we have to make a run for it, I don't want to abandon any more than we must."

"We're keeping that in mind," Randy said. "We'll be able to put the anvils into the Beast, but they're very heavy. We're saving them for last. At this point, we'll probably be able to fit the bellows into the Beast as well."

"Do the best you can," he said. "I'm not sure how long it will take for us to scout ahead. Certainly a couple of hours. Worst-case scenario, we come hauling back in twenty minutes with a howling horde of people on our heels. Be ready to repack the moment we call or if you start hearing gunfire."

Rachel shook her head. "Nika will be monitoring you via the drone. We will know if you are in trouble. If so, some of us will get everything packed while the rest provide cover for you."

Tom turned to where Nika was sitting near the fire. Since she was wearing her goggles, he assumed she was using one of the drones to keep an eye around them.

"How long has she been doing that? She really needs to get some sleep."

"I will swap out with her while you're gone. Poppa can help Randy. I will make her show me how to control these things. She said they were very automated. We will find out. I will send her to bed and only wake her if I run into a problem that I can't figure out.

"Once we get on the other side of I-5, I will make certain that several of us learn how to run those things. We have been on the run for less than a week, but they have been lifesavers."

He nodded. "I wish I could say that we'll have the time, but we won't. It's going to have to wait until we get to my place."

"Just how far away are we?"

"If it wasn't the apocalypse, we could be there in about three hours. It isn't normally a strenuous drive, even going slow with something like the Beast. Now? Several more days. Possibly more, if we run into significant trouble."

"Are there any obstacles between here and there that you think might cause us trouble?"

He grimaced. "Yes. There's a federal prison directly between the coast and us. I've never visited it, but I'm going to assume there are other unsavory people inside. It's always possible that the place is still under control, though."

She laughed. "With our luck, do you think that is likely?"

"You're right," he said tiredly. "We have to assume the inmates are loose. I can't even remember the name of the place, much less what kind of convicts it had. I don't think it was a maximum-security facility, so maybe we won't get the worst of the worst."

Rachel stared up at the aurora. "Sometimes you cannot tell who the monsters are going to be. It might be the mild-mannered, quiet people. It might be the intellectuals. Until now, we have run into those accustomed to using force to get their way. In the long run, I suspect we will have more trouble with people that were never criminals in the old world."

She frowned, staring up. "Is it just me, or is the aurora dimming?"

Now that she'd brought his attention to it, the colors were definitely faded, though they still covered the entire sky.

"Maybe the CME is weakening. It's been going strong for days now. Longer than I'd expected, frankly. The one back in the 1800s lasted a couple of days. We have no way of knowing until it ends."

"It must be the prettiest mass murderer in history," Rachel said softly. "It is hard to believe something like that could cause so much death."

He nodded. Even though he knew that a CME alone probably wouldn't have brought civilization down completely, he agreed with her.

The idiocy of the people in power that used EMP weapons and then nukes had been what truly slit the modern world's throat. The CME wouldn't have been nearly as bad on its own.

"Well, do what you can. All this stuff would be useful if we can get it to my place. To *our* place. I suppose if we have to, we can stash it somewhere and try to come back, but I'd rather not take that chance."

She looked him right in the eyes. "I will make it fit. I give you my word."

He glanced over and saw that Greg was waiting for him. "See you in a couple of hours," he told Rachel.

"Be careful. We need you."

Without warning, she leaned forward and kissed him soundly on the lips.

Shocked, he could only stare at her back as she walked away. Where the hell had that come from?

Greg stepped up beside him. "I had no idea you two were a thing."

"Neither did I."

The other man clapped him on the shoulder. "We're always the last to know. Let's get moving. I'll fill you in as we go."

They'd examined the ground via drone before Tom had gotten any sleep, so he knew the rough features they had to cross. There were a few dark houses between the shop and the wide pasture beside the freeway.

Even though they thought those houses were unoccupied, it made sense to avoid going too close. With the power out, someone inside with a shotgun could really mess up their day.

The two of them swung wide and crossed the road between the shop and the field beside the highway. The fence was made of barbed wire. Rather than posts of wood, the fence used metal rods sunk into concrete. Pretty secure.

Tom knelt down and examined one of the posts. "We're going to have to dig up at least one of these to get the Beast through. It's too wide to fit through the gap between just two posts."

"That would be a pain in the ass if we actually had to do it," Greg said. "You're forgetting that big winch on your front bumper. It can pull ten thousand pounds. More than enough to uproot one of these in a jiffy."

Well, that was embarrassing. He'd completely forgotten about that capability. It would make doing this a lot easier.

The two of them slipped between the strands of barbed wire. One had to plant a foot firmly on the bottom strand and yank the topmost high into the air to allow the other person through.

Once they were in the field, Tom tried to get an idea of how soaked the ground was. If the soil was loose and saturated, they might as well turn around now.

Optimistically, he thought it was pretty well packed. It might be possible to drive across the field without turning this into a huge mud pit.

The two of them started toward I-5. It was obvious that someone used this pasture for cattle on occasion. There were none in evidence right now, but he saw a central windmill that drew well water into a tank.

Greg stopped next to it and looked around in a circle. He pointed off to the left. "There's a road leading from here to the highway. If we come in this way, the ground will be less prone to turning into muck. That gets us halfway to where we want to go."

Tom stared up at the windmill. "I'll bet Randy can build something like this to keep our pump working even when the power is off. One more thing I should've thought of ahead of time. I have a hand pump and a lot of stored water, but this would be a hell of a lot easier."

They continued their stealthy walk toward the freeway. They became more cautious the closer they got. The ground was still thankfully flat and hard packed. It was beginning to look like this crazy plan might work after all.

The dirt path they were following had a gate at the freeway. A set of cattle guards inside the gate made certain no bovine prisoners escaped.

A wide gravel road crossed over metal tubes and led to the asphalt. The culvert beside the road was made of concrete and did have some water flowing through it. The sides were fairly steep.

Dead cars choked the highway, packed bumper to bumper. Looking carefully, Tom could see no sign of occupation. Everyone must've made their way to the makeshift camps. Off to the south, Tom could hear the sound of car alarms.

Quite a few of them, actually. Someone had to have set them off recently, too. Otherwise, the batteries would have been dead by now.

"Well, that's one side of the freeway," Greg said. "We need to look at the median and see what the other side has to offer. It won't do us any good just to get on the freeway. We have to be able to get off again."

Now things were going to get dangerous. With all those cars out there, the chances that they'd run into someone who could sound the alarm were much higher. It was time to consult a higher authority.

He keyed his radio. "Eye in the sky, what have you got for us?"

The response came quickly into the small headset he wore. It was Rachel's voice. "Things look quiet in that section. I do not see anyone near you.

"There are a few people to the south, but it seems as though they are just looting the cars closest to the overpass. So long as you keep a low profile, they should not see you. They probably will not be able to hear you over the noise, either."

"Do you see any way for our vehicles to get over the culvert on the other side of the freeway?"

"About a hundred yards to the north," she confirmed. "It looks about the same as the one in front of you. There is also an emergency vehicle crossing on the median right in front of it. Basically, if we can get through the cars in front of you, then turn right and go about a hundred yards, we can cross the median and get to the other side."

Tom eyed the vehicles in front of them. If they could clear the road enough—particularly given the Beast's turning radius—it was possible they could make the run across before anyone caught up with them.

They'd have to clear the path in advance. If they tried to clear it as they moved, they'd have hordes of people all around them before they got across.

"What does the field on the other side look like?" he asked.

"Just like the one you are in. You will need to look at the ground, but it looks passable. Obviously, there is a gate right beside the freeway. It leads to an area where cattle can eat. I don't see any paths leading further down towards the back of the property, though."

"Does it run up against the highway on the other side of that encampment?"

"Hang on while I go look."

A few minutes later, she spoke again. "It does connect. In fact, it looks as if there used to be a gate there. The fence is solid now, but there is something across the culvert that would allow a vehicle to pass. It is somewhat narrow. I am not sure if the Beast can make it across, but the rest of the vehicles should be okay."

He turned to Greg. "We'll have to go look. If we can't get every vehicle through, then we don't try."

The two of them made their way cautiously across the freeway. They examined the cars and trucks that they'd have to move when the time came. It should be possible, though getting them moved without making too much noise might be a challenge.

Crossing into the field on the other side revealed exactly what Rachel had said. It was just like the one they'd crossed. It would support the weight of their convoy.

They made the trek to the back corner of the other property. Now they were very close to the refugee camp, so they kept low and slow. This last leg of driving was going to be the most dangerous. People from the camp could run this far in just a few minutes.

With everyone driving a vehicle, that would leave only the motorcyclists to respond and hold them back. The problem was that desperate people did desperate things.

The place at the back of the property where a gate had once been did let out to the road. As Rachel had suggested, it was too narrow for the Beast, but it should be able to support the width of the rest of the vehicles.

Whether it would support the weight of the fuel tanks or not was another question. He thought that it would, but they wouldn't know until they actually tried it.

The culvert here was only dirt, but it was fairly wide. There was water flowing through it, but it might be passable.

Tom had Greg hold the barbed wire apart for him so he could go take a closer look.

He stepped down onto the sloped surface beside the slow-moving water. It felt compacted, but he didn't weigh as much as the Beast. It was possible his vehicle would get part way across and then get stuck. If that happened, they'd have to abandon it and everything inside it.

Or they'd have to use their weapons to keep the refugees at bay while they unpacked it, pulled it out, and repacked it. That didn't sound as though it would be easy, or even possible.

He went back to the crossover and gave it a second look. The total wheelbase for the Beast was too wide to fit on top of it, but maybe just the interior wheels would fit if he was *exceedingly* careful.

The risks of trying it this way were that he would fall off to one side or the other, or the crossover would collapse and dump him on his side.

None of those options sounded good to him, but they didn't exactly have much of a choice. This was the best chance they had of getting across this obstacle and onto the road home again.

As much as it made his stomach churn, they were going to have to take it.

"The mission is a go," he told Rachel. "We're going to head back that way, so finish packing up. We'll pull out as soon as we get the highway cleared."

"We are done packing. Amazingly, we made everything fit. I think we are completely out of space at this point, so try not to find anything else interesting."

He laughed. "Wake Nika up and put her back on drone duty. She'll keep watch while we clear vehicles."

"Copy."

After he cut the fence and tied the wire safely out of the way, the two of them retraced their steps back to the freeway. He repeated the work on the fence there. This side was open.

Now came the most ticklish part of the operation—breaking into the cars, getting them into neutral, and pushing them out of the way. They couldn't make too much noise, or it would draw the attention of the refugees. Yet one did not break glass silently, or trigger car alarms.

Tom was just about to step out beside the nearest cars when Greg grabbed his arm and yanked him down to the ground. Following the other man's gaze, he saw the problem immediately. The looters from up the highway were coming their way.

They'd split into four smaller groups, one on each side of both lanes. They were looking into the cars as they passed, occasionally smashing windows and taking possessions. The closest group was less than a hundred yards away and heading straight for them.

23

Tom inched backward slowly, grateful for the camouflage clothing he wore and the relatively dim light coming from the aurora. He made it back into the ditch without any of the looters spotting him.

Thankfully, the men were focused on robbing cars, not looking off into the ditch. They continued their random destruction and looting as they swept past where he hid. The scent of alcohol on them was strong.

Once the men were several hundred yards away, Tom stealthily slipped across the highway and waited on the far side to see if they noticed his movement. They didn't. Greg quickly joined him. They cut the chain securing the gate but left it closed for the moment.

Once they made it back to the windmill, he activated his radio. "Nika, we just about ran into some looters. Is something wrong with the drone?"

"I had to pull it back to swap out the battery. They weren't anywhere close to you when I moved. They must've sped up."

Thankfully, it hadn't ended badly. "It worked out okay this time. In the future, let us know if the drone is going to be relocating. That'll help us plan better."

"Will do. I'm sorry. It won't happen again."

"Good enough. We'll head back as soon as we cut the last fence and dig up a post."

He looked over at Greg. "With all the nighttime travelers, I think we'd best do this by hand."

Greg sighed but didn't argue.

Digging the concrete-secured post up was backbreaking work, but they got it done in about twenty minutes.

They arrived back at their temporary camp exhausted. Tom gratefully took a bottle of water and a food bar from Annie.

Everyone gathered around him. He took a few bites and then proceeded to fill them in on what they'd discovered.

"So the bottom line," he said after he'd finished his rundown, "is that we should be able to get across, but we're going to run the risk of someone catching on and chasing after us. We're going to have to move quickly.

"I want to stress that we have to do everything carefully. One mistake and we'll get a vehicle stuck. That means we'll have to abandon it and anything that's in it. I'd rather not do that."

Rachel gestured at the vehicles. "Everything is packed away. There were many blacksmithing tools inside that shop. I have no idea if they belonged to the dead man, but they are going to be very useful in setting up a full-blown shop of our own.

"The owner also had quite a library on primitive blacksmithing stashed away in a couple of boxes," Randy said. "All safely wrapped in protective bags.

"He even studied under a couple of people that still did it for a living. There are several notebooks filled with his observations. Solid gold."

Tom was impressed but worried. "While that will be useful, I'm really concerned about the extra weight. We're going cross-country here. It's going to be obscenely easy to get the Beast stuck."

He sighed. "We'll just have to do the best we can and pray. Nika, it's critical that you keep a good watch over both refugee camps and the area around us. I realize that's a lot of coverage, but we don't know where trouble is going to come from. If it comes, it's going to come fast."

The young woman smiled. "I've been working on that. Rachel is more than capable of flying a drone on her own under circumstances like this. The software-based protections will keep her from crashing. And I've found an excellent backup drone pilot."

She gestured towards Adam Baker.

Tom smiled skeptically at the nine-year-old boy. "Really?"

Nika nodded emphatically. "Without a doubt. I gave him a test drive after his sister told me that he was amazing at video games. It turns out that he can control a drone as well as anybody I've ever seen. Nancy will have a second pair of goggles and keep an eye out on what he's looking at.

"I'll fly the big quadcopter over you guys, Rachel will take one of the small drones to the south, and Adam will do the same to the north.

"If there is any movement, we'll let you know. If anyone has to take a break to come back for a battery swap, we'll let you know. I won't make that mistake again."

Tom had reservations but not a lot of choices. They had a very few people trying to do a whole bunch. Everyone had to pull their weight, and that sometimes meant having to trust someone to carry out a task even if you weren't sure they could.

If Nika said they had it covered—and he'd seen her skills at work —then that was as good a recommendation as he was going to get.

He checked his watch. They had about two hours until dawn. He really wanted to be on the road before the sun came up. They'd best get moving.

"We'll head back on foot and clear the cars," Tom said. "Once we have things cleared, we'll come back. Be ready."

The two men retraced the steps they'd taken earlier, bringing Randy with them. There were three lanes on either side of the freeway. The stalled cars were bumper to bumper.

They not only needed enough space for their vehicles to cross, they had to go far enough down to provide for the wide turning radius the Beast required. That meant relocating several dozen vehicles on each side.

It would've been simpler to drive directly across, but while the Beast could probably make it, he wasn't sure about the other vehicles. If he was wrong about the big vehicle, they'd lose a lot of their supplies.

Thankfully, the looters had smashed the windows in on a number of vehicles, even the ones they obviously had no intention of taking anything from. Some people just liked destroying things.

That had set off what sounded like hundreds of car alarms. It seemed the EMP didn't affect those as much as the vehicles' engines.

That would do wonders masking any noise the convoy made as it worked its way up onto the freeway. As long as they kept their acceleration low, all the loud horns would mask their travel.

It looked as though looting had an upside.

No one had left their keys in the abandoned vehicles. That meant they had to use brute force to get the vehicles in neutral and break the steering wheel locks.

This was where Randy really showed his worth. The young engineer had no problem figuring out how to bypass whatever lockouts kept the vehicles in park or getting the wheels to turn like they wanted. It meant spending a moment under the hoods or under the cars, but he made it look easy.

The young man grinned at him. "My professors would be horrified if they knew I was using their teachings to break into cars."

"You might be surprised," Tom said. "Right about now, I'd imagine a lot of them are doing something similar, if they're smart."

It took about half an hour to create a gap wide enough to allow the Beast to cross and turn on that side. They then repeated the process on the far side of the highway.

As counterintuitive as it seemed, some people had been heading toward Portland. He suspected they thought it was better than what they'd experienced in Salem. Desperate people did unexpected things.

Any time the drones had to return to swap out batteries, the three men took a break—if, by taking a break, you meant watching for possible intruders.

It took longer than Tom had planned to clear the freeway. By the time the three men got back to the convoy, it was about forty-five minutes until dawn. The sky was just starting to gray in the east.

They wasted no time and set out. Greg led the way on his scout motorcycle. Rachel and Randy had their four-wheelers close behind him.

During the first part of their travel, Tom had the Beast in front of the other vehicles. He had already lowered the air pressure in the tires to give him more traction. Once they got safely away from I-5, he'd have to take time to get it back up to road pressure with his compressor.

He made sure to keep the truck's engine revving as slowly as he could while still moving. He didn't want the Beast to roar.

It turned out they hadn't quite cleared enough of a turning radius on that first section of highway. The Beast went part way into the median before he stopped. He called a halt while he got out and investigated his options.

Even with rear-wheel turning installed on the Beast, it wasn't going to be able to make the turn to get onto the shoulder. He was going to have to chance crossing the median.

He motioned for Greg, Rachel, and Randy to join him. "I'm going to have to cross here. Let's clear a few more cars on the other side so I can get to where I need to be."

The four of them quickly did what they could to clear a path for the Beast. Things went smoothly enough until Tom set off a particularly loud car alarm.

He could only hope that it was far enough away from the encampments to avoid drawing any attention. Or, if it did, they'd assume it was just someone looting.

By the time they finished moving the extra cars, the sky had brightened enough that they could see into the distance. Any early risers in the refugee camps might see them now.

He returned to the Beast and drove it slowly across the median. The ground there was somewhat wet, but the big tires and powerful engine pulled the massive truck across, even with its heavy payload. Unfortunately, that meant he had to make some engine noise.

Once the Beast was out of their way, the rest of the vehicles shot up the shoulder on the original part of the freeway and slipped across into the field on the other side. He brought up the rear and made the turn off the highway. Barely.

The trailer caught on a car bumper and dragged a little Smart Car off into the ditch as he made that final push. That, too, made more noise than he really wanted anyone to hear.

Nika looked over at him. "We're starting to get some looks from the refugee camp to the north. The one that is set up on the same road that we're going to come out on. There are a couple of dozen people staring in our direction."

Tom grunted. "Can't be helped. We're just going to have to push on. Tell the other vehicles to get onto the farm to market road. We'll bring up the rear. Either the Beast is going to make it or it's not."

She stared off into space after she passed on his instructions. "It looks like about a mile between where we'll come out and the refugee camp. Those people are on foot. Even if we get stuck, we might be able to get you back onto the road before they get to us."

"That would be nice, but we can't count on it. Cross your fingers."

They continued across the open field and made it to the other exit just as the sun began rising. They'd run out of time.

None of the other vehicles had any problem getting onto the roadway, even Moshe's extended-cab truck with the trailer. They pulled a little bit ahead of where the Beast would come out and climbed out to watch him make the crossing.

"We've definitely got some eyes looking our way now," Nika said. "It looks like a bunch of people are jogging toward us. I'm not seeing any Olympic sprinters, so we have maybe fifteen minutes before they get here."

"Here goes nothing," Tom muttered.

He lined up his wheels as carefully as he could on the thin bridge going across the drainage ditch. He put the Beast into low and began the crossing.

"Edge just a teeny bit to the right," Nika said.

She obviously had a better view than he did, so he did as she instructed. The big truck made it across far enough for his rear tires to get on the pavement before he started making the required turn.

The left trailer wheel dropped off the crossing and yanked the big truck to a halt. It didn't flip, thank God. He gave the Beast some gas, but the trailer was stuck.

24
─────────

Cursing, Tom climbed out the Beast. The trailer was wedged good. The axle was clear, but the culvert had trapped the tire on the left side.

Greg stepped up beside him and looked down at the trailer. "We're going to have to cut it loose."

Tom hated to do that. He started looking considering other options. He immediately rejected being able to raise it up off the ground with the support jacks. They didn't have time. With the refugees headed their way, they *really* didn't have the time.

He looked up the road, and an idea began forming in his mind. Well, desperate times called for desperate measures.

"Get further up the highway. I'm going to try something potentially stupid."

He released the hitch binding the trailer to the Beast and removed the safety chains. The wheeled support kept the tongue up off the ground.

Tom climbed into the cab of the big truck. "Nika, make sure you keep a close eye on those people running this way. I'd like to have at least a couple of minutes warning that they're about on top of us."

The young woman nodded. "They're running faster now. I think we have less than ten minutes before the more athletic people get here. A couple of them look like they have guns."

Tom stuck his head out the window. "Greg, Nika says we have some armed folk coming up behind us. I'd like you to dissuade them without killing them, if at all possible."

The young man nodded, jumped on the scout bike, and headed towards the refugees.

Without the trailer holding the Beast back, he was able to get it on to the highway without any trouble. He drove about fifty feet up the road to the next property entrance. This one was on the other side of the road and was significantly wider and sturdier looking than the one he'd just crossed.

He carefully backed the Beast into the drive and stopped. He set the brakes and jumped down. At the front of the vehicle, he began unwinding the cable from the winch. It was heavy, but he was able to get it back to the stuck trailer.

Once there, he used the trailer's safety chains to help bind the cable to the tongue. This would be either a really good idea or a really bad one.

He turned to his companions. "I want everyone else to get as far up the road as you can. If this cable snaps, it could kill someone. The way the trailer is wedged, it's entirely possible that might happen."

"Just leave the trailer," Rachel said firmly. "We will make do."

He shook his head. "I'm too stubborn to just abandon it. I'm going to give this a try."

A few shots rang out from down the road. He hoped those were warning shots to keep the refugees back. He could hear what sounded like pistol shots, too.

That would be the refugees firing back. He sincerely hoped this didn't turn bloody, but if the choice was between Greg and the refugees, he'd pick Greg every time.

Once he was back at the Beast, he engaged the winch carefully. It used the engine's power for torque, so it would be able to pull roughly ten thousand pounds. That was more than enough to move the trailer if the damned thing came loose.

The trailer turned toward him as the cable tightened. Once it was taut, Tom increased the pull. The line strained, and he tried to stop imagining it snapping and cutting him in half.

Slowly, the trailer inched forward until the stuck wheel popped free. The trailer skidded onto the highway.

He let out a breath he hadn't realized he'd been holding. He gave the cable some slack, went and disconnected it from the trailer, and then respooled it.

Tom pulled the Beast back out onto the highway and backed it up to the trailer. It took several of them to get it safely latched onto the hitch. He wrapped the backup chains around their securing points to hold it in case it somehow came loose.

Greg came zipping up on the scout motorcycle. "They're still advancing. I decided I wasn't going to be able to stop them without killing someone. We've got a couple of minutes before they come around the bend back there. There are hundreds of them now."

Tom felt badly for those people. Unfortunately, he couldn't save the world. No one could.

"Everybody mount up," he said. "We're going to go two miles up the road, and then we'll stop to check all the vehicles to make sure everything is good. I need to use the compressor to inflate the tires on the Beast, too."

They got away from the refugees without him having to see all the desperate people chasing after them. Most of them were going to die within the week. Lack of water, illness from drinking water from where they shouldn't, and violence were going to take a quick toll on them.

As they got away from the freeway, the number of stalled cars began dropping off quickly. The only people that left major thoroughfares under normal circumstances were the ones that lived in the area. Once the freeways had jammed, getting off them wasn't even possible for most vehicles.

They found a conveniently deserted stretch of highway that they could use to take a well-deserved break, inspect all the vehicles, and allow him to pump up his tires.

The Beast had a system that could theoretically have done it all at once, but the damned thing was notoriously unreliable. He'd disabled it on the advice of the man who'd refurbished it for him.

Nika took over the fixed-wing drone and set it to circling above them. She was working with Adam and Nancy to show them everything they needed to know about flying the device.

Tom had to admit, the children had really come through. The adults had kept them too busy to fall apart over the deaths of their parents so far, but he was smart enough to realize that was still coming.

Once they'd eaten a cold snack, they headed to 219 and went north toward the bridge he'd selected to cross. They didn't push it, so they didn't get into the area until early in the afternoon.

The roads out here were mostly clear of disabled cars, though they did spot a few people driving. He gave the others plenty of time to stop and turn around when they showed concern at driving near his convoy.

He knew that was going to allow word of their presence to spread ahead of them, but it couldn't be helped.

The bridge was what the military called a chokepoint. Anyone wanting to get to the other side of the river would have to cross it. Considering that there was a city on the other side, it was almost certain the residents had blocked it to protect themselves.

Once they got there, they'd have to negotiate with whoever was holding the bridge. He wanted to avoid violence, because the odds were that the other side would be entrenched well enough to severely injure or kill a number of them if they tried to force a crossing.

Besides, this city wasn't so far away from his home. He might have to deal with them in the future. It was far better to leave friends in one's wake than enemies.

His caution proved warranted when they got the drone over the bridge. There were a number of police cars on both sides of the structure. It certainly appeared as though they had a dozen or more people covering the approach.

Rather than bringing his convoy close to the bridge, Tom decided to stop about a mile back, close enough for the police to see him coming once he came around the final bend, but far enough back to conceal their numbers. If things went wrong, the rest of them could turn around and look for other options.

Tom borrowed the scout bike from Greg and drove around the curve toward the bridge. As he got closer, he could see that the police vehicles were from either the City of Newberg or the Yamhill County Sheriff's Department. He really wished he knew some of the officers there.

Hell, he wished he knew anyone that lived there.

A single man on a small motorcycle apparently didn't intimidate the police, which was kind of the point. Three of them stepped out beyond the cruisers, and the center man raised his hand.

The cop was a young man with a jaunty hat. He wasn't close enough for Tom to read his nametag, but his uniform was still in good shape.

"That's far enough," the man said. "The bridge is closed."

Tom carefully set the motorcycle on its kickstand and took two steps toward the police. He kept his hands away from his belt and made certain that he wasn't in a threatening posture.

"I have to come through here to get home. I live in Otis, over by the coast. I've got some friends just around the curve. We were off getting stuff in Portland when all this went down. It's either this bridge or the one in Salem. Trust me, going through Salem is a bad idea."

The man smiled a little. "I imagine it is. I feel for you, friend, but the mayor has laid down the law. No one goes in or out of Newberg. Only residents."

"I'm willing to trade for our free passage."

The man scratched his chin. "I've heard offers like that before. Mainly folk offering money. I'm afraid that paper ain't worth the numbers printed on it anymore."

"No. I'm talking hard trade goods. We picked up some things here and there before all this went down. Some of our folk are professionals, too. We might be able to work a passage. I'm just looking to come to some kind of agreement in principle so that we can negotiate."

The man considered him for a long moment. "I wouldn't be too confident of a positive answer, stranger, but I'll pass your offer up the line. I want to see your driver's license, though.

"One of my boys is on the other side of the river with a scoped rifle. He's a damned good shot. I'm going to come on out there and look to see if you're telling me the truth. Then I'm going to back off and call my boss. Are we good with this?"

"Sure. I need to reach into my pocket and pull out my wallet. Tell your friend not to get too excited."

Once the cop spoke on his radio and nodded toward him, Tom reached into his front left pocket and pulled out the small wallet he kept there. He'd gone to one that fit into his front pocket when he'd started carrying a pistol regularly. That way he could get at it without exposing his weapon.

He extracted his driver's license and handed it to the cop, who had advanced to within a few feet of him. He could read the man's nametag now. The cop's name was Jenkins.

The man looked at the license carefully. "Well then, it looks like you're telling me the truth about where you live, Mister Morgan. That might help your case. I'll be right back."

Jenkins backed up a few feet and read off Tom's information to someone on the other end of the radio. Tom couldn't hear the response, but the cop came back close enough to return his license to him.

"I'm going to return to my friends, and when I get an answer for you, I'll come back out."

Tom used his radio to pass the information back to the rest of the convoy. Personally, he more than half expected the cops to shut them down. Why should they let anyone cross through their territory? They were a city. Surely, they didn't have much they needed to trade for.

"Tom, I'm seeing some movement in town," Nika said. "Half a dozen cars are leaving what looks like the city center and headed your way."

"It sounds like maybe they're at least willing to talk," he said. "That's better than an outright no."

Once the cars arrived, he started to reevaluate that initial assessment. The man that climbed out of the lead car was big and beefy, and his expression was fierce. He had another dozen armed men behind him. Reinforcements for the bridge, perhaps.

The large newcomer stopped out away from the bridge toward Tom. Half a dozen men armed with rifles trailed closely behind him.

"Officer Jenkins told you we weren't allowing traffic across the Willamette," the man said harshly. "The mayor is serious about that order. He told me that again just five minutes ago. No one crosses into Newberg."

25

The large man glared at Tom for a moment and then continued. "If I'm going to argue with my good friend, you're going to have to convince me that you're worth it. My name is Anton Green, and I'm a city councilman. The mayor picked me to be his personal envoy and to make sure that we protect Newberg in these uncertain times.

"One of my associates says that he thinks he knows you. That you're some kind of writer. Is that true? What do you write?"

Tom smiled a little. It always surprised him when someone had read his work. Even making more than enough to live off still meant most readers never heard of him. That was the way it was.

"Ironically enough, I write postapocalyptic fiction. End-of-the-world stuff. I write other science fiction, too. Whatever appeals to me."

The man nodded. "I thought as much. My associate showed me one of your books. You do bear a striking resemblance to the author.

"This is where opportunity knocks. We need more information about how things will work in this new world we find ourselves in. Things we can do to increase the chances the good people of our city survive."

He pointed at Tom. "That's where you might come in. You've studied this sort of happening in a theoretical way. We need to know what kind of steps we can take that will have a real impact. The kinds of skills we might need going forward. The dangers we might we face. Do you think you might be able to shed some light on those topics?"

Tom nodded. "I can. I could give you a verbal rundown, but the real resource is my library at home. I have a lot of books about postapocalypse survival skills and any number of useful topics. The problem being, I'm over here."

The man smiled. "While it's still quite a trip from Newberg to the coast, at least you have a straight shot with just a few cities between you and it. The odds are very good that we'll be trading with the cities on the coast for fish. That means there's going to be some kind of communication back and forth.

"With that communication comes the opportunity to consult with you on problems that our community might face. Sure, we've got libraries full of books. I'm just not quite sure how Nora Roberts is going to help us at a time like this."

Tom laughed. "You might be surprised. Keeping a positive attitude is important. I don't imagine many of us will have a lot of reading time, but Nora Roberts at least writes something that would uplift those inclined in her direction. Frankly, once you get past the formula, she writes really well."

"Be that as it may, we're talking about a deal between you and the City of Newberg."

Tom nodded. "As I said, I've got quite a library. I have solar power that I can use to scan and print these books. It would take time, but I'd be more than happy to provide you with copies of the best ones in exchange for our passage and your assistance in getting us as close to home as you can."

The man gave him a searching look and slowly nodded. "I suppose that's the best anyone can hope for. You seem like a standup sort of guy."

Green extended his hand, and Tom took it. His grip was firm and his eye contact direct.

"Let's bring your people across. We can sit down and have

something to eat. I'll send some folks to get you to the outskirts of McMinnville. We've had conversations with them about mutual support, so I believe they'll pass you through without any harassment.

"The sheriff is working with us to help secure the river and to divert the refugees from Portland. That's why we have some of his deputies here."

"That would be terrific," Tom said. "I'll head back to get my people. I'm driving one of the vehicles, so they need me."

"I'll be waiting on the other side of the bridge, and we can go to a café I know. The owner still has a few things that he's fixing for folks. He's a determined sort, so if anyone can make the transition to the new world and keep his business open, it's him."

Tom nodded, returned to his motorcycle, and drove back to the convoy.

Everyone except Greg huddled around him as soon as he arrived. Greg was watching a couple of cars that had pulled in behind them. The newcomers were keeping their distance.

"I've made a deal for safe passage across the bridge and on to the next city toward the coast. McMinnville," Tom said. "One of the city bigwigs wants us to have lunch before we go."

"Is that safe?" Rachel asked. "They could just be luring us in to take everything that we have salvaged."

Tom shrugged. "The offer was made without them knowing what we have. There's no real way to know for sure, but the guy acted like a straight shooter.

"Do we really have a choice? If we don't cross here, we have to go down to Salem. I don't need to tell you how poor our odds of crossing the Willamette are down there."

Rachel slowly nodded. "We will keep guards out. Trust only goes so far."

"Everyone mount up," he said. "Let's get across the river. Nika, recover the drone. Let's keep that little secret to ourselves."

"Already done. The battery was low when you started back, so I stored it right before you arrived."

"Excellent. Let's go."

The police had moved the patrol cars far enough to the side to allow them to pass. They had to move them a little farther for the Beast to get through.

Jenkins grinned and waved as they passed. "You sure are full of surprises!"

"I try," Tom called back.

They slowly made their way across the bridge. From this side, Tom could see several hardened firing positions that covered the bridge and beyond. Rushing it would've been suicide.

Green waved at them and got into a vehicle just ahead. He led them to a restaurant with a large covered patio. Someone must've moved all the cars away from it, because the road was completely clear.

There was enough room to park the convoy if they used both sides of the road.

Tom climbed out of the Beast and looked at Rachel. "I want you and Greg to keep an eye on all of our stuff. If there's trouble, let us know. I'll send someone else out to relieve you in a bit so you can come in and eat."

She nodded. "If they have something hot to drink, could you send that out in advance? All this rain makes me feel cold."

The gray skies had been dropping water on them pretty steadily all day long and he had to admit that the temperature was fairly chilly.

"Will do."

Once Nika was out of the Beast, Tom dug into the box under her seat and retrieved a thumb drive in a case.

Green was waiting inside the restaurant. The owner had dug up some oil lamps to provide lighting. It looked old-fashioned, but Tom knew this was the new normal.

Oil lamps would make good trade goods, now that he thought about it. Candles, too. He'd have to devote some time to thinking about the new economy that was going to develop in the postelectrical world.

Tom made introductions all around, and they took their seats. He held out the thumb drive to Green.

"This might make a good down payment on what I promised. I assume you still have access to some computers and printers."

The man took the drive and nodded. "Charging up the power used by the damned things is a pain in the ass, but we can do that. What's on this?"

"That's one of my backup drives. I kept them scattered around in case I had some kind of fire or hardware failure. It has electronic copies of all my books and many pieces of research material that I found on the web. Topics ranging from preserving food to medicine in the field.

"None of it is professionally produced, so you'll have to take it with a grain of salt. Still, it should give you some things to start thinking about until I can start making copies of the books."

The man nodded and pocketed the drive. "While we wait for the food, what's happening on the other side of the river? We had to block 99W toward Portland. Refugees overran Sherwood."

"We had a guy with heavy equipment rip the road out and make a barrier that cars can't cross. That doesn't slow those on foot down, but we keep them out of the city. It makes me sad, but we have no choice."

Tom certainly understood.

"Seattle caught a nuke, and the one meant for Portland flew over the Cascades," Tom said. "That probably explains a lot of the terror you're seeing. I've heard rumors that Los Angeles and San Diego caught shots, too, along with other major cities deeper in the country. Washington, DC, is a smoking crater."

Green grunted. "No loss there. This country would've been in a hell of a lot better shape if someone had detonated a pocket nuke underneath Congress about forty years ago."

That was hard to argue with.

The restaurant owner came out with some baked fish for everyone. He'd found something to add to the children's plate that they seemed to enjoy. For Tom, the salad was a fine side dish.

He filled Green in, but he expanded on what his friend from Washington, DC, had been able to pass on about global events, as well as what Randy had learned. He didn't mention that they had access to a high-frequency radio. He attributed all the information to his Washington contact. He'd rather keep his capabilities close to his vest.

About halfway through the meal, he sent Randy and Moshe out to relieve Rachel and Greg. He made introductions as the owner brought fresh food out. They topped everything off with some excellent whiskey.

The ladies opted for wine, with the exception of Annie, who also went with the whiskey. The owner found a couple of warm soft drinks for the kids.

It was only few hours before dark when they finished. Green stood and shook his hand. "It's been a right pleasure making your acquaintances. I'm hopeful that the information you're going to provide us will help more people survive this tragedy.

"Once trade with the coast is opened up, we should have some kind of regular transportation back and forth between here and there. I'm hopeful that we will meet again."

He gestured towards the door, and Officer Jenkins stepped inside.

"Since you've already met, I've decided it would be appropriate to send Jenkins to head your escort. He'll take four men in patrol cars to be absolutely certain that no one molests you on the way to McMinnville. Two of them will be Yamhill Sheriff's Deputies. Once there, he'll speak with their people and arrange for your safe passage through the city.

"I wish you the very best luck in making it home. I hope that you and the knowledge that you have can make these dark times just a little bit brighter."

Tom shook his hand. "We'll do our best, Councilman. Good luck."

He only allowed himself to relax a little once they were clear of the Newberg city limits. To the confusion of the officers, he pulled off to the side of the road and stopped the convoy.

"Nika, go ahead and launch the drone. Make it the one with the FLIR camera. If there's an ambush ahead, I want us to see it before we get there."

The young woman nodded. "I'll fly that one and let Adam control the fixed wing. It can keep a better watch over our front and rear. I'll focus in on any heat sources that look suspicious."

Officer Jenkins stepped over and watched them launch the drones curiously. "Those things have cameras? We've got to see about getting some for Newberg. That would certainly make keeping an eye on the other side of the river one hell of a lot easier."

Tom smiled at the man. "It did let us get the lay of the land before I came out to meet you. If you have any toy stores, you might be able to find some there. I'm told they're not that difficult to fly."

"You can bet your ass that I'll look." Jenkins inclined his head towards Nika. "Pardon my French."

She smiled at the police officer. "I may have used the word a time or two."

After the drones were up, the convoy resumed its forward movement. They encountered no trouble. About an hour before dark, they saw police blocking the road ahead.

Jenkins made the approach to the McMinnville police, and they had a brief discussion. After the two men shook hands, Jenkins headed back toward the convoy.

"I'll be handing you off to Sergeant Conroy. He's agreed to pass you through the city. I've known him for ten years. He's a good man, and I trust him."

He held his hand out to Tom. "It's been a pleasure meeting you. I hope we'll meet again one day."

Based on the glance that the man sent Nika's way, Tom had a better idea of who the young policeman would like to strike up a friendship with. Based on the way she was looking back, that wasn't completely out of the question.

The McMinnville police opened up the road and allowed the convoy to pass. They put a car in front and a car behind to see them safely through the city. Based on the lack of stalled cars between Newberg and McMinnville, someone had been clearing the roads.

Every time Tom had driven past McMinnville before, he'd passed around the city. This time the officer led them right through it.

McMinnville was about half again larger than Newberg. The fact that it was closer to the coast probably also meant he was more likely to see people from here in the future. He made sure to take a good look.

"You're recording all of this, right?" he asked Nika.

She nodded. "Sure. We might need to know what's here later."

"Excellent."

On the other side of the city, he found out who was moving the stalled cars. A group of men was pushing them off the road and into a huge parking lot. One of those big grocery stores. Cars filled it. The men doing the pushing wore orange jumpsuits.

Once the convoy passed the police presence on the far side of town, the escort pulled over, and the man Tom thought was probably Sergeant Conroy walked up to the Beast.

The man was older than Jenkins was, and based on the excessive redness of his face, probably had some type of blood pressure or other medical issue that wasn't going to serve him well in the next few years.

"As you probably already know, Sheridan is the next sizable town on your way to the coast. We've spoken with the folks there, and I don't think they'll give you any trouble. That said, you need worry about FCI Sheridan."

It took Tom a moment to realize that the man was talking about the Federal Corrections Institution. He'd warned the others about it, but it had slipped his mind with everything else going on.

"Why?" he asked. "Are the convicts loose? What kind of inmates do they have there anyway?"

"It's a medium-security facility with a minimum-security camp adjacent to it. Last I heard, the guards still had the facility locked down. With the situation deteriorating though, I'm not certain how long they'll be able to keep the upper hand.

"A bunch of convicts have already escaped from the minimum-security camp. It's not as bad as if some maximum-security facility let everyone loose, but those are not nice people. If they can cause you trouble, I suspect they will."

Tom nodded. "We'll be careful. Any idea how many people were talking about?"

The man scratched his chin. "If I remember rightly, they had a bit more than five hundred convicts in the minimum-security camp. Probably twice that in the prison itself."

"Thanks for the warning. We'll keep our eyes peeled for trouble."

The man stepped back. "Safe travels, friend."

Tom waved for Greg to resume the lead as the convoy headed out on the highway. They were on their own again.

He grabbed his radio and made sure that everyone knew they might have trouble ahead. They were almost home. All they had to do was get through these last few obstacles.

Privately, it had him worried. This was the part of the book where he'd throw in one last massive plot twist. Like the convicts taking over the town. He hoped that for once this disaster was less apocalyptic than his fiction.

26

Highway 18 split just before Sheridan, with a business spur serving as the main road through the town itself. The prison was beside the main branch. That posed a bit of a conundrum for Tom. Which way would be safer?

The sun was already nestling in the mountains ahead. It might be best to find a place to pull off the road and set up camp. Taking the winding road over the mountains in the rain at night wasn't his preferred plan.

In fact, with the minimum-security convicts on the loose, it sounded too damn risky even to try.

A couple of miles short of Sheridan, Tom spotted a likely side road. He signaled everyone on the radio, and they turned off the highway. If they couldn't find a decent place to turn around, he'd have to cut some holes in the fences in the morning.

He found a field with adequate access to get all the vehicles safely inside and decided to use it. They might have some trouble with the owner. Or maybe not. They were a large group and well armed.

"There's a house just to the north," Nika said. "Based on the big gate between this field and that property, I'd be willing to bet those are the owners."

"Do you see anyone in the house? Getting a local source of intelligence might be useful."

"One of the windows has a teeny bit of light, and I see some smoke coming out of the chimney. Someone is home. How are you going to approach them without getting shot?"

"That is the question," he said wryly. "Very carefully."

He considered the possible hostile responses and decided that him just walking up to the house would be asking for trouble. On the other hand, sending someone that didn't look threatening to negotiate might work.

It would probably work better if they could do this before the encroaching darkness made seeing everything problematic.

He made his way over to Rachel. "I'd like you to go say hi to our neighbor. I'd really appreciate it if they didn't feel the need to come out and shoot at us tonight.

"I'm more than willing for us to pay for the privilege of sleeping here tonight and for any intelligence Farmer Jones can provide us about the situation in Sheridan. This close to town, he may have heard something."

"He might already have had trouble with convicts," she said. "Including pretty little lady convicts, if they had any."

Tom shrugged. "If it were easy, it wouldn't be the apocalypse."

She sighed. "Why not. What could possibly go wrong?"

Tom would accompany her part way but stop in plain sight. He'd be present if Farmer Jones wanted to talk but not close enough to be threatening. He'd have Greg cover them, just in case.

As soon as he had Greg set up behind one of the trucks, out of direct sight of the house, he followed Rachel over to the gate. The daylight was dimming, and Tom could see the first hints of the aurora. They'd only have another fifteen or twenty minutes of decent light.

He stopped at the gate and let Rachel walk ahead alone. She'd found an undershirt to attach to a short pole. She conspicuously waved it as she slowly walked forward. Tom knew that she had a pistol stashed at the small of her back, but he hoped she didn't have to use it.

The front door opened, and an older man in blue coveralls came out with a shotgun. "That's far enough. You're on private property."

Rachel stopped and planted the pole on the ground. Her response was loud enough for Tom to hear.

"We do not want trouble. We are just going home and had to stop for the night. We are willing to pay for disturbing you. If you have news about Sheridan that you would be willing to share, we would pay even more."

The man grimaced. "The way I hear it, money ain't worth nothing."

"How about food or ammunition?"

The man's expression sharpened. "You have any 30-30? I'd be willing to talk for something like that."

Rachel nodded. "How about five boxes for us staying here and the news about Sheridan?"

The man considered that. "I could do that, but I'd like you to throw in some food as a sweetener. Food's always good."

She turned back to Tom. "Go get five boxes of 30-30 and a sealed container of freeze-dried food."

Tom didn't like the idea of leaving her there alone, but he went. It only took Moshe a couple of minutes to dig out five boxes of 30-30 ammunition. While his friend was doing that, Tom found an unopened plastic pail full of freeze-dried breakfast meals.

The situation had not changed when he arrived back at the house. He slowly approached Rachel and handed her the ammunition and pail. She carried it part way to the house and set it down before backing up to stand beside Tom.

The man cautiously came down the steps and examined the items.

He straightened up and looked at them. "Well I'll be damned. Keep your hands out where I can see them and come a little bit closer. My eyes aren't as good as they used to be."

Tom and Rachel walked forward, keeping their hands out to their sides. They stopped a dozen yards away from the man.

He looked them over carefully. "Can't say you look like convicts, but you never know. Why don't you tell me who you are, what you're doing here, and where you're going?"

"My name is Tom Morgan," he said. "I have a place over by Otis. We got caught in Portland in all this mess. My friends and I are just trying to get through to safety."

"Otis, huh? I've been there a time or three. You ever go by the market?"

"The Salmon River Market? Sure."

"What's right across the road from it?"

"The Otis Café."

The man relaxed a little. "That's not exactly the kind of knowledge I'd expect a federal convict to have, so I suspect you're telling me the truth. Keep your hands out to your sides and come over here where I can get a really good look at you."

They advanced to within a couple of yards of the man. He eyed them closely. "Nope, you're not convicts. The ammo and food will pay for your night here and what answers I can give. Let's go up on my porch."

The man was rightly cautious, sitting them at one end while he was a little bit off with a shotgun in his lap. He set the freeze-dried food and ammunition beside him.

"Before anyone gets any ideas, I'm not alone. My wife is inside, and she's right handy with a shotgun. Just in case I'm wrong about you folks."

Tom nodded. "I absolutely approve of being cautious. What's going on in Sheridan?"

"Nothing good. I've had to run off a couple of convicts already. People that should probably know better than to come up on somebody that don't trust them. Even so, they didn't seem like hardened criminals. Probably from that minimum-security camp.

"I've also heard a lot of gunshots coming from that direction. Maybe it's the guards. Maybe it's the townsfolk. No way to tell. The prison's the biggest employer in town, so the guards are local. They've got a vested interest in keeping the hard cases locked down.

"With all these people scattered about, that's going to start getting really hard. The convicts almost equal the town's population of honest folk. When that dam breaks—and it probably will—there's not going to be any way to put the water back inside."

Tom nodded. "How dangerous do you think it would be for a group of people like us to try to go through town?"

"Can't rightly say. With the convicts on the loose, you might find yourself on the wrong end of a gun. Worse, the townsfolk themselves might not want you traveling through. There's really no way to know."

"Is there a way to get around town? My maps don't show anything, but I've discovered over the years that local folk often know a lot more about the lay of the land than any map."

The old man considered. "Might be. Depends on how rugged your vehicles are. If you keep going up the road, there's a lane on the left. It's not marked, but it leads around past town. It's not paved, and it goes through some rough terrain. You'd also have to cross a creek."

"How deep are we talking?"

"A foot or two."

Getting the four-wheelers through that would be a pain in the ass, but they could probably get the other vehicles across easily enough. He'd have to see it in the daylight to make that kind of assessment.

"I'd appreciate it if you could write down the directions for us. You could leave it out at the gate, and I'll swap it with a parting gift when we leave in the morning. Something your wife might appreciate."

The man smiled a little. "You sure know how to convince a fella. Fine. I can do that."

Tom stood slowly and walked down the steps with Rachel at his heels. He turned back to face the man.

"If you find yourself down near Otis, ask for Tom Morgan. I'll do what I can to help if you need it."

The man nodded. "I appreciate the offer."

Tom and Rachel headed back toward the campsite.

"You think he'll be safe here?" Rachel asked.

"I doubt it. He's far too close to town. Still, maybe he knows this place better than we do."

The others had started a fire and set up a basic camp while they were gone. It looked as though Annie was boiling something.

Nika waved them over as they approached. "I have some news from town. It's not good."

"It never is," he said with a sigh. "Tell me."

"I sent the small quadcopter over to take a look. The town is within range. It's pretty dark, but there are a lot of fires. It looks like eight or ten inside the city limits. I saw more than one shootout taking place. I'd say the prison is in enemy hands."

Tom sighed. "Perfect. I can't say I'm surprised, but I wish they'd have waited one more day. We've got to find our way around this town. Going through it just came off the table."

He made his way over to the fire. "As soon as we finish cooking dinner, we need to extinguish this fire. Nika says the convicts are loose. If any of them come out this way, I don't want them seeing a fire and coming over to investigate."

That certainly cast a pall across their dinner. Annie took the boiling water and added it to some freeze-dried stew. That made a hot, filling dinner. They ate in relative silence under the shifting aurora.

Once they finished, he set Nika to patrolling the area with the FLIR drone. If anyone tried to sneak up on them, she or her relief would let the night watch know. Due to the danger, they were going to have two people on watch at all times. That meant less sleep but more security.

He volunteered to take the first shift with Rachel. Nika was running the drone.

The two of them moved away from where the rest were sleeping so they could speak softly. They set up a couple of chairs facing away from each other so they could keep watch into the darkness.

"Do you think we are going to make it?" Rachel asked after a few minutes.

"I think so. I have to think so. We haven't come this far only to fail."

"Even if we get away, these convicts are going to be a problem, aren't they?"

He nodded even though she couldn't see him. "Probably, but that's a problem for another day. Right now, we need to focus on getting home."

"Tell me about your place."

"I think I'll let you be surprised. Even as a writer, I've discovered that words occasionally don't do things justice. Sometimes you have to see things for yourself."

Tom spent the next two hours worrying about how they were going to evade the convicts and get back on the road home. By the time he went to sleep, he still had no concrete answers to any of his questions. They just had to pray for the best.

He drifted to sleep in his sleeping bag after his watch only to wake an undetermined time later when a shotgun blast split the night.

27

Tom jumped to his feet, grabbed his AR, and started walking toward the farmhouse. Whatever was going on, running wouldn't help. He'd probably break a leg in the dark.

Rachel and Greg fell in beside him. Several more shotgun blasts erupted from in the house, and then a few handgun shots went off. Someone was attacking the old man. It looked as though the separate garage was on fire.

"I'd rather not get shot," he said. "Keep your eyes open and your heads down. If you see a threat, eliminate it. I hope to God the old man doesn't shoot us."

When they got to the gate, Tom saw two men in orange jumpsuits out in front of the house. They squatted over the prostrate form of another man. Another couple of shots came from inside the house. There was some yelling, but Tom was too far away to make out the details.

Tom lined his AR up and took sight on the men. He was using his suppressed .300 AC Blackout. The people inside the house might not hear anything over their own noise.

There was just enough light from the aurora and fire for him to line up on the men. He guessed at the range and squeezed the trigger.

He was a little off. Instead of a body shot, the slug took the man in the neck.

He swiveled to the other target while the man was still gaping at his dying friend. Another subsonic round took this one in the chest. That one flopped back and tried to rise, earning him a second bullet.

With the obvious targets eliminated, the three of them advanced on the house. Tom put a shot into the third man just on general principles. With the damage from what looked like buckshot, he might as well not have bothered.

Greg led the way into the house with Rachel right behind him. Tom brought up the rear, looking for threats coming from unexpected directions.

Someone had kicked the front door in, so there was no trouble moving silently into the house. Another body lay just inside the foyer. The old man's shotgun had claimed another convict.

A deep male voice shouted something from upstairs. Two more pistol shots sounded, then another shotgun blast, followed by a scream of pain.

Tom was more than willing to bet it wasn't the old man feeling the hurt.

Greg pointed toward Tom and then the living room. He pointed at Rachel and then the kitchen. The ex-Army sniper started up the stairs slowly, keeping his feet to the sides of each step. Probably to minimize any creaking. He kept his AR aimed up at any possible threats.

Tom split away from Rachel and entered the living room. He didn't see any sign of intruders, but he moved to clear his side of the house as efficiently as possible. He'd have to trust that the others did their job.

A burst of automatic gunfire sounded from upstairs, and then a pistol thundered from somewhere toward the kitchen. An AR fired several rapid-fire shots in the kitchen.

He resisted the urge to abandon his area and continued clearing it. When he was sure it was safe, he headed toward the kitchen at a run.

The room was bloody. A dead man in orange lay sprawled on the floor, his head a ruined mess. Rachel leaned against the counter, her hand pressed against her side. A side stained red.

"It is a flesh wound," she said as he came in. "Back Greg up."

Tom raced back toward the front of the house. He headed up the stairs, leading with his weapon. A pistol boomed, and then an AR fired several more shots. Greg was fighting someone.

He got to the top of the stairs just in time to see the barrel of the shotgun come out from behind a cracked door and shoot a huge shaven-headed man leaning out of another room. That memory would no doubt haunt his dreams for some time to come.

Greg was in the closest room. He must've been exchanging shots with the convict. The man in orange had allowed himself to get fatally distracted.

"Morgan?" the old man's voice asked from behind the door.

Tom's ears were ringing. He was going to be deaf by the time the apocalypse was over.

"It's us," he confirmed.

He jerked his head at Greg. "Rachel is in the kitchen. She's hit, but she says it isn't bad. Go check."

The young man raced down the stairs as the door in front of Tom opened slowly. The old man peered out, leading with his shotgun. He lowered it when he saw Tom.

"These bastards came out of nowhere. It's a good thing that I was worried about you sneaking in. They set off my little homemade alarm."

"I think we got everybody inside the house," Tom said.

"I surely do appreciate you coming to help me. You didn't have to."

Tom smiled a little. "When you accept somebody's hospitality, you feel obligated to help if they get in trouble. Far be it from me to tell a man his business, but if you have friends you can stay with, you and your wife might be safer a little further away from town."

The man grunted. "I lied about the wife. She divorced me years ago. Ran off with a trucker. Bitch."

Tom smiled in spite of himself. "I'm going to head downstairs and see about my friend. We need to get out of here. I'm afraid they set fire to your garage."

The man started cursing.

"We're leaving at dawn," Tom continued. "If you want to travel with us, we'd be happy to have your guidance getting back to the highway."

"That fire could spread over here before we know it," the old man said. "Go check on your friend. I'll pack some clothes."

Tom headed down the stairs but slowed when he saw someone coming in the door. It was Moshe.

"Is everything okay?" his friend asked. "Nika doesn't see anyone else in the general area. The burning building is too close to this one. We need to get out of here."

Tom saw that his friend had his radio. "Call Annie. Tell her to bring her bag. One of the bad guys shot Rachel in the side. She says it isn't bad, but I think that a doctor should make that call. She's in the kitchen."

The worried man proceeded to do so as he rushed into the house. Tom followed more slowly.

Greg had convinced Rachel to sit down at one of the chairs. The red stain on the side of her shirt was larger. He was slowly pulling the fabric away from the wound.

"Just barely caught you," Greg said. "More like a graze than anything else. Didn't even penetrate the abdominal wall. Passed through the layer of fat."

She glared at him. "Did you just call me fat?"

The younger man laughed. "Hardly, but that's what took the hit. You're going to be fine."

"We'll let Annie make that call," Moshe said repressively. "She's on her way. We need to get out of the house."

Seeing that things were well in hand, Tom picked up the revolver the convict had dropped and the bucket of freeze-dried food sitting beside the counter. The 30-30 ammunition was still sitting on top of it.

Waste not, want not.

He headed up front to keep an eye out. He passed Annie on the way in. She handed him his radio.

"You left this by your bag. Nika wants to talk to you."

He put the headphone over one ear and settled the radio on his belt. "Go ahead, Nika."

"I'm so sorry. I was looking one direction, and they came from the other."

"You can't watch every direction," he said softly. "These people probably came up through the woods. They didn't see us in the dark. They were going for the house. Don't worry about it."

He knew that she would. Experience was a harsh teacher. After the highway and this, she'd be much more cautious going forward, and that was probably a good thing.

Tom searched the dead men out front but didn't find anything worthwhile. They weren't even armed.

His watch told him it was about two hours before dawn. They might as well get everybody moving. At least they could have a hot meal before they got back on the road.

"Nika," he said over the radio. "Stoke the fire and have someone start making breakfast. Dealer's choice. I think the old man is going to be coming with us, so make extra."

A minute later, Greg and Moshe came out of the house with an annoyed Rachel held between them. She wasn't pleased about them helping her walk, but they weren't giving her an option. Annie came out behind them.

"Head back to camp," Tom said. "I'll get the old man." The fire was burning high and threatening to spread to the house. It was really time to get out of here.

He headed back up the stairs. He found three dead convicts lying in various locations. All had carried pistols, so he collected them, too.

The bedroom door opened, and the old man came out with a bulging suitcase. "I have all my clothes. I figure everything else can be replaced."

"Grab your 30-30. I bet you're going to need it before long. And your shotgun, of course."

"Bet your ass I'm taking them."

The two of them exited the house and watched the other building burn. Embers drifted to the house and set it ablaze, too. Nothing they could do would save it.

"Well shit," the old man muttered. "You need a farmer or rancher? I've done both and find myself in need of a new place to stay."

"I'm sure those skills will prove useful," Tom said. "Let's get out of here."

By the time they got back to the camp, breakfast was ready. They all sat down and ate in relative silence while they watched the house burn.

Once Tom had taken the edge off his hunger, he turned toward the old man. "I don't think I caught your name."

"Reckon not. Calvin Sumner. Thanks again for saving me."

"Look like you were well on your way to saving yourself," Tom said. "All we did was speed the process along. You're pretty handy with that shotgun."

"One does what one can."

Calvin stared at the burning house. "I've lived here all my life. My parents raised me here. I'm going to miss this place."

He turned to Tom. "Even though I'm mainly a farmer, I do have some cattle. I'll open the barn before we go. The windmill will take care of the water. My neighbors will come and check, I'm sure. Some of them live too far out for the convicts to cause them trouble.

"If you have space at your place, we might be able to come back for them. Beef on the hoof would be a good thing to have around. After a while, nothing beats a juicy steak. I got some horses, too."

"Those will be very helpful," Tom agreed. "Once we get to my place, we might be able to get enough people together to come back and drive them over the Northern Oregon Coastal Range. Maybe buy some from any of your neighbors that have them and are willing to sell. It would certainly be a worthy project.

"A lot of the convicts are going to scatter. Some will stay. We'll have to deal with them in conjunction with Newberg and McMinnville."

They were able to put all of Calvin's belongings in the back of one of the Hummers. By the time Annie finished cleaning Rachel's wound and putting a bandage on it, the sky was growing light. It was time to go.

"I'm not sure that somebody with the wounded side should be driving a motorcycle," Tom said. "Nika, can you ride?"

The young woman nodded her head. "Well enough."

"Switch places with Rachel. She'll control the drone while we make our way around Sheridan."

The news didn't exactly please the young Israeli woman, but she didn't argue. Good.

Tom stuck the old man in the passenger seat of Moshe's pickup truck. They'd ride ahead.

When the old man had declared that the way was somewhat rough, Tom decided that he'd been understating things a little. The dirt road they turned on was barely wide enough for the Beast and was the roughest they'd traveled on yet. Bumpy wasn't even close to describing it.

This wasn't a public road. It had to be cutting through somebody's property. No wonder it wasn't on any map.

They stopped when they came to the creek. Tom got out and eyed it. He wasn't going to trust its depth without walking it. He took off his boots and socks and, with a look back at the trucks, his pants.

"No laughing," he warned them.

He grabbed a handy limb to probe ahead and forded into the ice-cold water. It came up to his knees, but no further. The track continued on the other side.

Tom got out of the water and accepted the towel that Greg had dug up for him. It took just a couple of minutes to dry off and redress himself.

Rachel gave him an amused glance when he got back inside the Beast. "Nice butt."

"I feel so used."

They took the vehicles across one by one. Moshe's pickup truck had the most trouble, but it made it. The four-wheelers made it across with no problems. Greg carried the scout motorcycle across on one of the trailers.

Once everyone was safely on the other side, they continued until they hit a paved surface. Calvin directed them through several turns until they made it to a road headed toward the highway.

Throughout the trip, Rachel had been watching over the convoy with the fixed-wing drone. She'd had to find a convenient landing place for it before they got back out of the woods, but they recovered it just fine. Once she swapped out the power pack, she sent it ahead.

"A lot of the town is on fire," she said. "It looks as though there is a war going on. The convicts definitely have control."

"Can you see where we're going to come out?"

She nodded. "Maybe a mile outside of town. At least we are on the coastal side of Sheridan."

"Focus on any activity between us and the coast. If the convicts are doing anything that would interfere with us, I'd like to know about it before we get there."

After about ten minutes, Rachel started swearing. That didn't sound good.

"Some of them are between us and the coast. They are setting up some kind of roadblock."

28

Tom stopped the convoy just short of the highway. Before he pushed forward, he wanted to have the best read on what they were facing that he could possibly get.

The convicts setting up the roadblock didn't see or hear the drone slowly cruising over their heads. Rachel had it far enough out and at its maximum elevation.

It looked as though they'd blocked the road with an eighteen-wheeler. Some kind of tanker truck. They'd picked a spot where the road went over a drainage ditch. That would certainly stop anybody from getting around them.

Multiple counts of the convicts put the number at somewhere between a dozen and sixteen. That was a lot of people to deal with, but not everyone was armed. In fact, most of the convicts had makeshift weapons.

Even those that did have guns probably didn't have much ammunition. That was going to be a real sore point with those folks that stole weapons from guards or took them from people's homes. Most people just didn't keep a lot of ammunition on hand. There was no need to under normal circumstances.

It was a damn good thing he didn't live here. They'd have found enough ammunition to keep going for years off what he kept stored under his house.

Getting past the blockade shouldn't prove difficult. All they had to do was set up several shooters in the woods nearby. They could catch the convicts in a crossfire and drive them off.

What they couldn't do was set the tanker on fire. They needed to be able to move it when the time came.

Tom didn't know anything about driving one of the big rigs, but it turned out that Moshe had some experience from his IDF service.

He'd never driven one over a long distance, but they'd cross-trained him to move one to get fuel to troops. His friend felt relatively certain he could figure it out well enough to get it moved.

"I've been looking at the town, and something is going on," Nika said. She'd taken over the drone duty while Rachel plotted with him. "It looks as though the convicts are herding a bunch of people together."

Tom took the pair of goggles she offered and slipped them on. There were a bunch of people down there. Men, women, and children. Hundreds of them. Maybe as many as a thousand.

Dozens of armed men in several clusters were herding them toward an open field. It would take a bit to get everyone there, but that was obviously what they intended.

"That doesn't look promising," he said flatly.

"Why are they moving them all into the open like that?" Nika asked.

"Because they're going to kill them. Change in plans, everyone. It looks as if the convicts are planning to commit an atrocity. Moshe, break out the big guns. I want everyone armed and loaded down with ammunition.

"Greg, you need to find a place with a good view. I want you to be able to take out anyone down on that field that you choose. I doubt we can drive the convicts out of the area, but I bet we can kill enough of them to allow the townsfolk to defend themselves."

The ex-Army sniper looked at him. "I thought you said we couldn't take care of everyone else."

Tom shrugged. "I can't stand by while something like this happens. Is the collapse of civilization going to kill a bunch of those people? Probably, but I don't think I could count myself as human if I just let it happen."

While they were moving to arm themselves, Tom went over to Rachel. "We're still going to need to clear out that roadblock. Let me show you how to use that high-tech sniper rifle. You can sit back off on a hill and take them out once the shooting in town starts. By the time we're ready to make a run for it, maybe you'll have run them off."

Tom wasn't going to give up his AR, but for something like this, he thought he might need just a little bit more firepower. He went over to where Moshe was handing out weapons, magazines, and ammunition.

"We're going to use your pickup to get in there quickly," he told his friend. "Let's clear out what we can from the back. We'll take all the loose guns we've collected and ammunition for them to give to the townsfolk. If we can free enough people, they'll turn the tide on the convicts."

The old man nodded. "Will do."

"Also, I'm going with you. I'll ride in the back. I think it's time to use the minigun."

The older man smiled coldly. "That's really going to ruin someone's day."

They quickly unloaded the cargo from the pickup truck. They left all the loose guns and lots of boxed ammunition to hand out to any townspeople who wanted to fight.

Moshe uncrated the minigun. He set up a big box of linked ammunition in the back next to where Tom would be crouched. It looked like enough ammunition to kill everybody in the town three times over.

They left the ladies to handle the roadblock and guard the equipment. The children stayed behind too, of course. Greg had vanished. No doubt he was off to find a position overlooking the town.

That left Moshe, Randy, Calvin, and himself to man the pickup. Randy rode in back with Tom.

"Are we really going to take on hundreds of armed criminals?" Randy asked.

Tom shook his head. "Hell no. We're not the Army. We're basically going to run in, smash them, and arm those poor people. They're going to have to do their fighting for themselves. We're not going on a suicide mission."

"Won't they see us coming?"

"Sure. We're not going to make any effort to hide ourselves. We're going to bebop right in and kick them in the googlies. Then we're going to ride around like wild men shooting the hell out of anybody that looks like a threat. Kind of like the British SAS during WWII.

"Criminals are cowards. They have no trouble ganging up on innocent people, but when the fight starts, a bunch of them will run. If we can break them, the townsfolk can save themselves."

Randy didn't look convinced. "Not all bullies are cowards. What if we get some fighters?"

"Then we fight. Channel your inner Arnold Schwarzenegger."

They hit the main road and drove toward town. Moshe stepped on the gas. As one might expect early in the morning, there wasn't a lot of foot traffic outside the city. But that didn't mean there wasn't any.

Off to the right-hand side of the road, Tom spotted a pair of men in orange jumpsuits with old jackets. They were walking towards the roadblock a few miles up the road. They'd do nicely.

Tom leaned over so that Moshe could hear him through the window. "Drive right up to those two."

The men watched the truck approach without any sign they were worried. Neither one of them was very old or—apparently—very smart.

As soon as the truck stopped, Tom and Randy stuck guns in the men's faces.

"Morning," Tom said affably. "I suggest you don't move, or my friend and I are going to shoot you."

The two men wisely stuck their hands in the air, suddenly terrified.

"We didn't have nothing to do with it!" one of the men said. "We're leaving town because we don't want nothing to do with it!"

"Good for you. What exactly are your friends doing?"

The two men stared at one another for a long moment before the first responded. "It's those crazy bastards from the medium-security lockup. They're going to kill a whole bunch of people. They say they don't have enough food and water for everyone."

"All we did was bounce checks and grow pot, man," the other guy said. "We don't want to hurt nobody."

Tom was inclined to believe them. They didn't have the hardened look he'd expect from career criminals. Of course, all criminals were liars. Some of them were really good at it.

"I believe you. Since you were forthcoming with me, I'm going to do you a solid in return. That roadblock you're headed for is going to run into trouble very shortly. You don't want to be anywhere near it. Not unless you want someone to shoot you."

"Now, before I let you go, I want those jumpsuits. Hand them over."

The two men stared at one another in confusion. "What?" one of them asked.

"If this was a Terminator movie, I'd tell you to give me your clothes and your motorcycle. I'll settle for the jumpsuits. Keep the jackets.

"Move it, boys. We don't have all day. My patience is running out, and I start shooting when I get impatient."

The two men shucked their jackets and their jumpsuits.

Tom dug into the supplies and found pants and shirts that looked as though they'd fit. He wasn't going to send these idiots off to die of hypothermia.

Once the two men had handed their jumpsuits over, Tom pointed at right angles to the road. "Things are about to get a little exciting. I suggest you start running. Damned if I know what's off that way, but it's got to be better than what's going to be happening here in about five minutes."

The two men wasted no time in running down the ditch, climbing through the fence, and hauling ass for the trees.

Tom took off his jacket and put the jumpsuit over his clothes. He wouldn't have to wear it for very long.

Calvin climbed in back with them. "I'll take charge of throwing guns and ammunition to my friends."

Tom nodded and hefted the heavy minigun but kept it behind the cab. He wanted it out of sight when Moshe drove up.

Once the crowd came into view, it was easy to tell which people were civilians and which were convicts. The convicts had bunched the townspeople together into one huge mass at the center of a field beside the road. The convicts were in clumps scattered all around them. The atrocity was about to begin.

Many of the convicts were armed. They had to be to keep control over so many people. Once the killing started, the people would run in every direction. The criminals would never be able to catch them all. He suspected that didn't matter to the bastards. They just wanted to kill people.

Moshe stuck his head out the window. "There's a bigger gathering of these bastards over by the road. I think we should start there."

"Remember, once the party starts, keep driving," Tom said. "And don't throw us out of the back."

"You want miracles? Everybody's going to be shooting at us. You just hold on as best you can."

Tom slid the smaller electronic earplugs into place. This was about to get really loud.

Bold as brass, Moshe drove off the road and placed his pickup between the largest group of convicts and the townsfolk. The convicts didn't appear perturbed, though some of them were obviously curious.

One of them, a huge, burly man with tattoos on his neck and face, came out to meet them. He had several people behind him. All had rifles.

Tom guessed that he was in charge. Even better.

"What the hell, man?" the guy asked.

Tom grinned. "Funny you boys should mention hell."

Since the only people on that side of the truck were convicts, he didn't have to worry about catching anyone else in the crossfire. He swung the minigun out so that its barrels aimed right at the bastard and depressed the trigger.

The six barrels began spinning and spitting fire. Spent brass fell into the truck bed like rain. The man and his lieutenants died instantly, ripped to shreds by more bullets than anyone could easily count.

Tom swung the barrel around and cut down just about the entire group in one sweep. It was just like mowing grass, only faster.

Tom lurched when Moshe put the truck into motion. Everyone was running. He used one hand to grab on to the top of the cab, aimed the minigun at the next group of convicts, and resumed firing.

The convicts were hauling ass, though some of them were shooting back. Tom heard bullets striking the side of the pickup truck. He hoped Moshe was okay.

The truck bounced up. It felt as though Moshe had run over someone. He probably had.

As they drove near the suddenly running townspeople, Calvin began throwing guns and boxes of ammunition out, shouting to them to fight. Things were flying everywhere.

A bullet struck Tom in his left arm, causing a blast of intense pain. He swung around and spotted the group shooting at them. In seconds, he'd turned them into hamburger.

The volume of gunfire behind them was increasing. Tom glanced that way and saw that the townsfolk had armed themselves and were shooting at the convicts. A lot of people were going to die today, both good and bad, but it was better than a slaughter.

When the minigun ran out of ammunition, Tom shrugged off the harness and set it in the bed of the truck. He brought up his AR and started firing short bursts at anyone that looked like a convict. He mainly stuck to those wearing orange. He didn't want to risk killing any of the townsfolk.

As he'd hoped, the convicts broke and ran in every direction. Vengeful townsfolk picked up weapons from the dead or got them from Calvin and pursued them hotly. If they were going to throw the convicts out of their town, today was the day to do it.

Moshe stopped the pickup and climbed out. Miraculously, he looked uninjured.

"Are you okay?" he asked.

"Maybe." Tom's arm hurt like crazy, but the bleeding wasn't as bad as he'd expected.

The sound of rifle shots in the distance drew his attention back to the chaos around them. That had to be Greg. He was calmly shooting any convict he could. He seemed to be focusing on those who were armed.

That was smart. The fewer guns the convicts had when this was over, the less danger the town was in.

Randy jumped down from the back of the truck and helped Calvin down. The two of them assisted Tom. Neither of the other man was injured. It was a bloody miracle.

The truck, on the other hand, was peppered with bullet holes. Two of the tires had gone flat, and the engine was making funny noises, too. Tom suspected it was going to die in just a moment and never start up again.

An older woman, her face covered in mud and her hair in wild disarray, walked up to them.

She glanced at the local man. "Calvin. I see you found some friends."

The older man nodded. "Abigail Johnson, meet Tom Morgan. He's from over in Otis. Tom, Abigail is our mayor.

"Tom and his friends stopped some of these convicts from killing me. They burned my house down, so I'm going with them. I'll come back for my cattle and horses."

She nodded and extended her hand to Tom. "It looks as if you've saved more than just one old man today. I can't begin to tell you how grateful we all are that you showed up. Those monsters were going to kill us."

Tom was impressed that she didn't seem disturbed by the blood all over his hand. "I couldn't sit back and watch this happen."

"Well, whatever your reasons, the town of Sheridan is in your debt. I can't imagine where you got all those guns, but they're going to let us get rid of these bastards once and for all. Is that one of your friends shooting them while they run?"

Tom nodded. "His name is Greg, and he's an ex-Army sniper. I don't doubt that some of them are going to get away, but he's going to make sure a lot of them don't."

"Good. Now, let's see to that arm. There's no way we're letting the hero of Sheridan bleed out on my watch."

29

In the end, it took most of the day to drive the convicts completely out of the area. Some of them holed up in buildings inside the town, and they had to force them out.

Tom let the townspeople do the heavy lifting. The more difficult nut to crack was going to be the prison. A fair chunk of the convicts escaped back inside its walls. There was no getting into that building without the convicts shooting someone up.

On the other hand, the food inside wouldn't last forever. Hell, it had probably already spoiled. Water was also going to be an issue for the bastards.

The townsfolk were now well armed and would be able to deal with any issues the convicts presented going forward. At least he hoped so.

Rachel hadn't had any trouble clearing the convicts away from the roadblock, so her father went down and moved the big rig. Interestingly, it held five thousand gallons of propane in the big tank.

Based on the logs in the cab, it was originally supposed to go to some place down the coast. It would never make it there now.

Moshe's pickup was a complete loss. That saddened the old man, but the townspeople dug him up a replacement. The original owner hadn't made it.

Annie came into town with her equipment and started saving lives. Tom wasn't going to try to tear her away from that. He felt lucky that someone had slapped a bandage on his wound. There were plenty of people in worse shape.

They ended up staying in Sheridan until late the next day. That night, the aurora bloomed into bright color again. Perhaps even more so than before. Earth must have caught a second CME, this one stronger than the earlier one.

Why not? At this point, it couldn't hurt them anymore.

Annie had stolen a few hours of sleep and was finally ready to go. They gathered all their gear and lined up on the road just outside of town.

Some of the townsfolk even helped him recover the brass from the battlefield. There was a lot. Reloading it was going to take a while, even with the high-speed presses he had.

Abigail Johnson was there to see them off. "When things calm down a little, you and your folk should feel free to come back and see us. The town of Sheridan owes you. You have only to ask, and we'll be there to help you."

He shook the woman's hand. "We appreciate it. I suspect things are going to get grimmer before they get better. I don't know if there's anything else I can do to help, but feel free to come to Otis and ask. If I can help, I will."

They set out with about three hours of daylight left. When they got to the old roadblock, Moshe climbed out of his new pickup truck and let Rachel drive it. He climbed into the big rig and started it up.

"I remember you said your generator used propane," he said out the open window. "And that you have a big tank that needs filling."

"It does and I do," Tom agreed. "This will make things easier."

It would make things a lot easier, actually. He had just short of seven thousand gallons in capacity at his place but only two thousand gallons of propane. This tanker would fill the commercial tank he'd picked up from a bankruptcy sale last summer.

Tom's whole-home generator used a bit more than two gallons an hour to run everything in the house and the nearby workshop. Since he didn't need central air-conditioning, he only had to use the generator at half power. It used about three and a half gallons an hour when running full out, but he seldom needed that kind of juice.

Running the generator for a couple of hours every day to keep the freezers going wouldn't really put a dent into this supply for years. When he added in the solar panels that he'd bought from Randy, they might not even need to use the generator that much.

He wasn't going to argue with having that kind of capability, though. It might just save their lives.

They got on the road and headed up into the coastal range. Under all the trees, shadows obscured the road. They were lucky to have the road. Walking the rough terrain would take them days and be as hard as hell on them.

They traveled slowly, ready to react to any ambush. Adam flew the quadcopter with the FLIR ahead of them, looking for trouble.

The next worry was the Spirit Mountain Casino. It sat just off the highway.

Cars filled the parking lot, and armed men stood near the road. Tom was certain they were going to attack, but a tall man in a dark suit waved the men back. He smiled at Tom and gestured for him to proceed past them.

Tom was sure that meant there was an ambush ahead, but they didn't meet anyone until just before they arrived at the town of Rose Lodge. He thought they were about at the point the Treat River met the Salmon River off to their left.

They slowed down when he saw a couple of Lincoln County Sheriff's Department vehicles on the highway outside of Rose Lodge. Besides the uniformed deputies, there were half a dozen other men with guns.

Tom stopped the convoy well short of the roadblock. He took off his jacket and handed his pistol to Greg. He made certain that the deputies could see that he was disarming himself.

With his arms out straight at his sides, he walked slowly toward the men until they told him to stop.

One of the deputies came out to meet him. His nametag said

Walker. "You need to turn around and go back the way you came. This road is closed."

There were back roads that he could use to get around the roadblock, but Tom had no idea if the semi could use them. He'd save that for a last resort.

Tom smiled. "I'm hoping that I can talk you into opening it for us. My name is Tom Morgan, and I live in Otis. Just a couple of miles up the road. We've been trying to get home since all this started."

The man gave him a hard stare. "I don't suppose you can prove that, can you?"

"I'm going to get my wallet and hand you my license. Could you ask your friends not to get too excited?"

"Move slow." Walker turned his head just enough to shout. "He's getting his wallet."

Tom retrieved his wallet, opened it slowly, and showed the man his license.

Walker took his wallet and examined the license. "Well I'll be damned. You really are from Otis."

Tom retrieved his wallet and put it away. "All I want to do is get to my house, Deputy. My friends and I have gone through hell to get here."

The man stood silent for a moment. "The sheriff won't be too happy, but since you're a local, I'll make an exception. I don't want to see one of our citizens stuck out in that hell.

"We're going to move the cars out of the way. Drive through and go straight to your house. I'm going to tell the sheriff that I let you through, so I'd imagine he'll come by at some point to find out what's happening out there. Where did you come from again?"

Tom sagged a little in relief. "We were in Portland when the hammer came down. We had to drive around our elbow just to find a way through. Oh, the convicts at Sheridan got loose. They're probably going to be all through these woods in a few days."

Walker shook his head. "Can't say I'm surprised. Go back to your vehicle and get moving. I'm calling for backup, and I don't want you in the way."

Tom walked back to the Beast and climbed in. He wasn't going to relax until he made it home, but they were almost there.

Once the deputies pulled their vehicles to the side of the road, he ordered the convoy to continue. He waved at Walker as they drove through.

Apparently, the men hadn't gotten a good look at how many vehicles were in Tom's convoy. They looked somewhat bemused, particularly when the eighteen-wheeler drove past them.

Tom called ahead to Greg and made sure he turned when they reached the right road. It took them another fifteen minutes of driving and several more turns onto progressively smaller roads before they arrived at the gate leading to his place.

Tom jumped down out of the Beast, unlocked the gate, and swung it wide. Because of his vehicle's turning radius and the fact that they'd had to bring in a lot of construction material to build his house, the turn-in was big enough to allow the eighteen-wheeler to make it.

Just barely.

His house wasn't visible from the road, so he couldn't see it until they'd gone a couple of hundred yards deeper into the property. He came out of the trees and drank it in.

They'd made it.

The front dome was certainly a welcome sight. He could barely see the workshop off to the left but couldn't see the rest of the house because of the slope. There was a large gravel parking area between the two buildings that was big enough for them all to park. Even the eighteen-wheeler.

When all the vehicles were finally in place and everyone had shut down, Tom climbed out of the Beast and whooped. Everyone else circled around him and added their voices to his. He found himself shaking with relief.

Just audible from the other side of the house, he could hear the generator running. It wasn't loud enough to carry to the road, so no one else would've known the power was on here. Just the way he'd wanted it.

Rachel stared at his house. "What the hell is this?"

"Concrete domes," he said. "With foam insulation and large amounts of crushed stone packed on the outside."

He'd gone with a light brown as the color because it kind of blended in with the rest of the landscape most of the year. At least it didn't contrast too badly when everything was green.

"I built it after my father died," he continued. "The construction bill would've sent him through the roof, but it's what I'd always wanted. I put a lot down in order to get a mortgage on the rest. I suppose I came out ahead on that deal. The bank probably doesn't exist anymore.

"Basically, it's a circle of domes with interior dividers to make rooms for various purposes. The central area is a Japanese garden. Not a very big one, but enough to relax in.

"I had them add some platforms to the top of the front dome so that I could go up at night to watch the stars or during the day to look over the property. It's a little more elaborate than that, but that's the gist of it."

She shook her head. "Well, I am glad to see it. I was beginning to doubt we would make it here at all."

"We're not quite here just yet. We need to unpack everything and get it put away. The rain has let up for now, but it can come back at a moment's notice. We can take everything into the workshop there. It's where I normally park the Beast. There's plenty of room in there to get it all laid out until we decide where it needs to go."

He turned to face the rest of them. "There are a couple of deep freezes in the workshop. I can't think of anything that we have that needs to be frozen, but someone needs to make sure that they didn't thaw out.

"You'll find a cup of frozen water inside each. There should be a penny on top of the ice. If not, it thawed and the penny fell through before the power came back on.

"In that case, we'll have to throw all the meat out. I'm pretty sure that the backup power worked the way it was supposed to, but let's be sure."

He singled out Annie. "We need to get the refrigerated drugs—

including all your insulin—into the refrigerators. We'll move everything out of the one in the basement and use it for medical stuff. We can get more units if we need to. With no power, I expect no one will care.

"While you all do that, I'm going to go into the house and start getting things ready for us to move in. There's plenty of room for all of us, though I don't have nearly enough beds. We'll find some of those over the next few days, too."

Tom looked at them one at a time. "You've all done miraculous things. I am so proud of each and every one of you. Thank you."

He headed up to the front door and unlocked it with his key. Inside, his cats were waiting for him. He didn't relax until he'd seen each of them and given them love.

They weren't going to like having so many new people around, but they'd adjust. Life was going to change for all of them, people and pets alike. Civilization might have ended, but the struggle to live went on.

Getting home was only the first of many fights. Survival wouldn't come easily. The hard times were just beginning.

They had the tools and supplies to make it through the grim future that lay in front of them. Now they just had to do the hard work to make that happen.

* * *

WANT to get updates from Terry about new books and other general nonsense going on in his life? He promises there will be cats. Go to TerryMixon.com/Mailing-List and sign up.

DID YOU ENJOY THIS BOOK? Please leave a review on Amazon. It only takes a minute to dash off a few words and that kind of thing helps Terry make a living as a writer and gets you new books faster.

· · ·

WANT MORE BOOKS BY TERRY? Flip to the next page and grab one.

VISIT TERRY's Patreon page to find out how to get cool rewards and an early look at what he's working on at Patreon.com/TerryMixon.

ALSO BY TERRY MIXON

You can always find the most up to date listing of Terry's titles on his Amazon Author Page.

Note: the links below (ebook only, obviously) redirect you to my website where you can click a button to go to Amazon. This allows me to participate in Amazon's associates program and earn a little more. Sorry for any inconvenience.

The Last Hunter

The Empire of Bones Saga

Box Sets

The Empire of Bones Saga Volume 1

The Empire of Bones Saga Volume 2

The Empire of Bones Saga Volume 3

The Empire of Bones Saga Volume 4

Humanity Unlimited Publisher's Pack 1

Humanity Unlimited Publisher's Pack 2

ABOUT TERRY

#1 Bestselling Military Science Fiction author Terry Mixon served as a non-commissioned officer in the United States Army 101st Airborne Division. He later worked alongside the flight controllers in the Mission Control Center at the NASA Johnson Space Center supporting the Space Shuttle, the International Space Station, and other human spaceflight projects.

He now writes full time while living in Texas with his lovely wife and a pounce of cats.

TerryMixon.com

amazon.com/author/terrymixon

facebook.com/TerryLMixon

patreon.com/TerryMixon

bookbub.com/authors/terry-mixon

goodreads.com/TerryMixon

www.ingramcontent.com/pod-product-compliance
Lightning Source LLC
Chambersburg PA
CBHW052026020726
47501CB00004B/1273